CORA CRANE

PAUL FERRIS

HarperCollins*Publishers*

HarperCollins*Publishers*
77–85 Fulham Palace Road,
Hammersmith, London W6 8JB

www.harpercollins.co.uk

This paperback edition 2004
1

First published by HarperCollins*Publishers* 2003

A catalogue record for this book
is available from the British Library

ISBN 0 00 651443 X

Set in Sabon

Printed and bound in Great Britain by
Clays Ltd, St Ives plc

Some of this story is true

For Dick and Jeannie

1

A blonde American woman is in her big but poorly furnished bedroom at an English villa called Ravensbrook, overlooking a garden that could do with a gardener. Strictly speaking she is a Mrs Cora Stewart, but hardly anyone knows her as that. Her hair touches her shoulders; the remains of breakfast for one are on the bed; a drawer in an oak chest that has jammed open contains flannel shirts and a long-barrelled revolver. The man of the house is believed to be in Cuba – Cuba! – and she is desperately lonely without him. She is also upset that he went in the first place.

Cora sits at the bay window, writing, in a fat manuscript book with a lock, about a man she once married, a Captain Donald Stewart, and wishing in the nicest possible way that he was dead. Small hopes of that, since he isn't yet forty, a well-fed son of Empire whose only disability was – presumably still is – a limp, thanks to a campaign of 1880 and an Afghan tribesman whom he described to her once as 'wieldin' somethin' sharp.' In his way he was a sweet boy, while it lasted, which wasn't long, with sandy hair combed over a premature baldness, and a curly moustache that barely moved when 'I'm damned if I will', a phrase he was fond of, came out between his teeth, as in 'I'm damned if I'll give you a divorce.'

Scribbling at her vast secret memoir that no one ever bothered to look at, in which Donnie was a mere twig, a twiglet, she tried to mimic the voice by writing 'I'm demned if I will, and you're demned if I won't.' Eternally demned.

A dog at her feet, a mongrel called Sponge, whimpered in its basket and she offered it slivers of rare beef from a basin under a cloth, talking to it in the way dogs liked, man-to-man, none of that baby-talk, telling it about the Surrey rabbits that were queuing up beyond the hedge in this fine weather to have their necks bitten. Sponge licked the taste from her fingers. 'He's pining for his master,' was the veterinary's considered opinion the previous evening. 'Me, too,' she said, which made him stare at his feet in embarrassment.

The dog slept instantly, and she went back to brooding on her husband, five foot nine of soldier, now civil servant in pith helmet, ruling hapless black men on the Gold Coast. For light relief she dwelt on their first night together. Two ghosts, a Donald and a Cora, in a bedroom with purple hangings like a funeral parlour. Outside, the gas-lit street, Harrington Gardens, London S.W., silent, patrolled by policemen walking close to the houses at two and a half miles an hour, alert for open windows and cries of distress; inside the bed, naked-ness and confusion. She gave a polite groan, thinking it was expected of her, and he told her savagely to be quiet. Perhaps he was afraid it would alert a policeman. He was rough, too; verging on the cruel.

The sleeping Sponge waggled its paws, trying to swim. Recovery meant she could go back to her rented rooms in London that evening. So did non-recovery, assuming there was time to fit in a burial. It would be the second dead dog to be deposited under the rhododendron. She wouldn't dare cable the news to Cuba. Anyway, she had no address except care of a tugboat or a newspaper. He liked to disappear. 'A weakness,' he said; explaining, not apologising.

Cora heard the butler's voice downstairs, back from visiting Mr Figg the butcher with an order. He came streaking up and stood by the open door, a young Greek with blue-black hair and the satisfying name of Adoni; a sort of war refugee from Athens, part of her plans for an English country life.

'Mr Figg say nothing doing till he see the colour of money.'

'I despair of you,' said Cora. She could tell he was waiting for her to smile, and tried hard not to. 'It is not the butler's job to rush about the house. Strictly speaking it is not the butler's job to go shopping, but we are short-staffed. Now walk downstairs – *walk* – and give a message to Rose. When you're back home earning vanloads of drachma on account of being trained in England, you will say, "Thank you, Mrs Crane."'

Because of Figg, Cora had to get dressed earlier than intended. Rose heated water for the tub and stood looking the other way.

'You are doing very nicely,' Cora said, when the girl was helping her dress, 'but we are two women together, and you must learn there is nothing wicked about proximity. When Mathilde is dressing me, as she has done most days for the past seven years, she doesn't cast her eyes down. But I have left her in South Kensington.' In the mirror she saw the girl grinning. 'I suppose we shall have the village saying "You won't believe the things she told Rose Wellington."'

'Shan't take no notice,' said the girl, and Cora kissed her on the nose and said it was time to start brushing her hair and pinning it up.

Oxted was a short walk away, a village with a street and a railway station. Cora marched through the dust and came to a cottage, a cobbler's shop, an infant in rags crawling towards a dead bird, which she moved out of range with the toe of her boot. The Greenwich Meridian was said to run precisely through the spot, according to the cobbler, who thought the fact was good for trade.

A telegraph boy in his blue outfit shot down the street on his bicycle, pedalling furiously in the direction of Ravensbrook, making her heart thump. They pedalled like that as a matter of course, but there was an additional furiousness about this one, suggesting the postmistress had said it didn't matter if he knocked a few people over on the way. But she pressed on up the street to Figg's, where a customer was being served, as she hoped would happen. It was the stationmaster's wife, having kidneys wrapped in greaseproof paper. They exchanged Good Mornings.

'I do adore kidneys,' said Cora. 'We have a dish in Boston that uses breadcrumbs and Tabasco. Not that Mr Figg approves of good English offal being tampered with, I daresay.' The butcher rolled the package tight. 'So is it true, Mr Figg, that you are declining to send meat to Ravensbrook because our credit is no longer satisfactory?'

He wiped a rag down a dirty knife and mumbled about comings and goings. The stationmaster's wife was slowly rearranging items in her basket to make room for the kidneys.

'I didn't quite catch?' said Cora.

More rag and knife work. 'Said I was given to understand the house was shut up, Ma'am, as good as.'

'Let me tell you the dispositions, since they interest you so much. Mr Crane has gone to Cuba to write about the war that we Americans are having there with the Spanish. You might like to know he is wearing a money-belt full of Spanish gold. I will see if I can obtain a copy of the *New York World* with one of his despatches, and you can use it to wrap somebody's beefsteak in.'

'My sincere apologies,' said the butcher.

'Be honest, you thought we had run off to Timbuktu, but you can't say it in front of customers because that would be slander.'

'Custom greatly valued is all I can say, Mrs Crane.'

'I accept your apologies. Now please have the following sent round. A crown of lamb. A pair of chickens. Two pounds of best pork sausages. Most important, a large piece of sirloin steak cut half an inch thick for an invalid.' Fingers hesitated over purse, where two sovereigns were ready if a gesture was absolutely necessary. This time it was not. The bill could balloon a bit more before he complained again. But he looked so glum that Cora changed her mind at the last minute. She put the coins on the counter, and the stationmaster's wife, realising the drama was over, moved away from the door.

The telegram was in the hall at Ravensbrook, in a clay dish that came from Mexico. A rose petal had fallen into it. Adoni watched her slit the envelope.

'Good news has come?'

It was over in a second. Inside was 'EXPECT HAROLD AND ME AT NOON FOR DRIVE AND LUNCH', signed 'KITE' in error for 'KATE'. She could breathe again.

'So the boy has got into Cuba,' said Harold, when they were on their way. He spoke over his shoulder, having hired a trap but not a driver, and was charging west along lanes in the general direction of Redhill, ignoring the possibility that someone else might be charging east. 'We have to hope he doesn't try and get himself killed. He has a predilection for it.'

'Hush,' said Kate. 'We all know you're as fond of Stephen as if he was your brother.'

'His considerably younger brother,' said Cora.

Harold waved the whip. The trail of dust was thickening by the second. 'That boy needs to be kept an eye on. Did he rip up the story I warned him about before he left?'

'"The Monster"? He did not. He hopes the *Century* will take it.'

'A Negro with his face burned off? They'll lose half their subscribers.'

'It's about compassion.'

'I'm sure. Let's not argue. Stephen and I are in the same mould. We are the finest fiction writers of America.' Cora nodded vigorously; it was half true, anyway. 'But I'm cursed by having to write yards of journalese about Europe,' said Harold, 'and he's cursed by his itch for gunsmoke and heroics.'

Some of that was true, too. The gaunt, stubborn boy had gone off swearing he meant to join the US marines. When that didn't work, turned down because of something unrevealed – lung, heartbeat, pallor? – he settled for being a newspaper correspondent again. Going off to the boat, he had looked as though he needed a week in bed; only the eyes seemed nourished.

'I have been to see a house in Sussex which I'm thinking of taking,' announced Cora. 'Brede Place, in the most wonderful countryside, not far from where William the Conqueror landed.'

'What's that got to do with anything?' shouted Harold.

Unperturbed, Cora informed them that the house had been built in the shape of the letter E, in homage to Queen Elizabeth.

'I thought we were all good republicans,' sang Harold over his shoulder.

'Do stop teasing her, there's a dear.'

'I would simply like it explained to me why Stephen and Cora want to ape the English.' Twigs and nettles whizzed through the air as the vehicle clipped the hedges. 'I have asked Stephen more than once, and all he does is put on his best Bowery accent and say, "Aw, rats, t'hell wid English dis an' American dat, I don' take no sides."'

Two women carrying jugs flattened themselves against a gate. Harold shouted that he hoped it was something stronger than ginger-beer, ha ha, then the sons of the soil would reward them suitably.

Why did men suppose that women liked having nonsense bawled at them? To be fair, it wasn't what Stevie supposed. But Stevie wasn't a yardstick for anything.

'It would serve him right if he got hurt,' said Harold. 'Nothing serious, a graze from a bullet or a bit of shrapnel. That would bring the boy to his senses. Pray for a scratch, Cora.'

'I take each day as it comes. If war is what Stevie wants for his books, who am I to complain?' She couldn't resist adding, 'Did I mention that I had a very pleasant letter from Helen Hay at Carlton House Terrace, after I sent round two of Stevie's books for her father?'

'Helen Hay?' asked Kate.

'Cora's aiming high. John Hay is our new ambassador in London.'

'It was Miss Hay who asked for the books,' said Cora sweetly. 'I expect they will ask for yours as well, Harold.'

'I am sure they have them already.'

'I shall mention it when I speak to Miss Hay, just in case.'

'She is only provoking you,' said Kate.

'Don't worry, I can take a joke,' roared Harold, and the whip caught the horse again.

At Redhill they entered the yard of the newly done-up Bull Hotel, which Harold had heard was sumptuous. It was crowded with vehicles, including a steam motor-car that hissed and dripped water, guarded by a chauffeur. A wedding party had taken over the place, a challenge for Harold, who showed his card to waiters so they would know they risked turning away Mr Harold Frederic, London correspondent of the *New York Times*, not to mention the wife of Mr Stephen Crane, author of that well-known work, *The Red Badge of Courage*.

They were all famous except Kate, who was looking into the dining room and the bride at the top table.

The management gave in. A table was found in the farthest corner of the room, behind lacquered screens that Harold soon folded back so he could give encouraging nods to anyone who caught his eye. He picked at his lamb chops, but made up for this by drinking a bottle of Burgundy, raising his glass whenever there was a toast and applauding the speeches.

'That bride's no chicken,' he whispered.

'No,' said Kate, 'she must be nearly my age.'

Cora whisked her off to the cloakroom, where they looked at their hats in smoky mirrors and washed their fingers in bowls of lukewarm water.

'Has something happened?'

'His wife has been talking to him again about a divorce, which he won't hear of, naturally. I don't know what he tells her. He tells me that our lives together, his and mine and the children's, are pure and sacred enough as it is, and that I am his wife in the eyes of God. I daresay the National Liberal Club and the *New York Times* as well.'

'Divorce would compromise him. One can't get round that.'

'I suppose if she lived a thousand miles away it would matter less. Cora, dear, I think I'm going loopy. I keep imagining love nests all over the place. How do I know it stops with Grace and me? How many more mothers of his children do we suppose he's got tucked away? Somebody in

Hampstead? A lost soul in New York? All pure and sacred, I'm sure.'

'Stop being silly. You and I happen to lead equivocal lives, that's all. It was our choice.'

'At least you know that Stevie would marry you tomorrow if he could.'

'Oh, I'm sure,' said Cora. 'So why did he have to go to Cuba?' Her hand reached for Kate's, and for a second in the mirror they looked like sisters posing for a portrait against a background of white tiles.

At the table, Harold had drawn a couple of men away from the fringes of the wedding party, which had broken down into informal groups. A bottle of champagne was in a bucket. The men stood up for Cora and Kate, then sat down again uneasily.

Harold had sweat in the lines of his cheeks. 'This was in South Bend, Indiana,' he was saying. 'A fellow was studying a poster showing pretty girls outside a vaudeville theatre. He asked the proprietor if it would be all right to bring a lady to the show. "Can I be perfectly safe in bringing *my wife* to this theatre?" he wanted to know. "Sir," replied the proprietor, "it is no portion of my business to inquire whether she is your wife or not, but if she comes in here she's got to behave herself."'

Harold shook with laughter. The men looked uneasier than ever, and one of them said, 'I suppose he wasn't married at all. That's very good. But we mustn't intrude. I sincerely hope you enjoy your stay in England, sir.'

Ushering the women out and leaving money on the table, Harold said they had better not hang about in case they were arrested for upsetting the natives with American jokes.

No one could take vehicles from the stables while the yard was full of guests. When the couple appeared in travelling clothes and made their way to the steam car, the crowd began cheering. Harold started waving his hat and shouting 'Hurrah! Hurrah!' Cora and Kate looked at the ageing bride, the confetti falling, the chauffeur saluting. They didn't speak.

2

The gang were rounded up early in the morning, while they were still packing the copper plates into barrels of sawdust. Bags of assorted currency were already on the back of a dray carrying false name-boards that was standing by to whack the evidence out of Seven Dials, and the driver, once he realised what was happening, moved off smartly and might have got away with enough roubles and marks to paper a bank if Detective Inspector Fred Hooper hadn't braved the wheels, leaped aboard and poked him in the eye with the handle of his whip.

It was a shame that their leader, who was also the engraver, a Pole called Wilk, escaped through a window into an alley, Fred having forgotten to post a man there. Nobody was perfect. 'Not the end of the world,' he said. But he knew that Mr W. was worth all the others put together. Poles were geniuses with copper plates and acids. And Fred believed as a general principle that losing any foreign villain was worse than losing a home-grown one. Crime by aliens was on the increase. The anarchist bomb affair at Greenwich in '94, when he was a sergeant, had given him a lesson in the things that lawless

11

foreigners, who were often not quite right in the head, could get up to.

London wasn't as invulnerable as it seemed; nothing was. Detectives at Vine Street, headquarters of 'C' division, regarded Fred Hooper's views on aliens as odd but harmless. He wasn't keen on women either. Colleagues pulled his leg, making him shake a finger at them and say they would find out when it was too late.

By the time the rest of the gang (one Belgian, one Russian, two Englishmen) had been charged, questioned and left to stew until they came up before the magistrate next morning, there wasn't much of the day left for writing his report.

An unknown person had left a copy of the *Police Review*, the weekly trade paper, on his desk, with a humorous article about Vine Street ringed in red. This held him up, too, trying to work out who the anonymous author was. 'The Vine Street premises make an ideal home-from-home for officers who need a change of air,' it said. 'There is a charming view over the stables, and water for making tea is available from the kitchen, which is open for as long as half an hour a day.'

The important bit came at the end. 'Foreign visitors are guaranteed a hot welcome from a certain detective inspector.' Fred underlined the words, tore out the article and pinned it to the notice board in the inspectors' room, where he was the only occupant apart from Simmons, a new man. Simmons, who looked very young to be an inspector, walked over to have a look.

'Are you the "certain detective inspector"?'

'I am. I believe I am being made fun of. But I regard it as a compliment.'

'Hear you had a big success at Seven Dials today.'

'A routine operation. You've come from Canterbury, I hear.'

'I have an uncle who knows the Commissioner, served under him in the Army. He wangled it for me. I was in the Kent Constabulary but I fancied London. More opportunities.'

'Wangled, eh.' The newcomer had a comically small moustache. It was a well-connected face. 'Good lad,' said Hooper. 'Call me Fred.'

'Tom.'

'I can show you a thing or two about London, Tom. Excuse me while I write a report.'

It was a quiet evening. Under the distant clatter of traffic, London possessed a stillness that in Hooper's view reflected the character of the nation, its virtues of concealment and restraint. Fred's birthplace was in Norfolk, a village by a marsh, but years ago he lost any affection for the place. London consumed him from the start.

He got going at last, his 'Empire' nib writing '12 July 1898' and scratching slowly down the page. According to Belle, his sister, who had views about everything, nibs would be lucky to survive far into the twentieth century. She was a typewriting lady at a furnisher's and draper's, Arding & Hobbs in Clapham, claiming to type at a rate of forty words per minute. Fred wouldn't know. Like the telephone, it was a device that showed no sign of coming to Vine Street.

About nine o'clock, when he was reading through his report, a message came from the front desk to say they had a foreign woman brought in for importuning. The station was warming up. Pickpockets and drunks were being booked. A man with blood on his face, handcuffed to a constable, was asking to be unlocked so he could kneel down and pray.

'Thought you might be interested, Mr Hooper,' said Reilly, the desk sergeant. He provided details of the arrest. 'The matron has seen her. She is in the vicarage, having a weep. Refuses to give her full name.'

Some wag, the kind of man who sent jokes to the *Police Review*, once remarked that the communal cell for holding women of the street before they came up before the beak would never do for a vicarage tea-party. Tonight's occupants so far were two regulars – thin-boned girls with scraps of fur on their coats – plus the newcomer, sitting well away from them on the bench; a capable-looking woman with a bold face, hair dark, eyes brown, age mid-thirties. A short, tight jacket contained a high bosom. She was angry as well as tearful.

'She can't half grizzle,' said one of the girls. 'Teach you a lesson, bunging up our pavements. They ought to send you back to your gay Paree.'

'I am from America,' said the woman.

Her accent sounded as if she was, and Fred, full of anticipation, took her off down the airless corridor. Only the other day he read an article about crime syndicates in the United States, and how they might soon extend their operations overseas.

The woman was taller than he realised, with a swinging walk. In the interview room he opened a 'Record of Interrogation' pad and said, 'Full name and address, if you please.'

'I have done nothing wrong. I am warning you, let me go.'

'I give the warnings round here. Let you go? Have you pop up somewhere else? Tell me how and why you're working the West End, and I might consider going easy on you. Might, might not. You will have to see if I've got a forgiving nature.'

Females were a danger in this respect. Stick-and-carrot was the usual method with prisoners, but when the felon was a woman, she had a carrot of her own. Certain policemen looked the other way in return for favours. Fred believed he was past all that. At forty-six, he didn't give much thought to bosoms.

'No use sitting there like the Sphinx,' he said. 'Why did your fellow prisoner say you were from Paris?'

'Stupid girl heard me say I was called Mathilde. She jumped to a conclusion.'

'It's a French name.'

'I had a French grandmother.'

'Have you worked as a prostitute in Paris?'

'Oh, do help me!' cried the woman.

Fred found that as a rule, Lombrosian methods of finding depravity in faces worked well with women. This one's features had no vital indicators. But she was foreign and she was uncooperative.

'You were observed,' he said, 'by two plain-clothes officers in the Haymarket, smiling at men and approaching them.'

'I asked one gentleman for directions because I was lost. I am not familiar with the streets.'

'You are not helping me.' Fred put her purse on the table. 'Contents, one key to a Yale lock and coins to the value of four shillings. The bare minimum, which is what women of your profession find prudent. If you are innocent, why have secrets? We shall find out about you in the end.'

'I don't wish to embarrass the lady I work for.'

'Ah. We are making progress.'

He prised a story from her. She was employed as a companion, but she had come up to the West End alone to see the sights.

Was that how American women behaved, wandering about cities by themselves at night?

'I am capable of looking after myself. I lost my way, that was all. I needed the Underground railway for South Kensington and had to ask.'

'Four encounters were noted,' he said. 'One gentleman was heard to say, "That's a bit steep, my dear," to which you replied, "The proof is in the pudding." Following the fourth soliciting you were arrested and cautioned.'

'Will these men appear in the courtroom?'

'They don't have to, the officers' evidence is sufficient. Mr Mead at Marlborough Street will fine you five bob in the morning and tell you that henceforth you will be identified as a common prostitute. The newspaper reporters who hang about there will take notice because you're an American, and the case will be worth a paragraph in the evening editions. They will christen you "Mathilde, the mystery woman". Then the Home Office will deport you, just to be on the safe side.'

She said her throat was dry, and he gave her a drink of dusty water from a carafe, and asked if she would like to see the matron.

'The horrid woman who looked in my hair? I wanted to bite her finger.'

'That would have been a mistake. I am trying to help you, Mathilde, but you will have to cooperate. We had some French girls over here two years ago. Is it starting up again? Are you the thin end of a wedge?'

'If I show you my passport and the apartment, will you be kind to me?' She smiled at him. 'The lady I work for is away. I can show you anything you like. Anything at all.'

'We had better get round there at once,' said Fred, and ten minutes later they were in a police cab, heading out to west London. There would be questions next day about the use of a vehicle. But he was sure he was on to something.

The woman was calmer now. She told him that she was a Mrs Rudy. After her husband left her she worked as a house-keeper at a hotel, where she met her present employer. She had been 'larking about' in the Haymarket, nothing more.

16

The address was in Milborne Grove, a short street, dark with trees. Six or eight houses ran down one side, behind small paved yards decorated with pots of geraniums, sickly in the gaslight. The key opened the front door of No. 6, and they were inside a hall with lights burning.

A drawing room on the left had sofas, green wallpaper, pictures of churches and horses, and a square bookstand on wheels beside an armchair.

'Wait here and I shall fetch the passport,' she said. 'We occupy four rooms. It is in my bedroom.'

She left with the same swinging motion, and presently Fred heard her moving about above him. He pulled back a curtain to look out at the empty street. The cab and its driver were visible on the corner.

The bookstand contained a few novels, which he glanced at in the way he glanced at the contents of any house he went into – at framed certificates, or medals in cabinets, or family portraits (none here), or any letters that might be lying around (none of those, either).

His late wife had been a reader of novels. She got them from the penny library and devoured them in bed at night. These were American. Mrs Rudy was still prowling overhead. He opened a book called *George's Mother*, where a spidery hand had written, 'To an unnamed sweetheart. S.C., Jacksonville, Fla. Nov 4/96.' Out of habit he copied the inscription into his notebook.

Fred's guess was that she would reappear after five minutes, and he was nearly right. It was a shade more than four.

'I have looked high and low. I know it's there,' she said. She had removed her jacket; the blouse and naked arms gave her a businesslike air. The cheeks were flushed, either with the effort of pretending to look or because she had rubbed something in them. 'Perhaps we could look together.'

17

'I thought we were never going to get there.' He didn't so much as glance at the bosom. 'I could charge you with trying to pervert the course of justice, but I'll settle for your passport, the name of your employer, and how and when I can be in touch with her. And be quick about it. Otherwise you'll find yourself back in Vine Street, and I shall tell matron you need a full examination. You wouldn't enjoy that. Be a sensible girl.'

It was midnight before he got home. The Wandsworth streets were silent. His sister had fallen asleep in the parlour, where she must have spent the evening with her friend Miss Crumm. A half-finished watercolour of the local stream, the Wandle, was on the walnut table, on a sheet of oilcloth. When he woke her, she gave him a bleary smile and said, 'This will never do.'

'Go to bed. Mrs Monge will tidy up in the morning.'

He sat by himself for a while, exhilarated by the day and the American tart. Not the tart as a woman, of course. Merely as a means to an end.

3

The up-train, with men making for London offices, gave the impression of not having wanted to stop at Oxted in the first place. Shouts from porters, guard consulting his watch, stationmaster with whistle between his lips like a silver dummy, swept two or three sombre suits and Cora from the platform and onwards to the glass and smoke of Victoria station, as if the Brighton and South Coast Railway was rounding up stragglers whose late arrival might upset the smooth running of an imperial city.

A close day, damp cloudy air like a lid over everything. Cora walked quickly, as men did, as fashionable women didn't. Had she seen a pretty woman like herself plunging down the steps to the District Line, light grey dress slightly askew, hair shivering under a feathered hat, she would have ruled out obvious things – the shopping trip, the Academy visit with a friend – and made up a story.

Watching that woman emerge from the Underground at Gloucester Road station at a quarter to ten, beckon a cab and once inside inspect her face in a pocket-mirror, seeing the wheels disappear along streets of prosperous houses, she

19

would have run through exciting possibilities, a fashionable governess going for an interview, a relative summoned to a millionaire's death-bed, best of all a jealous wife who knew the exact time her husband would be leaving his mistress, and had a lady's revolver in her handbag.

The real Cora paid off the vehicle at the western end of Harrington Gardens, and looked across at No. 73 for the first time in eight years. She noted shutters on many of the windows that went up five floors, including the windows of the bedroom where she and Donnie had spent their first night thrashing about like fish in a puddle. These ponderous Kensington dwellings tried to make a virtue out of blankness, as though quarried from solid stone and laid end to end along the country lanes that were there before them. A vase the size of a barrel on a balcony contained stale-looking delphiniums. They weren't a family that went in for flowers.

Up four steps to the porch, and here were the stained-glass birds and fruits on either side, and there was the lever that made bells ring and indicators flip over on panels in half a dozen places, ensuring that a front-door caller would be attended to within a quarter of a minute.

The first hurdle was an Indian in green tunic and turban. There was no point in saying it was urgent that she see Colonel Stewart, since the system was designed to remove personal inclinations. Sending in her card and a languid request got her as far as a side room in the hall. This was the polite equivalent of waiting on the doorstep: two chairs in flaky gilt, a hatstand, a foot-warmer, and a table with an *Illustrated London News*.

Whispers would be running through the house already. A bell rang for a servant, a door opened, footsteps came and went. Rules would exist for dealing with an unwelcome wife who turned up years later, asking for her brother-in-law.

A woman's head came round the door. 'I'm Norah,' it said. 'You must be Cora.'

The rest of her came in, draped in a smock. 'You won't remember me. I was thirteen, the youngest. Do you remember me? I had the silliest pigtails.'

'I'm delighted someone wants to see me.'

'I'm Mrs Jenner now, I was married last year. Leo is in the Rifle Corps. They'll kill me if they know I'm talking to you, but I would have been on your side if I'd been older, which they would definitely have killed me for. We are going to live in Aldershot after I have the child. Leo is in Home Forces. It is due in October.'

'Lucky you,' said Cora.

'Did you go back to America? I would simply adore to go to America.'

'I can hear someone coming.'

'I'm a married woman. I can talk to whom I like. Goodbye, Cora Stewart.'

She scuttled out of the room, saying 'Hello, Elvira, I was just passing.'

Cora didn't recall an Elvira among the daughters-in-law. The face was unfamiliar: beaky nose, light blue eyes, the iron lips of an Army wife who was proud to be as free of sentiment as her soldier-husband.

'Colonel Stewart is not at home. I thought it better to tell you myself.'

'That's very kind,' said Cora. 'And you are?'

'I am Mrs Stewart.'

'I get confused, there are so many of us.'

'I am Mrs Norman Stewart. Now if you will excuse me. Ramu will show you out.'

The last time Cora saw Norman's wife she was pudding-shaped and called Ada, lacking the killer mouth. She was vague

21

and fluffy, and had made Cora think more kindly of Norman in the brief time that she knew him. Now Ada must be dead and Norman had married someone more appropriate.

Cora waited till she was in the hall. Then she asked if she might use the bathroom.

'I really don't *think*,' said Norman's wife, looking around her as if the great rugs, the wall-ornaments (banners, shields, scimitars), the stuffed tiger grinning sheepishly in his mausoleum of glass and walnut, made it unnecessary to finish the sentence. 'Ramu!'

'I mean the WC,' said Cora, who knew they wouldn't remove her by force without sending for a policeman. Her voice was loud enough to carry beyond a baize door or two. 'The water closet. As I remember, the house had four.'

Cora liked to think she was the first person in the history of 73 Harrington Gardens to be standing amid the glories of Empire, inquiring about WCs. All Norman's wife could do was let the iron lips say, 'I will find someone to attend to you.'

It wouldn't take her long to return with a female servant. Cora made for the staircase. The Indian flashed past and waited for her with his arms flapping, like a child pretending to fly. 'Oh, Madam, please, Madam,' he croaked. But he didn't dare make physical contact, and kept walking backwards, up and up as the staircase curved around.

A familiar canvas showing a soldier bent low over a wild-eyed horse came into view, the scene foaming with smoke, dust, blood-coloured clouds. Cora knew what it was, a family icon, portraying an event of forty years before. The rider had become Sir Donald, first baronet and field marshal, the head of the family. In the painting he was the young officer making a name for himself during the Indian Mutiny, carrying despatches through hostile country. Her Stevie would have approved, would have relished the squirts of smoke from the muskets of villainous natives who were trying to murder him. Stevie liked wars as much as the English did.

'Did you serve with Sir Donald?' she inquired as they reached the top.

'Dear me!' cried the servant. His face was like melting chocolate. 'I beg of you, kind Madam.'

Corridors branched right and left. Cora was looking for the library, which was up there somewhere. But invading Stewart territory in South Kensington was as hopeless as Indians having a mutiny. By now No. 73 was in a state of high alert. The air vibrated with messages, reinforcements were on the march; Cora wouldn't have been surprised to hear a bugle. She persisted out of principle, hers and Stevie's. There was just time to rattle a couple of doorknobs and find darkened rooms with dust sheets. Then the Indian was calling 'This way, hurry please', and the insurrection was over. Two brawny women came at her from the staircase. But they stopped when a voice behind her said, 'You may all go back downstairs. Cora, you had better come into the library.'

One more door and she would have found it. Norman Stewart, elder son, waved her into a leather chair beside a terrestrial globe, but before Cora could sit in it, Iron Lips was there, whispering to her husband. He shook his head. Then Cora was alone with him again.

'I didn't know about Ada,' she said. 'Not until I met Elvira downstairs. I'm very sorry. I liked Ada. I believe she liked me, too.'

'She was very fond,' said Colonel Stewart, spitting out the words.

He stretched his arm and gave the globe a push, staring at it as crimson Africa gave way to crimson India. No doubt domestic death was an embarrassment, compared to death in a fort or a gully.

23

'I apologise for my shirt-sleeves,' he said, and offered her coffee from the pot that was with the remains of breakfast on a tray about two yards long. Her husband used to laugh at him behind his back – 'My brother the son and heir likes a book with his breakfast.' That was how she knew his morning habits.

'So you are still the same old Cora,' he said. The same old Cora had a palpitating heart. She let herself be drawn away from the violence under the surface.

Stevie said once, 'What in hell do the white men care about Africa? They hang a native on a tree and go in to eat their breakfast.'

A toast crumb had lodged in Norman's moustache. 'I don't know I would have had the pluck to arrive on the doorstep,' he said.

'It wasn't difficult. You could have made it easier by seeing me at the start.'

'You were being unkind to yourself, coming here. How did you know I was in London?'

'There was a paragraph in the *Times*. You have been in India, you are going to China presently, you will command a brigade of infantry.'

'No peace for the wicked. I wouldn't mind settling down one day. The Father has, I'm sure you know.'

Stevie said once, 'The English stand me up against walls with a teacup in my hand and tell me with infinite politeness that I'm a rascal.'

'I saw that he was Governor of the Royal Hospital. And promoted to field marshal.'

'You see? You know everything about us, and I know nothing about you. I imagined you were in America.'

'I was, for years. At present I am living in England, where I am known as Mrs Crane because the man I live with

24

is a Mr Crane. You have a nice label for it over here, a common-law wife.'

The colonel rang a bell and rolled his palms together while a servant took away the tray. He said, 'Cora, my dear.' Then he looked at the ceiling. Then he said he hoped she hadn't come to discuss her marriage.

'Why else do you think I'm here?'

'I didn't know your circumstances.'

'You thought I was after money? It's much worse than that, I want you to talk to your brother. Ada would have understood.'

'I'm sure she would. Ada knew all about sentiment.'

Again that puzzling manner. 'When did she die?' asked Cora.

Norman pushed the globe again and the Americas rose over the horizon, a red layer of Canada on top, assorted pinks and olives at the bottom, the colours of second-class nations.

'She didn't. Ada is alive. I had to divorce her. It was a ghastly business. I would have preferred not to tell you.'

'I'm sure.' If she was outraged, she couldn't help being entertained as well. 'So your marriage was dragged through the divorce court, as the saying goes, but you don't see any reason why Donnie's should be.'

'Ada committed adultery and I was perfectly entitled to divorce her.'

'Forgive me, but Donnie never stopped seeing women. I know that wasn't the only thing. Our marriage was a mistake from the start. But your brother was a Grade A philanderer.'

'The law says—'

'I know. I do know, Norman, I have read it all up. If the woman is the one who's aggrieved, there must be some other offence by the man besides adultery. Convenient, isn't it? Could you not ask him to admit to cruelty?'

'Be sensible, Cora. It will never happen.'

'As if it matters to Donnie, where he is now. Show it me on the globe.'

Africa reappeared, and the red stains under the shoulder of the continent. 'There,' he said, 'the Gold Coast, but you know that already. You've written to him, I know.'

'The letters come back, return to sender. I am begging you, tell Donald how unhappy I am. Tell him I want to marry an American called Stephen.' She stared down at the rug. 'Tell him I love this man. Tell him we both hate the pretence. Tell him Stephen is a writer of books, who works himself to the bone, who hates deceit, who can't settle down, who isn't like anyone else, who is killing himself. Undoubtedly killing himself.'

'And all this would be different if you and he were married?'

'Stevie needs a change in his life. Do you know where he is now? He has gone to Cuba to write about the war. He wouldn't have gone if his mind wasn't always seething.'

'Men are fond of wars, even writing men, I daresay. I'm sure he'll be back.'

'Certainly he'll be back. There was never any question of him not coming back.'

'Of course, my dear Cora. Of course.'

The same old tricks, innuendo and condescension. She left at once, before she stumbled into more indignities. It might have been wiser not to come, except she had promised Stevie, one night when he was raving and smoking and firing his revolver at bottles in the garden at Ravensbrook. He needed a promise of something to calm his violence – always the hint of violence, as if he had wars going on inside his head. 'I will visit Norman Stewart, the brother-in-law. He is a decent man. Will that make my mouse happy?'

She was back in the street. A flower-seller had arrived at

the corner of Harrington Gardens, hoping to do some trade before the police moved her on. Milborne Grove was only a few minutes away, and she walked there to take Mathilde by surprise.

'I suppose,' wrote Cora, 'there *are* more idiotic women than Mathilde Rudy, who has only herself to blame if she reads this when my back is turned. It was bad enough when she had an aberration in Florida, while we were in the state capital, and she cut loose and went with a senator in a rooming house. It is not as though she is a woman of passion – thank goodness, who wants passion in a companion? Passion is what Mathilde thinks is her God-given right, with that surprising bust. If she *had* passion she would find someone worth sharing it with. *My* problem was always finding the someone. In the meantime, and what a long time it was before Stevie came to rescue me, I kept myself busy and nobody laid a finger on me, although the fingers were always ready and waiting if I had mistaken the *other thing* for passion. For Mathilde to say that she was intoxicated by the West End of London and succumbed to a "moment of madness" when she saw a man with nice eyes in a silk hat is so ridiculous that I laughed out loud. "Oh, Ma, it was like the old days," she said. What old days? I told her, if she was younger, or I was older, I would lay her across my knee and paddle her behind. As for the detective, I said it would serve her right if she was sent to the penitentiary, but I had my own reputation to think about even if she hadn't, and so I would find a way to take care of *him*. As a result I have invited this detective to tea. I have sent her back to Ravensbrook with instructions to take Sponge for little walks and feed him by hand, which is what he likes. Or what Stephen likes, he being crazy about animals, as I am crazy about him.'

Cora obliterated the last six words in case Stevie ever read them, because he didn't go in for gush.

Miss Helen Hay, the ambassador's daughter, arrived at Milborne Grove without ceremony. She wore a plain hat and was still new enough to London to feel purposeful about her duty to her father and the American flag, which was to make herself agreeable to the society, some of it exciting but much of it turgid and inexplicable, that she had come to live in.

The particle of modern Britain that had invited her for 'Tea, English style' was American, in the shape of Mrs Stephen Crane, assisted by a maidservant of about seventeen who put her thumb in the butter, having earlier had a go at a curtsey that was more like a stumble. Miss Hay wondered if the child had been instructed to do that kind of thing. There was an odd grandiloquence about the silver utensils, massed cake-stands, lace cloths, and obscure blends of tea from a grocer in Piccadilly which had a royal crest and 'By Appointment' on its jars.

But it was unkind to think like that. The invitation had come at short notice, with a note from Mrs Crane to say that she 'sometimes felt a little alone, now that Mr Crane is being a War Correspondent,' and looked forward to helping the American community in London. The woman wasn't quite as anticipated. As the wife of a rising young author with a Bohemian reputation ('a bit of a devil, I hear,' said Ambassador Hay), she might have been expected to sound Bohemian herself, or at any rate less ladylike.

'Are you a literary person, Mrs Crane?'

'I scribble from time to time. I have even written for the newspapers. Stephen was in Greece a year ago when the war with Turkey was on. He covered it for the Hearst papers, and I went with him and wrote under the name of Imogene Carter

– editors are impossible when it comes to wives and husbands sharing the same page. It was after Greece that we decided to settle in England for a while.'

'I am getting fond of England. I daresay you feel the same.'

'The countryside in particular. Our house is in Surrey at present but we have plans to try Sussex. There is a very distinguished property called Brede Place that we have our eye on. Do try an eclair. Carrie, give Miss Hay the tongs.'

Presently Mrs Crane asked to be called 'Cora', which made the ambassador's daughter 'Helen'. The maid brought fresh tea; in the late-afternoon heat, plates and knives acquired a stickiness. Cora asked if it was true that a society of American women in London was being talked about. Yes, and Helen would put her name forward to the committee. Helen asked whether Cora had met Stephen through a newspaper connection. No, she kept a hotel in a southern city, name not given, and Stephen, the travelling journalist, came in through the door one afternoon in 1896 and changed her life. That was more like it, thought Helen. It pushed Cora in the direction of romance and mystery. Not quite bohemianish but not quite afternoon-tea-ish either.

They were discussing the Spanish war in Cuba – how Mr Crane was not only writing about the US marines under fire, but had been running around the battlefield at Guantanomo Bay carrying messages to company commanders – when the doorbell clanged, and Carrie scurried to answer it.

'How brave!' said Miss Hay. 'How terrifying for you!'

'Stephen tried to join the marines but they wouldn't have him. I'm glad to say he has promised me that this is going to be his last war. He plans to become an English gentleman of letters and live to be eighty.'

Miss Hay was considering why it was that some parts of Cora's conversation didn't seem to agree with other parts –

it was just an impression, hard to pin down – when a thin, severe man in a brown suit appeared and presented himself as Detective Inspector Hooper. Apparently he was there by invitation.

The tea-party came back to life. 'This is Miss Hay, daughter of our ambassador to the Court of St James. This is Detective Hooper of Scotland Yard.' The maid was hopping about. More hot water, more cakes, more thumbs in butter were on the way. 'Detective Hooper has found some defect in the papers of my travelling companion, Mrs Rudy, who incidentally has had to go down to the country to attend to a sick animal. I have a confession to make, Mr Hooper. I thought it might be interesting for Helen – Miss Hay – to meet a London detective. Her father is a great admirer of my husband's books.'

There was nothing for Miss Hay to do but agree to all that as being true, or apparently true; go on to have a polite discussion about the problems of policing great cities; discover it was after five o'clock, shake hands and depart for Carlton House Terrace, being curtsied at by the child, who was hoping for threepence (which she didn't get, Ambassador Hay having told his family not to encourage the insidious tipping habits of Europe). Detective Hooper was still there. She saw his face at the window, looking sceptical at whatever it was he was hearing.

4

The Pinkerton Detective Agency of New York had opened a branch in the Strand, which Fred came to know after his sister applied to work there as a typewriting lady. She was not successful because they demanded fifty-five words per minute. But she named Fred as one of her referees ('Det. Insp. F. Hooper, Metropolitan Police'), and the bureau chief, T.T. Davis, made it his business to contact him and suggest they might be of mutual benefit to one another.

Officially the London police regarded Pinkerton's with suspicion, and gave them no help. Fred took to Davis and saw the possibilities, America being such a lawless place. Boats crossed the Atlantic now in ten days. Crime had wings.

After his unsatisfactory meeting with Mrs Crane, who drawled at him unconvincingly about the pure-heartedness of her companion, Fred thought to try cunning, and visited the Pinkerton offices. Davis was in Dublin. Fred would have to wait a few days.

Meanwhile he had no shortage of work. A single man could devote more time to villainy than colleagues with wives and kiddies. If it hadn't been for Belle, he would have gone to

31

live in the West End, on his patch, instead of crossing the Thames to go home every day. An Italian shop and eating house in Soho, with jars of olive oil and macaroni like string in the window, had a flat upstairs, permanently empty, that Fred kept his eye on. Two rooms had a view of lime trees and a church. Downstairs was a cordial family from Naples, who would charge him twelve shillings a week and throw in free breakfasts at a marble-topped table. Being foreign was allowable as long as you registered with the police and spoke well of the Queen. Besides, Mr Armellini kept his ears open, and was a useful informant.

But Belle came first. She was years younger, their parents had passed on, and no one was hurrying to snap her up; at twenty-nine it was unlikely that anyone ever would. It was true that she went for walks with a solemn young clerk called Sidney, who suffered with his back, but she referred to him as 'Sidney the Kidney' and didn't take him seriously.

Fred had lived in the same house in Disraeli Street since he brought his bride there, a sturdy girl called Florence. She remained childless (Fred didn't mind), she fell ill one night with cholera after a dozen years of marriage, and she was dead in the morning. Life rearranged itself. Belle, who put people's backs up or charmed them according to her mood, but had always been fond of her brother, joined him in Wandsworth. She sewed buttons on his shirts. She stroked his bald patch when he flopped in a chair, whacked by a hard day fighting the underworld. They evolved ways of being under the same roof in a small house without friction.

The day that Davis was due back from Ireland, Fred planned to fit in a visit to Pinkerton's first thing. As usual, he and Belle ate breakfast together, prepared for them by Mrs Monge, a silent, hygienic woman devoted to her employer, who arrived every day at a quarter to six to light fires, boil water and fry

32

bacon. She was upstairs now, scrubbing the boxroom, because they were having a lodger.

Fred's mind was on a raid he had been detailed for. He wasn't aware that his sister had said anything that needed listening to until she rapped his knuckles with a teaspoon and he heard, 'The creature is arriving about five. Monjy will see him installed, but I don't think we should leave him alone in the house until we have had a proper look at him, even if he is her nephew. Can I rely on you to be home at a Christian hour? Freddie, dear?'

'I shall be going to live at Signor Armellini's if you go on like this,' he warned, polishing off the bacon fat with a crust.

'Why did you ever say yes to Monjy?'

'Because she asked me nicely. It's only for a month. He's a Birmingham business man, come to London at short notice. Don't ask me what she's doing, having a nephew like that. His name is Leonard Rukes. He will be someone to talk to in the evenings.'

The shriek of a factory steam-whistle half a mile away drove her, bread and butter still in her mouth, to find her hat and brush her skirt. Fred used it to set his new Rapido pocket-watch, as advertised in the *Police Review* last month. They left the house together.

Davis still wasn't in his office. A porter, polishing the brass plaque that showed an open eye above the words 'We Never Sleep' said the night ferry had been delayed, so Hooper left a message and went off to prepare the raid. Six men, a sergeant and a battering-ram were going to descend on a house of ill-repute in Maddox Street at eleven a.m., leaving Vine Street at 10.50. Fred was in charge, and he was taking Tom Simmons with him. Raids on high-class brothels weren't something they saw much of in Canterbury. 'Queenie Gerald, been in the business a few years,' said Fred. 'Changes her address. Currently living under the name of Tait.'

'Why this time of day?'

'High-class establishments see the customers by appointment, and daytime suits them as well as night, or even better. They turn up in closed carriages and don't have to go creeping about after dark. We do them in turn, these posh places. I expect the Commissioner lives in hope of catching an unpopular politician or a radical journalist *in flagrante*, and letting the word get out, but we never do. Don't tell your uncle I said that.'

Pinkerton's man looked in at the station – T.T. Davis, just off the boat train, soft hat on the back of his head, saying he would have telephoned, if only the finest police force in Europe had got itself connected by the National Telephone Co.

There was just time for Fred to take him round to Armellini's. He passed on a titbit about a dollar-bill printing plate, found in the Seven Dials raid, and came to Cora Crane. An American citizen, he said, I suspect with a history. He gave the bare details. A husband called Stephen who wrote books. A Jacksonville connection. If Pinkerton's could make a few inquiries, he would be indebted.

They stayed chatting about the Wilk gang, and Fred returned on the dot of 10.50, except that his damnable Rapido watch had lost several minutes, and Inspector Simmons had taken the men and left. Belle had told him the day it arrived that it had a suspiciously loud tick. By the time he caught up with the plain-clothes squad they were sauntering down Maddox Street, carrying the ram in a cricket-bag.

'You did the right thing,' he said.

'That's a relief, Guv'nor. I'm the novice round here.'

A brass plate beside an electric-bell button said 'Mrs Q. Tait, Muscular and Rheumatic Conditions. Ring. Walk up'. They didn't ring. The raid followed the usual course – silence when the door was knocked, then a couple of good thumps with the ram before a reluctant opening. Fred pushed aside a woman, about twenty, dressed like a nurse, whose pinched cheeks and black curls reminded him of Belle, and then there was the customary rush to secure evidence and separate furious clients from half-dressed girls. A fellow of Fred's age was sitting on a leather couch, and Queenie herself was massaging the back of his hand with a glass comb hooked up to a galvanic battery that produced sparks on the skin.

'He's a martyr to rheumatics,' said Queenie. The handle of a schoolroom cane was just visible under the sofa.

Fred had seen the inside of too many brothels to take more than a forensic interest. His own sexual life began and ended with Florence. Going through cupboards, breaking the lock on a writing bureau to locate the cashbox (six tenners, three fivers, ninety-one pounds in gold coin), hearing the new man, Simmons, tell a girl sharply to get her drawers on, he recalled one of the rare occasions when he saw Florence naked – when the screen she was undressing behind in the bedroom fell over, and he glimpsed breasts, limbs and puff of hair arranged together in a symmetrical fashion, rather than appearing as separate items. Her look of surprise added to the pleasure. The memory was more fond than indecent.

Fred counted the money in Queenie's presence. The new man could be heard admonishing constables who were laughing over a cache of Parisian pictures.

'Poor boys,' said Queenie. 'Nice to know they're human.'

She was only a girl herself, with green and white gems on her fingers, and stockings that glimmered like gauze below the hem of a flowery gown that she hadn't bothered to do up properly.

'Queenie Gerald—'

'Tait, if you please.'

'Queenie whatever you are, I am arresting you for keeping a disorderly house. You will be taken back to Vine Street and charged. Sit there and don't move. Inspector Simmons will come and keep an eye on you till I'm ready.'

The last of the clients was leaving. 'I'd tie my shoelace if I was you, sir,' Fred told a man in a cloak, 'or it might trip you up on the stairs.'

He had a look at the five girls being kept in a bedroom, glanced under beds, and went to the back of the apartment, down a passageway hung with coloured pictures of a medical nature. A constable was studying The Digestive System. He came to attention. 'Keeping an eye on the ablutions, sir.'

'In case they run away?'

'There is a woman inside has the door bolted, sir. The sergeant said to make sure she comes out.'

When Fred banged with his fist, there was no response. 'Use your shoulder,' he said.

'Sir.'

The wood splintered after a couple of shoves. The girl who looked like Belle was lying naked in a bath of reddened water. An open penknife was on the floor. 'Get Queenie in here,' Fred shouted, and groped for her wrists. As the left arm came out of the water, blood sprinkled a cuff.

'Tie!' he called, pressing his thumbs in the wound. 'Anybody! Give me your tie.'

The sergeant obliged, and Fred got a tourniquet on the forearm. The flow became a drip. They lifted her out of the bath, wrapped her in towels, waved smelling salts. An elderly doctor came – well-run brothels usually had someone on call – and got busy with iodine and bandages.

'Who is she?' Fred asked Queenie.

'A friend of mine called Blanche. I expect she slipped and cut herself by accident.'

'Why d'you think she did it?'

'There's a husband, I believe, but I never question my friends. I daresay she was afraid of being wrongly accused of working in a medical establishment.'

'I shall overlook the crime.'

'Why, do you fancy her, Inspector? I'm sure I could arrange something.'

It was always the same in Vice, an area Fred kept clear of when he could, shadow-games with shadow-people. In ten years' time, Queenie would still be at an address in the West End, still being tolerated between prosecutions. Unless, that is, she had married an earl, unlikely, or had retired to Biarritz on the proceeds, very possible.

Tom Simmons was impressed by his leniency towards the Blanche girl. Fred had a word with her before she was taken off to a nursing home in Wigmore Street, to be paid for by Queenie out of funds she produced from God knows where under her gown, winking at Fred.

'You'll be all right now,' he told Blanche. 'Take this as a warning. Give it up. Make a fresh start.'

Even with bluish lips and the pallor of shock, she still bore a faint resemblance to Belle. She nodded, but Fred knew she had no intention. They never did.

One thing the raid achieved was to bring the two inspectors closer. Simmons was a man that Fred believed he could trust. Something boyish and respectful about him provoked a fatherly feeling. When Queenie had been charged and bailed, and Fred's report had gone to the Head of Detectives, he asked on the spur of the moment if Simmons cared for bicycling.

'Not the strenuous variety.'

'I always go biking on my annual leave. Nothing heroic, just buzzing about the countryside. I was thinking of Surrey this year, end of August. I like a bit of companionship. Is there a Mrs Simmons?'

'Not as such. I am getting married next year.'

'Why don't you take an entitlement and join me for a day?'

'Flattered to be asked. But I'd only hold you back. They say you're a hard man to please.'

'That's a fact,' said Fred.

A note from Belle on the kitchen table said that Mr Rukes had arrived *with his luggage* and gone out again. Mrs Monge had left his supper to keep warm. Belle and Violet Crumm had gone painting by the Wandle and wouldn't be late.

When he had eaten, Fred went outside and attended to his cabbages and beetroot, taking salt with him to sprinkle on slugs. It was peaceful, watching them die. He had black and red currants in the tiny patch, which the birds stole shamelessly, but Belle pleaded against birdlime or even nets, in which the thieves routinely caught a claw and died upside down, and he let her have her way. Slugs had no protectors. They foamed and rolled over in dozens.

Back in the kitchen, getting more salt, he heard a persistent ringing from upstairs, traced it to the lodger's room and found the place like a warehouse – the bed surrounded by wooden boxes, hatboxes, tin trunks and canvas bags. The culprit was in a crate of alarm clocks. Fred cut his thumb, rummaging to find the right one.

In the silence, sucking the blood, he thought again of his wife, whose untidiness had been incurable. Months went by and she never crossed his mind. Now it had happened twice in a day. Queenie Gerald's must have started it, prompting that picture of her nakedness. Memories bubbled under the surface

– let them bubble, he thought, and heard the sound of Belle and friend coming into the house with their paints and easels.

'We want you to decide, Mr Hooper,' said Miss Crumm, a round young woman of Belle's age, and Belle's prospects. 'I say that there are things one doesn't paint.'

'Undoubtedly,' said Fred. 'Belle, have you seen the box-room? Am I going mad? What has Mr Rukes brought with him?'

'Isn't it a caution? It seems he had a fire – or a flood – or something, in Manchester. This is what he salvaged.'

'I thought he was from Birmingham.'

'Was he? He travels in goods, you see. Has samples, sets up stalls in places. I'm honestly not sure. Monjy was here, they had the carter bringing the things in, Mr Rukes never stopped talking, it was like a parrot-house. I did warn you, Freddie.'

'I shall be having a word with Mr Rukes.'

The evening settled down. Fred finished with the slugs and sat at the kitchen table, using a pin to investigate the mechanism of his watch. The women were in the parlour with their watercolours, but they came back to ask if they could disturb him for that opinion on art.

Fred was indulgent. They had done enough Wandles to float a liner if they were all poured together. Violet was the serious artist. Belle thought dabbling in paint 'a bit of fun'.

'This is mine,' said Miss Crumm. 'There's an otter. Can you see it?'

'She invented the otter,' said Belle. 'There's too much muck in the Wandle for otters.'

'I did not invent it, but let's not argue. Please, Mr Hooper, what can you see in your sister's painting? In the Wandle.'

Fred's eye swept over a willow with misshapen leaves, a dark stream, a darker object on the surface, stretched out.

'Is it a drainpipe?'

'That would be an improvement,' said Miss Crumm. 'It is in fact – it is—'

'A pair of trousers,' said Belle. 'You see all manner of things in the Wandle.'

'It makes the painting ridiculous. One doesn't *have* old trousers in paintings.'

Fred considered. They might be in a conspiracy to pull his leg. He said, 'If you want my opinion, Belle should turn it into a corpse. The river police pull several a week out of the Thames.'

'That's awful, Mr Hooper,' said Violet.

'Now you've put us both off painting.'

They stayed in the kitchen. Fred asked his sister to bring some sewing-machine oil, which he dribbled into the Rapido. After more work with the pin, the watch stopped altogether. He gave it a shake. Oil splashed across Belle's watercolour.

'Another masterpiece gone,' she said.

Someone came into the house. A man called, 'Anyone at home?'

'It's him,' mouthed Belle. 'Mr Rukes.'

A head came round the door. Broad face, lock of fair hair over one eye.

'Mr Hooper! Mr Detective Hooper, I gather. May I present myself. Mr Leonard Rukes.'

The rest of him came in – stocky, eleven stone two, five foot seven, well-kept suit with fancy waistcoat. Nothing sinister about the features, but on closer observation, a white scar below the left ear. Accent of an industrial town, unplaceable by Fred. Late twenties, younger than he had been expecting.

Miss Crumm was introduced. Rukes was invited to sit down, but declined, saying that he must behave as he meant to go on, and not infringe on the family. 'I have my own room,' he said.

'Which is impossible to get into, let alone sleep in. It's not what I was expecting. To be frank, Mr Rukes, I would like all that stuff put in store.'

'Understood, sir! There have been mishaps. A burglary, the ending of a lease, an arson attempt by a competitor. London is by way of new territory. This house marks the turn of the tide. I shall begin sorting out my stock this minute.'

He didn't move. He made a performance of noticing the watercolours, was told they were the work of the two ladies, and exclaimed, 'Ah. Done with horse-hair brushes, am I correct? Artistry of this order demands hog. Or even sable. I shall look in my stock.'

Fred knew the type from street-markets, flash and no scruples. He admired the man's nerve, grafting in his lodgings. But he would have to go.

'That watch,' said Rukes. The dismantled Rapido and the pin were still on their sheet of newspaper. 'Having trouble, I see. May I?' He picked it up, turned it slowly in the air, peered at the case, shook his head. 'I am familiar with the model. They assemble them in Sparkbrook. They use springs of inferior metal imported from Belgium. Impose on decent citizens with trade-names like *Chronos* and *Rapido*. They ought to be prosecuted. It makes me very angry.'

Without pausing, he flung the watch on the stone floor, where the mat ended. It burst in a shower of cogs and glass.

'I couldn't help myself,' said Rukes. 'Excuse me one moment.' They heard him running upstairs.

Fred didn't let himself be fussed. 'I see all sorts,' he said. 'Mental disturbance brought on by his business troubles, I should say.'

Belle was scraping the remains into a dustpan. 'I hope you give him his marching orders in the morning. I shall bolt my door.'

41

'Come round to us,' said Miss Crumm.

'Harmless enough, once you have his measure. We shan't see any more of him tonight.'

He was wrong. Rukes came back bearing a pocket-watch on a silvered chain with an enamel fob, which he presented to Fred, saying it was an example of 'the very best Birmingham craftsmanship, cheap but not nasty, will go for years, and comes with the compliments of Len Rukes, bachelor of this parish.'

Twenty-four hours later the watch was keeping perfect time. Also, Belle had been presented with a pair of delicate hog's-hair brushes, and another two for her friend.

Belle said that of course her brother was right, and Len Rukes was a flash-harry, not to be trusted an inch. At the same time he was an entertainment. They joked about Aladdin's Cave.

Fred had looked in at Pinkerton's. Transatlantic cable traffic was overloaded, and Davis said he was sorry but the inquiry about the Florida person hadn't even been sent. He promised to fit it in soon. 'Take it easy,' he said. 'If the lady has a record, we shall nail her.'

5

Cora wrote in the book with a lock whenever the mood took her. It was taking her more often, now that Crane wasn't there.

'I would like to pretend it is easy, but it is not. I would like to say I enjoy reading your despatches in the *World*, but the truth is that they are a form of torture. It is not made easier by Harold Frederic, who tells Kate to tell me what I know to be true, that there is no correspondent in Cuba who can make the fighting and the blood and the mistakes and the mockery come alive like S.C. does.

'What I can't bear is being conveyed into your presence when I read about the battles, and to be there like a ghost, ignored. You know me, and whatever else I may be, I am not a ghost, I am the very essence of flesh and blood. I would admire your despatches more if I was anyone but me. There you were after the Battle of San Juan, with our boys on the hill after they saw the Spanish off. "The large tropic stars illumined the sky." (I like to copy out your words.) "On the safe side of our ridge our men had built some little red fires, no larger than hats, at which they cooked what food they possessed."

'At once I am floating in a void because I can hear your voice, telling me about those crazy Fabians over at Limpsfield (the Garnetts have invited me there next week, as a matter of fact), where the men have big beards and the women wear medieval smocks – colours either buttercup or mud, according to you – dispensing wooden cups of mead that tastes of stale candy, everyone in a draughty room that contains a fire – which is – you were laughing when you came back to Ravensbrook – THE SIZE OF A HAT. Now I have to read about fires the size of hats in Cuba.

'Your flesh-and-blood Cora even tried telling herself that S. C. put the phrase in his despatch for her to recognise and be reassured by. She dismissed this as the delirium of a woman who has been on her own for too long. Your dog Sponge looked me in the eye one day last week and I swear he was wondering why you hadn't sent him as much as a bone or a new leather collar or even a kind word. It is no good my saying, S. C. sends you intangible pats and whistles, because he knows the difference between sham attempts to keep the spirits high and the true elixir of remembrance.

'At least Sponge has the advantage of not knowing how easily a letter can be scratched on a bit of paper, sealed up inside another bit of paper, and conveyed in a mail-bag via Old Point Comfort, Va., or wherever convenient, for onward transmission by steamer to Liverpool Docks and thence to Oxted, Surrey, where he sits pining in his basket.

'You forbade ME to write to YOU because, you said, you had to be as hard as steel to do your job. I am obeying you and writing this in my MS book instead. But I didn't expect the prohibition to extend to YOUR letters to ME.

'Do I touch your heart, Stevie? Alice Barr called here last week and said that Robert went over to New York in June, since when she had received a mere postcard and a message via his publishers. We agreed (can you hear the girlish laughter?) that writers are uncommunicative beasts where their women are concerned. I stopped myself saying, "A whole postcard? You don't know you're born."

'Even Mrs Rudy, who is being as Rudyish as ever, asks after you with tender solicitation, and says ominously that she had a great-great uncle (one of those Frenchmen) who enjoyed battles so much, he didn't go home for twenty years. How long was Ulysses away? A mere ten. Crane has been away nearly three months. Where are you, King of Ithaca?'

Kate Lyon was nine years older than Cora, but in her mind the difference was reversed. Their friendship was recent. The Cranes had arrived in England little more than a year before. Harold told her that another pair of Americans with secrets were coming to live in Surrey, and their common ground drew them together. Harold, well-established in England, saw himself as an elder brother to the nervy young writer. Kate warmed to Mrs Crane at once, but it never occurred to her that Cora was someone you took under your wing, even though Kate's own love affair had matured into a sort of marriage and given her three children in the process. There was a knowingness about Cora.

The two women sat by a bay tree in the garden at Ravensbrook, talking about the Gold Coast of Africa. British & African steamer from Liverpool to Accra, overland to Kumasi, and Cora, desperate and dishevelled, arrives at the Residency, where Captain Stewart jumps to his feet and says, 'My God, Cora, you're a plucky woman.' A native servant brings her lemonade and a footstool.

'And then?'

'He says if it means so much to me, I can have my divorce.' Kate shook her head at this fancy, which Cora has worked out in detail, down to the money she needs for the steamer tickets, which she thinks that Mr William Heinemann, Stevie's publisher in London, is 'sure' to advance her against the next novel.

Sponge was panting under the bay tree. 'I am dying in this heat,' said Cora. 'I am out of sorts altogether. I slept badly.'

'Lie back on the rug.' Kate tore off bay leaves and pressed them on her friend's forehead. 'Close your eyes. Everything is a condition of the mind. Allow Christ to heal you.'

'Your fingers feel lovely.'

'Never mind fingers. The mind is what matters.'

Cora opened her eyes. 'I thought you'd given up all that Christ-and-Science stuff.'

'It helped me when Heloise was born. Even Harold was impressed. I shall study it properly one day.' She pressed a leaf between her fingers to bring out the aroma. 'Now do as I say. Let your mind be receptive.'

'That's all very well,' said Cora, and sat up. 'I miss Stevie, is the trouble.' She ripped a leaf down its middle vein. 'We could always take our stockings off and paddle in the stream, which is one of the few things about this house I like. There's no one to see us.'

'You still mean to move?'

'Once Stevie is back. You must come and see it. We shall have vellum writing-paper with the address decently printed. Do you think it should be in capitals?'

Kate had no view on capitals.

'They give it authority. On the left I thought, "BREDE PLACE, BREDE, SUSSEX". On the right, "TELEGRAMS: CRANE, BREDE HILL. STATION: RYE". The house is enchanting, very old, very historical. Have I told you that before?'

'Often.'

'Promise me you'll visit us.'

Kate's own stationery, bought cheap from a man in Croydon, had no significance. The unremarkable residence she shared with Harold, built circa 1890, had cool rooms in summer and coal stoves for winter. The plumbing was sound; the chimneys didn't smoke more than most people's. 'Very old, very historical' sounded like a threat, not a promise.

'Come on,' said Cora.

They fumbled with suspenders, then walked on the bare earth where the lawn ended in a clump of firs, above the hollow where the water ran black and white over shadows a few feet down the bank. Kate looked back at the house and saw Adoni watching from a window.

'We are under observation,' she said.

'Adoni doesn't count. It isn't as if he leers. He just likes watching women.' Cora turned and waved, and the boy waved back.

In the hollow they were out of sight, and Kate didn't mind pulling up her skirt to stand in a pool. The water covered her knees. Cora saw a coin in the water and bent to pick it up, soaking the edge of her skirt.

'I thought it might be Roman,' she said. It was a halfpenny, stamped with Queen Victoria's head. 'There is a legend that the Roman legions were here. They watched where the ravens came to drink and found this spot. Isn't that a stirring thought? Julius Caesar quenching his thirst at the end of our garden. It makes a remarkable coincidence. The greatest writer on war in modern times, living where the greatest warrior of the ancient world broke his journey.'

'Harold heard all that from Stephen. He told him it was nonsense, a child of ten wouldn't swallow it.'

'And when you tell Harold that I mean to go to Africa, I expect he'll say that's nonsense, too.' The women stood side by side, sharpened by the water that swept their skin. 'Harold is a fine man but he doesn't have much imagination. He doesn't go in for miracles.'

'Do you? Does anyone?' said Kate, who saw endurance as the only answer to both their situations. 'I say my prayers, as you know, but all I ever ask for is the strength to put up with being Harold's wife on weekdays, and having to let him go off to Hammersmith at weekends.'

'Which he spends locked in his library. He hardly ever sees Grace.'

'So he tells me. For all I know he shares her bed. But if he does, he does.' She waded ashore and took off her wire-framed spectacles to rub her eyes, still burning from the sunlight. 'I have to accept it. Just as you have to accept that your husband is what he is, and get on with your life with Stephen. You would only make a fool of yourself if you went to Africa. You've told me a dozen times, Donald is as stubborn as a mule.'

'He could be sweet as well, when he tried.'

'He's a middle-aged man in a jungle now, not a loopy young officer in New York who was smitten by a blonde. Promise me you won't go.'

They trailed back to the lawn, a green bedspread with their stockings laid out. Adoni had gone from the window. 'I owe it to Stevie to do everything I can,' said Cora. 'He has a secret itch to be respectable.'

'You'd only be going there to impress him.'

'Isn't that enough?' cried Cora. 'Isn't that why we do things?'

Cora had a list of British & African sailings. Unfortunately, steamer tickets were not the only thing money was needed for. A year's rent was owing on Ravensbrook, and the piano in the drawing room that came from Whiteley's still hadn't been paid for. Presently these little problems were overtaken by a large one. Crane was ill. He had been carried aboard a hospital ship with a roaring temperature, begging for orange-flavoured ice-cream soda. They kept him on deck, away from wounded men, in case it was yellow fever. The ship had sailed for Hampton Roads, Virginia.

The report was more than a week old. Cora bombarded his editors at the paper with telegrams. Was he having the proper medicines? Was he well enough to travel to England?

She had received a copy of the *World* with the last despatch he wrote before his illness. Mathilde was told to read it, to comfort her mistress.

'The public wants to learn of the gallantry of Reginald Marmaduke Maurice Montmorenci Sturtevant, and for goodness' sake how the poor old chappy endures that dreadful hard-tack and bacon. Whereas, the name of the regular soldier is probably Michael Nolan, and his life-sized portrait was not in the papers in celebration of his enlistment.'

Mrs Rudy stopped. 'Who are these people he's writing about, Ma?'

'Never mind. Go on reading.'

'Just plain Private Nolan, blast him – he is of no consequence. He will get his name in the paper – oh, yes, when he is "killed". Or when he is "wounded". Or when he is "missing". If some Spaniard shoots him through he will achieve a temporary notoriety. Shame on those who forget Nolan – Private Nolan of the regulars – his half-bred terrier masterless at Reno, and his sister being chambermaid in a hotel in Omaha. Nolan, no longer sweating, swearing, overloaded, hungry, thirsty, sleepless, but merely a corpse, attired in about 40 cents' worth of clothes.'

Mrs Rudy's eyes looked over the the top of the newspaper.

'If you ask me, Ma, he wasn't himself when he wrote this. He was sickening for something.'

'He is sympathising with the common man. You are a goose, Mathilde. Take Sponge for a walk and don't let him get stuck in a rabbit hole.'

She took the newspaper but was unable to settle to it. She wouldn't have minded some of his sympathy for herself. 'Where are you, King of Ithaca?' no longer seemed amusing. Wicked thoughts occurred to her. Stevie couldn't marry her but at least he could acknowledge her. Why not stir things up? Suddenly descend on New Jersey where the Cranes came from, where Stevie's brothers and their wives lived in deep respectability, unaware that she existed.

'Hello. I am Cora Crane. Stevie and I were married in England last year.'

Why not tell them the truth? They would find it out soon enough.

'Hello. I am Cora Stewart – Mr Stewart was an English officer and a gentleman. I was formerly Murphy – Mr Murphy was a dry-goods merchant in New York. I was born Howarth – the Howarths are good stock from Boston. Stephen and I met in Florida in November 1896. We were inseparable ever after.'

Why not go the whole hog and pre-empt their unasked questions? 'I am *that woman* you'd rather not know about, twice married, once divorced, aged thirty-three, consequently seven years older than Stephen. What I am not is an adventuress. But if it makes you feel better to call me one, I don't give a damn.'

And even that was short of the entire hog.

One evening Mathilde brought her a telegram that read, 'ALL WELL AFTER FEVER EPISODE'. The only other thing it said was 'RETURNING CUBA'. Its place of origin was New York City, with no explanation of what he had been doing there. Cora told the dog what she thought of its master. The waiting went on.

People were kind. They were so kind they made Cora wince. She visited Stevie's publishers in London. Their nice Mr Pawling, the editor-in-chief (their nice Mr Heinemann was away in the Alps), agreed with her that the idea of collecting Mr Crane's short stories for magazines into a handsome volume, price three shillings and sixpence, was not to be sneezed at. He was kind enough to say he knew the stories well, 'The Blue Hotel' and 'The Open Boat' and, er, all the others. Once Mr Crane was back in England, the proposal would be high on the list of the firm's priorities.

He was even kind enough to take the package of typewritten pages that she handed him, weigh it in his hand like a grocer with a pound of sugar, and say that it was an interesting idea of hers that they publish Mr Crane's unpublished sketches of life in New York City, written when he was younger – 'Even younger than he is now!' smiled Mr Pawling.

Cora had written out the titles, and he read a few of them aloud. He made a humming noise after each – ' "A Dark-Brown Dog", Mm-m, "The Silver Pageant", Mm-m, "A Desertion", Mm-m.'

Nor was that the end of Mr Pawling's kindness. It had a late flowering in his dusty room, where the sheds and vegetable barrows of Covent Garden were visible through dirty windows – why did publishers never clean their offices? – when he glanced at the clock, and Cora said she wondered if her own writings, as 'Imogene Carter', when she was a war correspondent in Greece, and as 'Anon.' when she was writing a London letter for American journals, might appeal to the British reader. That struck Mr Pawling so forcibly that he could only manage a nod and some humming.

His parting kindness came when Cora, about to leave, mentioned that due to her husband's prolonged absence, certain financial embarrassments had arisen, and it would be a helpful act on the part of Messrs Heinemann if a favourable decision could be reached quickly and a sum of money paid as an advance on royalties. Mr Pawling rose to the occasion. Instead of saying 'No', he pressed her hand and pretended he hadn't heard.

Whiteley's department store, still in pursuit of the money for its piano, departed from the prevailing mood of sympathy. So did the Oxted butcher, the Oxted grocer and the owner of Ravensbrook, tearing his hair out for the rent. But the Cranes' friends made up for it. Mostly they were scribblers, on the wrong side of prosperity, so nothing much in the way of money was to be expected, even if Cora had asked for it, which she didn't. What they offered was the unspecific kindness that went with pity.

From the Barrs, Robert and Alice, she heard the latest second-hand news about Stevie. Robert, a Scotsman who liked America, was the scribbler who sent his wife a postcard from New York. Now he was back home, two villages away from Oxted, with the news that 'your old hub' (Why did they cut him down with jocularity? Did they envy him?) was last heard of aboard a tugboat with other correspondents, in search of the tail-end of the war.

She had called on a Sunday, the minute she heard that Robert was in England. 'We hadn't forgotten you,' he said, 'but my news is nothing definite. You probably know more than I do.'

The Barrs had taken her for a stroll, and they stopped to watch village cricket, a game Stevie once described as men in white clothes trying to keep them clean.

Cora wanted to know, had he recovered from his fever? Who had seen him?

'One of the *Journal* reporters, I forget who. You knew he had left the *World*? The financial manager fired him over some trifling matter. Idiots, aren't they?'

Cora pretended she knew what he was talking about. She asked what the reporter said.

'He thought the boy hadn't been looking after himself. "Legs like pipestems," were his words.' He broke off to clap a cricketer poised in an arabesque who had just done something with a ball.

'You may count on us,' said Alice, a stately young woman with prominent teeth. 'We shall all feed him up with beef and bananas once he's back. I hear the war's nearly over.'

Kind, kind, kind. Nothing but kindness, very cheap.

A normal life was all she wanted. Her definition was wide enough to accommodate men who jumped at you and offered figurative pearls, metaphorical rubies (or real ones, but that hadn't happened). Captain Stewart would have tempted any ambitious girl who happened to be earning the rent by wearing pink stockings and serving liquor in a New York dancehall. Ambition wasn't a felony. Years later Stevie came through another door in another place and nothing was the same afterwards. That, too, was a normal event in women's lives, or it was if you believed penny romances.

Sponge had a thorn in his paw. He whimpered in her bedroom as she was trying to draw it free with tweezers. Stephen would have commanded respect and been allowed to probe, but all she got was yelps, and the dog would have bitten her if she hadn't taken her hand away. 'Ungrateful cur,' she said, and left him to lick it out. There wasn't much point in being resentful of a dog. But Sponge's need for Stephen was another reminder of her own.

She sat on the bed, checking his clothes for moth and loose threads. Two pairs of yellowed under-vests had tags with 'S. Crane' in Indian ink. Could they have lasted him since he was at college? Knowing Stevie, yes. A flannel vest needed stitches under the arm, and Cora found a needle and thread and attended to it herself. A soft felt hat, with a hole drilled through after he used it in the garden for target practice, was beyond repair, but she packed it away in tissue paper.

God knows what he threw into his bag when he left for Cuba. The framed photograph of her, taken when they were in Greece, was still on the desk in his study – left behind, and why not? S.C. travelled light and followed the hard-as-steel principle. What did she expect him to do, wrap it in a nightshirt and display it in every tent, bunk, barn or slit trench where he found himself? Plant a goodnight kiss on the lips? Gaze into the eyes when he woke with a sandpaper throat and fever in his bones?

Anyway, the photograph made her look too heavy, almost maternal, broad in the beam, sitting on a boulder with her legs slewed to one side (identified only by the protruding boots). Skirt like an apron, dark blouse criss-crossed with leather straps supporting water-bottle, field-glasses and purse; her left fist jammed into the hip, elbow at an angle.

They had gone there a year earlier, when the Greeks were fighting the Turks – travelling as husband and wife, outside America at last. The photograph was one of a pair. It was meant to be a joke, but never was. Its companion, which she kept in her bedroom, showed Stevie on the same boulder, looking almost well-built in his high boots with buckled-on spurs and crumpled jacket, cowboy hat at an angle, revolver-butt showing in the holster that went from ribcage to thigh. He insisted they dress up for the occasion. It would amuse their friends. But no one ever smiled when they saw the gallant war correspondents, and if they had, Stevie would have jumped on a horse (had there been one handy) or gone to shoot tin cans or slunk into his Bowery mood – 'A pitcher's a pitcher. Cora and me wuz *there*.'

Actually, when the camera flashed they were in the studio of a Mr Boehringer. Gun and spurs were props from a cupboard. The boulder was wood and papier mâché. Across the picture of herself, Cora had written, 'To me old pal Stevie with best wishes – "Imogene Carter", Athens, May 22/97.' She would have preferred 'Love from Cora', but that didn't suit his humour at the time.

It was his first sight of a war. In the *Red Badge* he merely imagined what a war was like. He told her in Jacksonville that he got his facts from a book called *Battles and Leaders of the Civil War* and some old photographs. Everything else was in his head. 'I know what the psychologists say – a fellow can't comprehend a condition he's never experienced. Well, I was never in a battle. The Civil War finished six years before I was born. I got my ideas about fighting from the football field. I'm serious. Or else fighting's a hereditary instinct. Easy to make it up.'

His hand was outside the sheet, resting on hers. A train of wagons slowing in the railroad yards behind the hotel knocked against one another in irregular sequence. 'Like rifle fire,' he said.

If her history was correct, the Civil War was over by 1865, which made him twenty-five when they met, and she was thirty-one. She customarily took two years off her age, but never thought to with Crane, as if he had infected her with candour.

When they were in Greece, he wanted her to behave like a war correspondent, sharing his world of blood and willpower. He was initiating her. He approved when she went off on her own into the mountains, hoping to interview the Crown Prince of Greece, and ended up eating a supper of black bread and sleeping at Pharsala on a pool table in a coffee-house. She kept her skirt on all night. It enthralled him to hear how soldiers banged on the door because they had heard there was a woman inside, protected only by the elderly proprietor with a musket.

'How would you have managed if a Greek lieutenant with twirly moustaches had pushed the old man out of the way?'

'Pretended I was Scheherezade and told him stories about America till dawn.'

The scrap with the Turks (as he called it) was over almost before it started, and he missed some of it because of dysentery, but he made the most of what there was. He was seen at the Battle of Velestino lounging on an ammunition box while shells burst in the vicinity and bullets flew about – details varied – smoking a cigarette and giving his opinions on the psychology of infantrymen.

Much later he wrote a short story about a war correspondent, Peza, who decides to fight alongside Greek riflemen. They strip a corpse to provide him with equipment. *Peza, having crossed the long cartridge-belt on his breast, felt that the dead man had flung his two arms around him*. He hears the dead speaking of death and mutilation. Overwhelmed, he tears off the bandolier and runs away to the rear. A shepherd-child on a hillside says, 'Are you a man?' He has no answer.

When she read the story, Cora asked if he, Stephen, was the man who bolted. 'I wrote it in the hope of finding out,' he said, 'but I'm none the wiser. I have not been tested to the limit. Soldiers are forever asking themselves before a battle, "Will I do as well as the rest? Will I bear up when I see a man shot through the face, see the wound all blood and teeth?" Nobody ever made me go to a battle. I am a writer who chooses to go to battles. That's different.'

In Athens they stayed at the Grand Hotel d'Angleterre. He appeared early one evening, hard-bitten and Stevie-ish, closed the shutters and began to kiss her and fumble with her clothes.

'I thought we were dining with Harding and the other correspondents.'

'So we are, in an hour.'

'You needn't be so rough.'

'How do you know what I need?'

When she was naked on the bed, he took off his belt and flung it across the room, but he kept his clothes on, more or less. Afterwards he lay staring at the ceiling, cigarette in hand, talking about a postmistress at Melissokhóri who was violated by Turkish soldiers, according to someone at the American Embassy.

'You have a morbid mind,' she told him. One of her breasts hurt and she was badly in need of a bath, but he kept her there, quoting lines from poems, including one about a man in the desert, holding his heart in his hands and eating it.

> 'I said, "Is it good, friend?"
> "It is bitter – bitter," he answered;
> "But I like it
> Because it is bitter.
> And because it is my heart."'

'My goodness,' said Cora. 'Now I wonder who wrote that?'
Nothing about men was supposed to surprise her. There

must be other fish in the sea as strange as Stevie. But not many.

A visit to Brede Place had been promised for weeks; Kate was to be converted to the cause of moving house. The outing – which took place on a Saturday, and was described at length to Harold when he returned on Monday from Wife No. 1 – belonged to the Europe of ruined castles and tombs where visitors stood respectfully, contemplating the Past. 'We are tired of Ravensbrook,' said Cora on the painfully slow train to the south coast, which tipped them out at Rye, a little town on a hill, drowned in the haze. 'Stevie needs real countryside around him. There are too many distractions in Oxted. London's too close. This is a real manor house.'

Whatever that was. 'Expensive, surely?' said Kate.

'Pouf! Thirty pounds a year cheaper than our horrid villa.'

A trap took them miles into deep woodland, away from the coast, along a track with a deserted lodge, through an overgrown avenue of trees, then down a slope to ivied stone and tall chimneys (rank gardens adjacent, water gleaming in the valley below). A traditional English edifice, surely price twopence for admission, coated with history; where an old unshaven man came out of a ramshackle shed; where Cora said, 'Isn't it a sight for sore eyes?'

'Breathtaking,' said Kate, adding that she doubted whether she could live in it if she was paid to.

'Wait till you've seen inside.'

The man was deaf, and at first vaguely threatening, until Cora said she was MRS CRANE, DO YOU REMEMBER, MR MACK? who was going to RENT THE HOUSE.

While they were talking, Kate had a look at the wilderness. She found a patch of potatoes, and chickens in a curious hen-coop built with thin wooden pillars at each corner, before

Cora summoned her to the stone steps at the front. A door with iron studs led to more steps inside and the same style of door again; copies of copies by craftsmen, too far distant to comprehend.

'Behold!' said Cora. 'The baronial hall.'

It was inconceivable, like a rectangular field made of stone flags. Beautiful; absurd. Black beams far overhead streamed with cobwebs. Kate had been at town meetings for two hundred citizens held in smaller rooms.

'Stevie will have rushes on the floor and half a dozen dogs sitting around the fire.'

'I expect he'll roast an ox.'

'Do be enthusiastic. You and Harold will be our first guests. Wait till you see the bedrooms.'

The walls must have had the same chill in them for centuries. They tramped through chambers with decayed curtains, or none, or broken windows or a derelict four-poster bed or a table with jug and pitcher, long dried out. Kate, who had been brought up in the countryside, recognised an abundance of bat droppings.

They heard a stick tapping and an old woman, also deaf, GOOD AFTERNOON, MRS MACK, appeared, anxious to be of help.

'Take no notice of old Mack,' she said. 'Am I to get the maids a-sweeping? When are you'm a-coming?'

'NOT YET.'

'This here's a fine house for chillun. How many have you got, Missus?'

'None,' said Cora sharply.

'They'll like it here. Old Mack will learn them fishing.'

Cora said it might be late in the year before they moved, and the house would have to be cleaned from top to bottom. She would be writing to the owners, and in the meantime here was a half-sovereign for Mrs Mack, whose last words when they got outside were, 'You tell those chillun about Mr Mack.'

The man who brought them was asleep on the grass beside the trap. Before they left, Kate took Cora to see the hen-coop. 'I couldn't think what it was till we were upstairs,' she said. 'Do you see? The frame's a four-poster.'

'Smile as much as you like,' said Cora, when they were on the train pulling out of Rye station. 'It's for Stevie, you know that. He's a restless man. All I want is somewhere he can settle for a while. He needs space and dogs and horses – you know? Solitude to work in. For his health as well.'

'The West would suit him better, Texas and those places.' England rolled past: oblong fields, low hills, spires like needles. 'Dakota, anywhere. Harold says half his stories are about the West.'

'We did talk about it once. He says that when babies are born there, they take a great gulp of wind and then begin to *live*.'

'Much like they do everywhere.'

Afterwards, when Kate was describing the day to Harold, feeding his appetite for stories about the Cranes that proved their peculiarity, she felt uneasy. A better friend would have shown more sympathy for whatever it was that Cora desired so badly. But Harold was grouchy – there must have been arguments about money at Hammersmith – and she knew she could soothe him with Brede Place, letting him indulge his view of Stephen and Cora as children.

It was like bedtime stories – he was still hungry for them when he appeared in her room in his pyjamas and put his head meekly on the pillow, breathing into her hair. 'What does she really want, that Cora?' he said, after a preliminary fumble with Kate's nightdress that showed no sign of leading anywhere.

She decided to tell him a story that Cora had confided, about an English nobleman of the seventeenth century called Sir George Crane. A genealogist at the College of Heralds charged her three guineas for looking into the history.

'You are making this up,' said the sleepy voice.

'On my honour.'

Sir Georgie was in circulation about 1620, and the idea was that his collaterals, if persisted with, might lead them to a family of Cranes who might have emigrated to America; details were meagre at present, but if the correct authorities were consulted, the spidery writings properly deciphered and the requisite flow of guineas guaranteed, Stevie might (another 'might') find himself inheriting the title and turning into a baronet.

'Priceless,' said Harold, half asleep.

'I believe Stephen told her to drop it. But you know Cora. It would make her a Lady when they're married.'

'Glass coaches,' he mumbled, 'diamond tiaras. God save the Queen. Tell me it again. Good girl . . .'

She watched him sleep, afraid for the future. He did too much; wrote too many articles for the cable-office and the impatient editors in New York; filled too many hours brooding over the novels that were supposed to make him more famous than Stephen, who unfortunately was years younger; gave himself headaches trying to manage his work, his money, his women.

If comforting him meant being disloyal to Cora, it was a pity but it couldn't be helped. Kate would have done worse deeds than that.

6

Queenie went to prison for six months. Her apartment in Maddox Street was taken over by a fur-importer. Blanche, the girl who cut her wrists, was soon out of the nursing home – Fred made it his business to inquire, and was told she had left without telling anyone. Crime was all loose ends. Nothing was final. Blanche and her pals from Maddox Street would be redeploying, like soldiers after a skirmish. Queenie would pop up again. Wilk the engraver was etching a copper plate somewhere and looking for a bent printer.

The American case was still undealt-with, a fading hope. Fred perked up when the New York Pinkerton's said that a woman called Crane had been accused the winter before last of bribing a police officer in Tallahassee, the State capital of Florida. The charge was dropped. It wasn't even certain that she was the correct woman. 'I told 'em to try some more,' said Davis, 'but they're awful busy. You wouldn't credit the crime scene in the United States right now. Hope it never comes your way.'

'My point exactly,' said Fred.

He could prod about on the edges, but a full-scale investigation would need to be sanctioned, and he had nowhere near enough evidence. To be honest, he had no evidence at all. Even his private inquiries were not without risk. As an experienced detective, half the things one did could pass unnoticed. But you were never sure.

He thought no one had noticed his failure to watch the window at Seven Dials, thus allowing Wilk to escape, but he was wrong. When he attended at Scotland Yard for his triennial review, the Head of Detectives expressed disappointment.

'You are supposed to be one of our best men,' said the H.o.D. He was putting seed from a paper packet into a cage that contained a silent canary. 'It was an elementary mistake.'

'Unforgivable, sir.'

'Watchfulness, Hooper. Do you keep a cage bird?'

'Sir?'

'They never cease to watch. His little eye is fixed on me when I open a window. And on the window. If he were outside the cage, he would be through it in an instant. Gone. Be like the canary, Hooper. Keep alert.' He closed the cage. 'What do you have?'

'Sir?'

'At home, man, at home. It is important for me to picture an officer's circumstances. There is no Mrs Hooper, I gather.'

'Died some years ago, sir.'

'You are not in debt? Police officers are not allowed to be in debt, you know.'

'No, sir.'

'No fast living? A wife is a steadying influence.'

'My sister manages the domestic side. Shall I mention a canary to her, sir?'

'It would do no harm.'

It became a standing joke. 'Have you fed him, Freddie dear?' Belle would say of the non-existent bird, inviting such replies as

'He's up the chimney,' or 'He bit me. He's not having anything till he sings.'

Fred had one last go at the American woman. When a busy spell of night work came up, trying to catch cheque-smashers operating in the West End, he managed to fit in an hour of personal observation at Milborne Grove, to see who came and went. Nobody did. The house was unlit. At two o'clock in the morning he found himself having to show his warrant card to a suspicious constable. That was the last straw.

After the cheque-smashing business (one arrest, shared with Tom Simmons), Fred wangled a rest day in the middle of the week. This meant a long lie-in, which he was enjoying until he woke to a series of thuds. It was the lodger, who was still there, dragging boxes downstairs. 'For pity's sake!' shouted Fred. The house went deathly quiet. As he fell asleep again he heard the front door close with a click, and a horse and cart drive away.

It was afternoon before he was fully conscious. He went downstairs to see if there was any cold ham left, and found a birdcage on the kitchen table with a card on top to say, 'With sincere apologies for my thoughtlessness. I know you have been contemplating a canary. Leonard Rukes.'

'He is trying to bribe us,' said Belle. 'He gave me that imitation pearl necklace, which I asked him not to, and that china rabbit, on which I have now drawn spectacles and two black teeth.'

'Don't forget the sanitary fish-fryer. Monjy thought that was capital. He's a keen young businessman, who has explained to me that he will be moving to permanent quarters once the stock-in-hand situation is clearer.'

'Whatever that means.'

'He is merely being friendly. Be fair. He has moved out boxes galore.'

'And moved in another lot. You are too lax, Freddie.'

'I am an absolute terror on duty. This is my other side, at home with my sister. Is there anything I can do to make you happier?'

'Tell him to go. He gets on my nerves. I caught him eyeing me one day.'

'What does that mean?'

'You know perfectly well. The glad eye. The roving eye. Mr Barrington-Jones, the floor-walker in hosiery, is another one of them. They make me sick. I'm not a piece of scenery.'

'Well, Sidney is coming round on Friday for the brass band, I believe, so that will put off Mr Rukes, should he have any designs on you, which is unlikely.'

'Thank you, Freddie, you give a girl no end of confidence.'

He didn't pretend to understand her, or any woman. He didn't need to, unless they committed crimes.

The Wandsworth town band was to play in the evening on Clapham Common. The weather was hot. Violet Crumm, keen on the arts, had suggested the outing and bought four programmes, price one penny, which acted as tickets and guaranteed fold-up wooden seats, the kind that caught your fingers if you weren't careful. Fred had no objection to music. One sat there and dozed.

He was late leaving the West End, Pinkerton's having sent a message to say a cable re the Florida suspect was in from New York, in cypher, and was being attended to. He went round to the Strand, prepared to wait for it, but found Davis struggling with the code-book. The cypher clerk had been taken ill suddenly ('London shellfish, without an r in the month, he ought to have known better'), and it would be Saturday at the earliest before Davis reached Hooper's cable and put it in plain English.

* * *

Miss Crumm and Belle were waiting in summer dresses, and so was Sidney the Kidney, who had brought a cushion with him.

'I suggest Sidney and Vi go in front,' said Belle. 'If he holds the cushion up to his chest, it will make it look ceremonial. You can lay your umbrella on it, Sidney.'

'I have been caught out by thunderstorms before now,' he said.

As they were leaving, Fred was surprised to see the lodger on the pavement, looking smarter than ever in a cream-coloured suit. Rukes raised his straw boater as they passed, making their way to the High Street, to catch an omnibus that had the common on its route.

The day's smoke and dust were dying down. 'I was afraid you wouldn't be back,' said Belle, taking Fred's arm.

'We could do with twice as many detectives.'

'You never talk about your work. I'd love to hear the gory details one day.'

'No you wouldn't.'

'I was putting a shirt for Mrs Monge to wash, and there was blood all over the cuff.'

'Must have cut myself.'

'Men have all the fun. If they had women policemen, I'd apply tomorrow.'

'I think you would.'

'Anything to get away from Arding & Hobbs. By the way, we're being followed. Sherlock Holmes would know at once.' She turned her head. 'Why are you following us, Mr Rukes?'

'More a case of going in the same direction, Miss Hooper. I happen to be making for Clapham Common.'

He caught up with them. The suit made his face darker and more melancholy. The boater was raised again, there was a small bow, then a quick shuffle of feet as he fell into step alongside Fred. The narrow pavement meant he was walking in the gutter. 'I am partial to open-air music,' he said. 'My reward after a busy week. May I tell you what I shifted?'

'Not interested, thanks,' said Belle.

'Please do,' said Fred.

'Much obliged. One gross of alarm clocks, three canvas tents, a hundred of shiny bracelets, a hundred of quality hair-combs, two hundred of toby mugs, three gross of clay pipes and one box of clockwork mice imported from the United States for the purpose of giving young ladies frights. I would set it to music if I could.'

Belle was determined not to be amused. Was it simply the lodger, or did she have other troubles? Women were well-known for having troubles in categories that men didn't know about. Fred worried about his sister: the thin, quite pretty face, the eccentric way of thinking that wouldn't settle down, that made the likes of Sidney keep their distance.

They shoved their way on to a bus and proceeded to Clapham, joining the throngs that converged on the band-stand. Peeling green chairs were drawn up in two quadrants with an aisle of grass down the middle. Bandsmen in black coats and tall hats were already in position. The audience hummed with noise but was well-behaved, mainly clerks and artisans from the neighbourhood accompanied by their wives: what Fred saw as a typical English crowd, not one of those Continental mobs that he read about in the *Daily Mail*.

The order of sitting was Rukes, Fred, Belle, Sidney, Violet. Sidney placed his cushion in the small of his back for maximum relief, and when the National Anthem was played to begin proceedings, he stood clutching it to himself. Fred stood stiffly to attention, and was pleased to see that Rukes did too, boater held across his chest like a shield.

As the music got under way, the louder pieces sending pigeons and crows flapping around the sky, he settled down to doze to the sound of familiar tunes, bits of *Gondoliers* and *Pirates*, marches he had paraded to as a recruit, a waltz that Florence had been fond of.

Married life was as distant as boyhood, but the summer evening brought her back. They came here once, to the common, to hear a military band. He had forgotten it till this minute.

Half awake, he dug out the memory. Hadn't they arrived early? Sat near the front? Must have done, because Flo was close enough to be struck with a lad in a tight blue uniform who played the cornet. 'Look at him, smart as a pin,' she said. Hair like straw stuck out from under his pillbox hat. Later on she acted strangely, not for any reason he could see. Sad face. Tears when they were in bed.

'You must tell me what the matter is,' he ordered. 'I don't like tears, Flo. Tell me what's up.'

It was nothing, she said. But tears went on appearing in the candlelight. He wormed it out of her. It was the cornetist. She knew a boy who looked like him at Sunday school when she was a girl, that was all. Fred was mystified. 'I was soft on him,' she said. 'I used to save sweets in the week and give them to him.'

'And what happened to this paragon?'

'He joined the Army. I heard afterwards he was killed in Khartoum or somewhere.'

'You never told me.'

'There was nothing to tell. He wasn't my sweetheart or anything. He was just a boy in Sunday school.'

Fred gave up and the boy was never referred to again.

The concert was ending. The band obliged with an encore, a rendering of 'After the Ball'.

Show-offs in the audience picked up the tune. 'Many a heart is aching,' they sang, 'If you could read them all . . .'

Rukes himself had a go, slightly off-key, 'Many the hopes that have vanished, After the ball.'

Belle said, 'Did you have a nice sleep, Freddie dear?'

It was almost dark. People were drifting away. Sidney was squashing midges between his palms. Youths made paper darts from programmes and threw them at girls, who pretended not to notice.

Horseplay started as the crowd broke up. 'This way!' called Fred, but a moment later discovered he was only leading Sidney. Young lads were jostling and whistling. Girls squealed 'Push off!' and 'Does your mother know you're out?'

It was merely English high spirits. Fred was still in the grip of memory. How many years since his wife wept about nothing? He saw Miss Crumm borne one way and the lodger's creamy suit going backwards. Belle he couldn't see at all.

As he tried to pick her out, a gang of boys charged towards a knot of hats and blouses, which squealed and ran, but not too quickly. 'Give us a kiss!' yelled a boy.

'That's enough of that!' called Fred.

The crowd had become shapeless, a mass of shadows. The wave of lads swept on, and a moment later, from another direction, a woman screamed. It was a proper scream, not someone larking about.

'Make way!' he shouted. 'Police officer!'

He thought of Belle. Dismissed the idea. Saw a shape with two other shapes in attendance, and an outer ring of onlookers. Found it was Belle after all. Took her from a sturdy fellow with a watch-chain and a wife. Embraced her. Found her undamaged but shaking.

'Disgraceful,' said the watch-chain. They were close by when she screamed. They saw a man running, with another man in pursuit.

Fred knew that a police officer should have had more sense. Because Belle was sharp and self-contained, it didn't guarantee her safety. Sidney was about as much use as a stick of sealing-wax.

'You can tell another detective about it if you don't want to tell me,' whispered Fred. But that proved unnecessary. Rukes and his summer suit came out of the darkness, shoving a man in front of him.

'Makes me so angry,' said the lodger. 'Right, Mr Squirt. You are going to humbly beg this lady's pardon.' He whispered in Fred's ear: 'Saw him press up against Miss Hooper, sir, and put his hands around her anatomy. Won't do it again in a hurry.'

A gurgling noise came from the prisoner. Rukes lit a match. The man looked like a clerk or a shopkeeper, middle-aged, respectably dressed, smelling of beer. Blood still dripped from his nose and ran down his shirt-front. The jaw was lopsided. Red moustaches were scrawled around the mouth.

''ery 'orry,' was all he could manage.

Fred had no quarrel with rough justice when circumstances warranted. Few police officers would have. Charging him was out of the question, since that might mean Belle going to court. A pair of constables were found to take him to hospital. No questions would be asked, or if they were, they wouldn't be answered.

Belle was silent, looking at no one, except when Sidney offered her his arm, and she half smiled and shook her head.

Violet suggested taking her home to stay the night.

'Excellent,' said Fred, 'and I shall send a telegram to her workplace in the morning, to say she's not going in. You can spend the day together painting otters in the Wandle.'

'Or trousers. You're a brick, Mr Hooper.' Miss Crumm looked flustered, as if she had been too familiar.

Sidney and his cushion disappeared. Fred went back with the lodger.

Rukes was something of a mystery. 'Boxed a bit when I was young,' he explained.

'You're young now. You didn't half give him one.'

'Can't abide to see a woman distressed, Mr Hooper. Thought it was the least I could do, considering your kindness. You and Miss Hooper have been most patient with my comings and goings. I am glad to say that the stock-in-hand situation has been clarified. I have found premises. Everything will be carted off this weekend.'

'I shall be sorry to see you go.'

They were in the kitchen, where Rukes as usual remained hovering, reluctant to settle. 'It has been like a home to me,' he said.

Fred was amused by him. He made a change. 'You have only been here a few weeks.'

'Were I to tell you,' cried Rukes. His hanging lock of hair was almost in his eye. 'I have led a lonely existence since the age of thirteen – family troubles, matters I never discuss, paddling my own canoe. One puts a bold face on things. But I have felt at home here.'

'What about Mrs Monge? She's your aunt. I know her house is crowded, but she could have fitted you in.'

'Children, you see. Too many of 'em there. Due to my peculiar upbringing, I have a constitutional dislike of children. And may I tell you a secret? Mrs Monge is my aunt by marriage only, and I must admit I have never encountered a Mr Monge, who was the brother of a stepfather I never met. There are mysteries about families best not gone into. Which is by the way. My point is this. You and Miss Hooper

71

have suited me down to the ground. But all good things come to an end.'

'So what are your plans?'

'I have been looking at lodgings. I found one with odoriferous drains. Another where the man kept pigeons, which are unlucky birds. I shall persevere.'

'Stay here,' said Fred, feeling fatherly, and sorry for someone with such a confused family history, and Rukes replied, without hesitating, 'Thank you very much. Would you like a canary for the cage?'

Belle, when she heard the news next day, said she was moving out and going to live permanently with Vi's family, if they would have her. But it was only talk. After the incident on Clapham Common she spoke of Rukes in a different way. 'I am a tiny bit frightened of him,' she said, without any sign of fear.

The incident itself wasn't dwelt on. When Fred suggested she might like to see the local quack, Belle said, 'No harm was done,' adding that it only lasted seconds.

'It's all very well being brave. I've seen women deeply affected, especially if unmarried.'

'Silly old Freddie,' she said. 'I had a pair of stockings pinched off the line once by somebody who came in from the lane. I mean, I do know the sort of things men get up to.'

'A serious assault of that nature is not a laughing matter.'

'I'm sorry, of course it isn't. I was very grateful to Mr Rukes. And to you, and everybody.'

But somehow she went on not being properly disgusted. Fred added it to his collection of unpredictable behaviour by women.

On Saturday, late in the evening, came news of his American suspect. A bicycle messenger brought the transcribed cable from Pinkerton's, and a note in Davis's hand to say, 'News re the Florida person. Thought you should see it instanter.'

Belle and Violet were painting in the parlour. Rukes was upstairs with the canary he had bought in Wandsworth High Street, trying to make it sing.

Fred settled down with a glass of lemonade, reading quickly and then going back to certain passages, smiling to himself, humming bits of the tune from the concert, 'Many the hopes that have vanished, Af-ter the ball.'

Before retiring he went outside with a cup of salt for the slugs. 'Evil beasts,' he said.

7

Cora was on her way to a country weekend in Kent, at a house she hoped would offer useful tips towards life at Brede Place. Harold and Kate were taking her. A husband and wife called Bollitt had invited the Frederics at short notice, and Harold, out of kindness – out of pity? – asked if they could bring a Mrs Crane along.

Cora has no objection to being added on like a postscript, any more than she resents being taken for jaunts to restaurants or being invited to a month in Ireland, at Inchgela on Bantry Bay, where Harold, man of many connections, knows a wealthy woman who owns a house she rarely visits. They were all there the year before. According to Kate, Harold needs a holiday. A second visit is planned for the fall, but Cora knows that long before that, Stevie will be back in England. Then she will no longer be a woman at a loose end.

Waiting for Stephen is something she does proudly. She wants to give it dignity, to give no sign that she questions *why* he rushed off to Cuba in the spring, *why* he visited New York, *why*, now that the Spanish are collapsing and the war will soon be over, he remains in those southern waters, writing despatches, silent in her direction. She accepts his absence, accepts the social perception that without a man at her side she is lamed, not in working order. Mathilde is available, but having her in tow only emphasises the absence of the man.

So on the train for Sevenoaks, locked into a first-class compartment by the guard in return for Harold's sixpence, there were just the three of them.

'Don't expect too much in the way of high society,' said Harold. It was a Saturday morning; women with live chickens and baskets of roses waited on platforms, going to market. 'I only met Bollitt a few weeks ago, and he has already informed me what repairs cost to the roof. Which isn't what an English gentleman is supposed to talk about. Not that I blame him talking about money. These big properties suck it up like a sponge. Beware of a house with more than five bedrooms. Cora wouldn't agree, would you?'

'I told him about Brede Place,' said Kate.

'So what's wrong with Ravensbrook, Cora?'

'It's perfect if what you want is a stockbroker's villa. But the English have the sense to live in nice country houses whenever they can. I am only following the custom. I am only doing what Stephen wants.'

'He should be in England in a month. Six weeks at the outside. Have you heard from him direct since the Spanish started running?'

'His letters are delayed.'

'Or he's too busy chasing the last man to surrender or the last man to have his legs blown off to write 'em.'

'I'm sure you're right,' said Cora.

She was used to finding comfort where she could. The Bollitts' mansion, Cranleigh Hall, was big enough to swallow four Bredes, but there were things to be noted – crunchy gravel and a boy with a rake standing by; the loose gown and cool hands of Sarah Bollitt, who waved aside a servant to greet them herself at the wide-open door; a big table immediately inside, littered with a convivial debris of caps, books, flasks, tennis-racquets, newspapers.

There wasn't much point in eyeing the system of hot-water radiators (newly installed, expense no object), or the electric lights, or even the luscious wild-silk curtains in Cora's suite. What she drew from the house was its style, the flowers like rolled flags in vases wherever you looked (she would harvest them daily in Sussex), the conservatory where peaches could be picked like blackberries (Brede Place was south-facing), the amiable way guests drifted in and out.

'We are a mixed bag,' said Mrs Bollitt, laughing, as if the arrangements were beyond her control. An ageing Lord Plumb was included in the bag, hairy-nostrilled and chatty, and a withered Lady Plumb, who didn't care for the heat. Mrs Tourbon, probable age fifty and a bit, was the widow of a banker; pursed lip, sharp tongue. Her son Charles, probable age twenty-six or -seven – the same as Stephen – was evidently a banker in embryo; fine linen suit and a flickering eye that rested on Cora's face, neck and breasts, and back again. Two further guests, the Miltons, who lived beyond a wood, were coming in for dinner.

Guests at Ravensbrook were mostly scribblers, friends or hangers-on of Stevie, but American authors or any authors at all were unlikely to be on the guest-list at Cranleigh. Satisfying, then, to be asked by Mrs Bollitt if *the* Stephen Crane was her husband, and be taken to the library where a case inscribed 'Fiction' in gold letters included English editions of two books by Stevie, the famous *Red Badge* and the rather less famous *Maggie: A Girl of the Streets*. Bollitt himself, a little orb of a man with chins, referred proudly to books as 'Mrs Bollitt's hobby', and said he hoped that Mr Crane would write a story about an ironworks, for which he would offer every facility.

Lunch was a picnic under awnings. Afterwards the men wandered off. Charles went to row on the lake. (Would Mrs Crane accompany him? Mrs Crane would not.) Arthur Plumb and his host went to inspect the new pumps and boilers underground. Harold borrowed a shotgun to go rough shooting, and said he was taking Kate with him; he sounded belligerent, as though waiting for someone to say 'How American!', but no one paid any attention.

Cora rested half-naked in her bedroom; changed to a square-cut frock for tea in a drawing room whose blinds were closed against the sun; was steered by Mrs Bollitt towards the subject of her famous husband. Lady Plumb and Mrs Tourbon were there, and so was the young Tourbon, back early because the boat leaked. He sat not taking his eyes off Cora, chewing scones, crossing and recrossing his legs.

Why not enjoy the company? She let herself be drawn into anecdotes. A mysterious figure took shape, a man apart, travelling in search of adventures that he could turn into stories, wandering through the American West, seeing a man shot dead in the snow in Nebraska, watching a sheriff take his bride home to a town in Texas where a deranged gunman is on the loose.

Were these events that young Mr Crane actually witnessed, or did he make them up for his books? Cora didn't say. The audience paid attention, all except Charles, who seemed to be trying to see through her dress as she presented the next scene – Mr Crane in New York City.

This was presumably factual because it came with names and dates. He was outside a restaurant late one night in September 1896 when he saw a detective arrest a chorus girl called Dora Clark who said she had done nothing wrong. The girl laid a complaint against the detective, Mr Crane backed her up, he gave evidence in public before the Police Commissioner, they tried to blacken his character. It was in the New York papers for days – 'Novelist Crane Risks All to Save a Woman.' He made enemies.

Mrs Bollitt's tea-party was impressed, except that Mrs Tourbon said, 'And what had she done, this little innocent Dora?'

'The police accused her of being a prostitute.'

There was a silence. Mrs Bollitt said, 'I am glad we are sufficiently enlightened not to close our minds to the Social Evil. I think it was a very wonderful thing for your husband to do.'

'Exemplary,' agreed Mrs Tourbon. 'Though it does rather depend on whether the woman was or wasn't what the detective accused her of.'

'Who are we to condemn?' said Mrs Bollitt, rather feebly, and the matter dropped.

Dinner was the next landmark, and Kate had an armful of clothes sent along to Cora's suite, so they could help one another dress. A bruised shoulder was making Kate wince, Harold having insisted she try for a rabbit. He said it was her own fault for not holding the gun properly.

Kate knew it was all in the mind, but at the same time the skin was going purple. 'I know, I know,' she said. 'Christian Science is very difficult. Some days I believe in it, others I don't.' She looked at herself in the triptych of mirrors; then at Cora standing beside her. 'Harold is in a vile temper. The Bollitts have none of his books in the library.'

'He only has to mention it to her, and she'll have them all sent down from Hatchards.'

'That isn't the point, is it?' said Kate, and Cora, who knew what writers were like, agreed that it wasn't.

When everyone assembled in the drawing room before dinner, Charles Tourbon made straight for her and Kate, and said he hoped they were to have more tales about the Bohemian Mr Crane. 'In that case I must rescue my wife,' said Harold, 'who has heard them before,' and he steered her towards Sarah Bollitt so they could talk about his novels.

'A no-nonsense chap, Mr Frederic,' said Charles. 'What interests me about your husband is you. I see you as the other side of his stories. Do you object to my doing that?'

She knew these budding men of the world who thought they were born with the gift of charming women out of their clothes. 'If it makes you happy,' she said. 'It sounds innocent enough.'

He looked down at his legs. 'I suppose you never accompany him on his travels?'

'I have done.' Cora hadn't intended to say any more about Stevie. But she loved to talk about the Greek adventure. The Plumbs came to listen as yet another Crane emerged, a man who understood the futility of battles, who heard civilians shouting 'Hurrah for war!', then saw a wounded soldier resting his head on a corpse. (Lord Plumb: 'My father saw butchery in the Crimea.')

'He rescued a puppy from a battlefield but it succumbed to the English weather.' (Lady Plumb: 'I'm glad Americans are fond of dogs.')

Cora wanted them to grasp the plainness and endurance of this unvarnished Mr Crane. 'He sent despatches to his newspaper when he was too ill to write,' she said. 'He had dysentery, poor lamb.'

Lady Plumb turned away. Charles said, 'A graphic detail, Mrs Crane.'

'A plain word for a plain illness.'

'And here they are,' said Mrs Bollitt.

The air was cooling at last. The Miltons said they had walked across the fields. They consisted of a retired General, gone to fat, and a straight-backed wife, still on active service.

'And here is someone you must meet,' said Mrs Bollitt.

'But we've met,' said Mrs Milton. 'Mrs Stewart, what a pleasant surprise.'

Cora had a faint memory of a luncheon at Harrington Gardens for officers' wives. 'I am known these days as Mrs Crane,' she said.

'Oh, I see.' It seemed to Cora that they were the only ones talking in the room. The woman said, 'Is Mr Crane here?'

'He is in Cuba at the moment. Or thereabouts.'

After that they went in to dinner with miraculous speed, and she found herself seated between Lord Plumb, who talked exclusively to Kate on the other side, and the General, who had evidently missed the fact that they had a scarlet woman in their midst.

'So what is your husband doing in Cuba?' he asked, when they had got past the Tortue Verte des Indes, and for the third time that day she trotted out the figure of Stevie, who, to suit the occasion, was now the daring newspaper correspondent in the thick of the fighting; strutting up and down the battle-lines in a trench-coat; complaining because the American Springfield rifles smoked like brush fires and gave themselves away; laughing at the Spanish shrapnel shells that exploded in the wrong places because the fuses were set too long.

'He sounds like a soldier himself,' said the General, towards the end of the long meal, when they were at the Fondu de Camembert and the fruit. 'I should like to meet him myself one day.'

'And I,' said Charles, who had been listening. 'A man's man, would you say, Mrs Crane?'

'You must come and see us in Sussex, General. We shall be moving there later this year.'

When the ladies left the table, Charles delayed her with some nonsense about joining him on the terrace for a cigar, and listening for an alleged nightingale in the woods. A maid showed her upstairs. The women were in a retiring room, all nooks and corners, pale-lit with candles. The chain clanked in a lavatory beyond. Voices murmured from around the angle of a wall, and she caught the word 'Stewart'.

General's wife and banker's widow smiled at her. 'Do join us,' said Mrs Tourbon.

'You must be dying of curiosity.'

'I am *never* curious. Mrs Milton and I were talking about the new colours. If one can't afford a variety of costumes, and I'm sure *I* can't, the couturiers are suggesting a dark green or a purple.'

Cora stood looking down at the two, disliking them, disliking herself. 'I hate being whispered about. Captain Stewart is a silly, worthless man to whom I feel no moral obligation.'

'One makes one's bed and lies in it,' said Mrs Milton, getting up, very erect; all she needed was a rifle.

Sarah Bollitt tried to sweep everyone out to safety, saying it was time they rejoined.

Banker's widow accompanied General's wife. Cora spoke to their backs. 'There are thousands in my position. I meet them all the time. They come and stay at houses like this, waiting to be singled out.' She felt Kate's hand on her arm. 'Is that right?' she called. 'Is that civilised?'

It was a disaster. Kate implied she had been a fool not to keep quiet, and said they would be wondering about her and Harold by now.

Telling her she was imagining things didn't help. She was in tears. 'You all but told them we aren't married.' More 'Kate, Kate!' only produced the accusation that Cora never thought of anything but her and Stephen. 'They always think the worst of American women,' she said. 'Well, Cora, you've managed to smash up the weekend.'

It was the quarrel with Kate that upset her most. Kate excused herself because of the shotgun bruise, but Cora stayed late, determined to sparkle. The hostess encouraged her; the other women had to follow her lead, and were probably curious as well, now that they knew her secret. Cora amused them with tales of domestic life in America (inventing bits where necessary), then giving way to the men and agreeing with what they said (nonsense, a lot of it), even playing some inexpert Chopin on the piano.

Without Stevie she had to put on acts. The weekend had reduced itself to a series of acts, performed with the sole purpose of keeping herself going. When the party broke up it was almost midnight, but she wasn't tired, and she used the stationery provided in her suite to write a few lines for copying into her manuscript book. In Cuba it was early evening. What was he doing at this second? She tried to visualise the cigarette stuck to his lip, the cowboy boots with dust on them. All she could see was a silhouette without a face.

Someone tapped at the door. She said, 'Come', and the banker's son put his head round. Even for a tipsy banker's son, this was silliness on a grand scale. 'How dare you!' she said, and rang for a servant, but he hung on, half in the room, saying that all he wanted was a chat. He was puzzled by her Mr Crane, who one minute was describing war as madness, and the next was marching up and down battlefields, trying to get himself killed.

'He is a puzzling man,' said Cora. 'Therein lies the attraction. Now run off before I tell your Mama.'

In the morning Kate wasn't at breakfast. Harold was there, scowling at a coffee-pot. The only bright spot was Sarah Bollitt, who made a point of getting Cora into the library and saying that she must visit them again, this time with her husband, whom she was careful to describe as 'your husband, Stephen'.

One or two guests discussed going to church; others planned walks. There was an absurd encounter with Harold, who cornered her by the peaches in the conservatory, and told her she had made a bad situation worse. Kate, in the background, wouldn't talk to Cora, who said, 'Don't let him intimidate you.' That did nothing except annoy Harold; which was something.

Cora stayed for lunch, then slipped away for Sevenoaks and the train, courtesy of Mrs Bollitt, who made the arrangements. No one saw her go except the wretched banker's son. He appeared on the gravel, just in time to blow a kiss at the carriage.

The heatwave persists for weeks. Mathilde Rudy, temporarily in charge of the household whenever Ma goes off on her own, is exercising her authority to have Adoni bring her a weak Bourbon and water; sitting on a sofa in the drawing room, bare-legged, reading *Tit-Bits*; Ma gone for the day to visit the family called Garnett down the road at Limpsfield, another of the literary set who swarm about this part of England, gabbling to one another about unfinished masterpieces and tight-fisted publishers.

The only writer Mathilde has taken to in England is a black-bearded Polish gentleman called Joseph who came from Essex in the spring with his wife Jessie and a baby. He kissed her hand and said she had the eyes of beauties he used to see in the South Seas, when he was captain of a steamship.

'Can I sit with you, Mrs Rudy?' asks Adoni.

'Certainly not.'

'Does your book have pictures of laughing?'

'It is called a humorous magazine.'

She turns the pages. Adoni perches inside the door on a stool.

'Will Mr Crane come home?'

'Once the war in Cuba is over.'

'He was at New York. I also will be at New York. Is it true they put cross of Christ into river on Christmas, and Greek boys jump in and find for one hundred dollars?'

'Probably not. How do you know about Mr Crane?'

'I keep ears open, like Mrs Crane tell me, to help speak English good. At New York is pretty actress. Who is Amy?'

The boy smiles innocently.

'If you work for someone, you hear all sorts of things. But you keep your trap shut. This is your trap.' She points at her mouth.

'Sure, sure. You have nice trap, Mrs Rudy.'

He isn't a boy at all, with his bow-tie and smudge of moustache. Voices had been raised about Amy all right. It happened after Christmas, when the house was full of bills. Money that Mr Crane was expecting from America didn't arrive because a New York actress said it was owing to her. Mathilde never got to the bottom of it. But she heard Ma say in a temper, 'I don't want to know who Amy Leslie is, but kindly get her off your back. You haven't been honest with me.' To which Mr Crane replied, 'Never said I was honest, Cora. Only said I was as honest as my weaknesses permit.'

These outbursts were rare. Ma knew the wisdom of letting men feel powerful by having secrets, which were always predictable; like little boys stealing toffee from a tin, she said once to Mathilde. But that was in Florida, before Mr Crane came on the scene.

'What is a tit bit?' asks Adoni.

'Something small, something nice, I guess.'

He creeps over and she pretends to be surprised to find him kneeling a yard away, trying to read the back of a page.

'I order you to go back to your pantry this minute,' says

Mathilde. 'Go on. Bad dog! I shall tell Mrs Crane what a nuisance you've been.'

'Most kindly Mrs Rudy. Tell me this pictures,' and a long delicate finger prods the paper.

'I am not a schoolteacher, and if I was I would make you stand up straight in a corner with a dunce's cap on, and all the girls in the class would laugh at you.'

'Please?' says the grown-up boy, looking puzzled. His finger keeps tapping *Tit-Bits*.

Mathilde sips her whisky and water and gazes through the window. England has little appeal for her, too parochial, too chilly, too old-fashioned, too unhygienic; when they came to Ravensbrook they found that the previous occupants had pasted thick paper over the ventilator in the dining room.

A white cloud drifts through the trees, as a cart trundles along the powdery Sevenoaks road beyond the garden. She pictures herself at Jacksonville, setting out in the victoria with Ma. Benjie the Negro coachman holds the reins, and the steep southern sun makes their parasols glow like lamps. Men look their way; soft-brimmed hats are raised. An evening breeze sets in from the east, from the sea. Mathilde could weep at how distant it all is.

'Adoni, you are a regular nuisance,' she says. 'They are pictures of . . . interesting things. You see this word here? "Cu-ri-osities." It says they are drawn from photographs, so people will know they are real. Do you follow?'

He looks at her admiringly. 'Yes, yes, Mrs Rudy.'

'It says that this is "a remarkable speaking-trumpet" and comes from Dorset, which is in England somewhere.' The drawing shows a tube with wings at the end. It could be anything. "It is used to call in labourers from the fields." Do you understand?'

'And this?'

A dead mouse, looking strangely clean-shaven, with its tail standing up at right-angles to its body, lies across what appear to be two lengths of string. '"An unfortunate mouse,"' she reads. '"The creature was electrocuted by electric-light wires at a house in Ealing, London W."'

'So these are laughing pictures,' says Adoni, and grins. By some means he has arrived beside her on the sofa.

'You have a lot to learn,' says Mathilde.

His hand rests on hers. *Tit-Bits* slides to the floor.

August without Crane dragged on. Cora sat where he sat, in the study, planning diversions.

'Ma?' she heard. 'Are you all right?'

'You can come in.'

'Brooding again,' said Mathilde, in the doorway.

'Put your hat on, go up to town and fetch a hamper from Fortnum & Mason's.'

'I hate London in hot weather.'

'Kindly do as you're told. Make sure it has game pie, French cheeses, bottled pears and three bottles of Bollinger champagne. It will go on Mr Crane's account. I shall give you a written authority for the manager, and a letter to post to Mrs Conrad. I intend to spend a few days with them. You remember the Conrads?'

'The Polish gentleman with gout.'

'The novelist would be a better description. You took a fancy to him. I always know when you take a fancy to a man. It makes you sly.'

The colour ran into Mrs Rudy's neck.

'If you behave yourself I shall take you with me to Essex, where they live. Otherwise I shall take Adoni so he can improve his English at railroad stations.'

The hamper was not for the Conrads. She had a box of toys

earmarked for Borys, their child of six months. Champagne and game pie were to tempt a greedy man. Stevie would have twisted his mouth and said, 'Aw, t'hell with it,' but she was doing it because of Kate, the greedy man's woman, not the greedy man himself.

Cora hadn't seen her since the weekend at the Bollitts' that ended in tears. It was no way for friends to behave, but all Cora could get from her was a note to say she was trying to persuade Harold to see a healer about his fatigue, and at present he needed her full attention.

In retrospect Cora had to admit that she might have managed things better at Cranleigh Hall – keeping her mouth shut would have helped – but Mrs Milton couldn't have been foreseen. What upset Harold was being reminded of the thin social ice they walked on.

There he was, with a loving mistress and three small children down in Surrey, and a somewhat less loving wife and four more in Hammersmith, a famous foreign correspondent who was himself the subject of magazine articles. They even printed photographs of the powerful face and well-filled waistcoat. Stevie had left a magazine on his desk that showed Harold against a wall of books, like a bronze head of a Roman tyrant except he had a pipe in his mouth. A wiggly line in Stevie's pencil ran down an accompanying paragraph that said, 'He lives a severe and disciplined life, taking little amusement beyond a daily visit to his club, and rarely going to the theatres. "I live wholly to myself because I like to live an unshackled life," said Mr Frederic.' That got two wiggly exclamation marks.

Crane, too, had his fears of moral condemnation. When it came to defending Dora Clarke and defying the New York Police Department, he knew he was opening himself to public scrutiny.

In Jacksonville, where Cora first encountered him two months later, he was still buoyed up with his defiance of what he saw as corrupt and hypocritical policemen. As expected, his own behaviour had been scrutinised. Police lawyers implied that he had smoked opium and lived with loose women. He said it was the writer's duty to dig about in awkward places and find the truth.

But there was evidently truth and truth. When it came to making a common-law wife out of Cora Stewart, he kept the secret as close as possible. Was it something deeper and graver than fear of offending his family: that he had dug about in himself and found another truth, this time nearer the bone, that Cora Stewart was not the woman he wanted to marry even if he could? Was that the real concealment?

If Cora wanted to talk about this with anyone, it had to be Kate, and Kate was under Harold Frederic's thumb. That was why she needed the hamper.

Her telegram said 'CLEAR DECKS FOR SURPRISE CHAMPAGNE PICNIC WITH CORA TOMORROW WEDNESDAY I SHALL BE AT KENLEY AT 10 PLEASE NO ARGUMENTS'.

The slate roof was still wet after a thunderstorm in the night when she arrived at the house. Kate answered the door to a background of child-noise and carbolic-smell. A kitchen drain had blocked and the housemaid was telling Barry to keep away or else. It was like a diversionary tactic to get Cora inside without Harold noticing.

The eyes were inflamed. 'Was I supposed to plead with you by telegram not to come? You can be just as difficult as he is. I am caught in the middle. I can't change Harold's mind. I can't stop him being Harold.'

'Stop feeling sorry for yourself and let me talk to him.'

'He's dictating letters to the secretary. Please go away. It only makes things worse.'

They were in the drawing room. A teddy-bear lay face down on the sofa.

'A day out will do him good.'

'He doesn't have days out any more. You think it's all so easy. "Let's have a picnic," and the sun begins to shine. You're lucky, you glide through life. He doesn't and nor do I, more's the pity.'

'Try pretending to glide. You'll find it works.'

'Oh, Cora dear!' said Kate. 'It's all such a muddle.'

Reconciliation was hovering, and then Harold appeared, his heavy features regarding them from the doorway.

'Harold! You look quite yourself.'

'I am not aware of being anybody else, Cora. So where are you taking us? I have decided to bow to Kate's wisdom and stop working myself like an old drayhorse. Otherwise she will have one of her healers in, disguised as a seamstress, and I shall have mumbo-jumbo practised on me without my knowledge. Isn't that right, Kate?'

'Are you truly better?'

'Well enough for game pie and champagne. Secretary Stokes will come with us, too, if that's permitted. And the surprise?'

'Is a surprise. We have to be at Warlingham Station for the four minutes past eleven. The trap is outside, with extra umbrellas in case it rains again.'

But the overcast sky broke up to give splashes of sunlight, and by noon the train was approaching its destination – 'By the Thames' was all Cora would reveal.

So far it was the picnic party as planned, except for the addition of the secretary, a well-connected young man who spoke ironically of the General Post Office, for which he worked when it suited him; who said, 'Ah, Gravesend,' as the train was pulling in, 'they have a postmaster here who personally took delivery of a satchel of mail that a transatlantic steamer sent off by pinnace, which he managed to drop in the river.'

'What river is that?' said Harold, waking from a doze.

'It floated, fortunately for him, and there was a boatman with a hook.'

'Come along, we get out here,' said Cora, and Kate said in her ear, 'You are a marvel. I am happy for the first time in weeks.'

Was it as simple as that? Minus the men, she and Kate could have hidden themselves away in a teashop and discussed forbidden subjects. That would have been happiness. Today's business was a means to an end, a picnic to disarm Harold. It seemed to be working. As he summoned the station wagon, Cora whispered instructions to the driver, and they trundled past shops and drab houses before reaching a lane where figures in white could be seen in a field, beyond fences and trees.

'Cricket,' said Cora. 'It is the county of Kent playing the county of Somerset.'

'I never knew Cora had a sense of humour,' said Harold.

'I have arranged seats in the stand and they will supply jugs of boiling water, and rugs if it gets chilly. Robert Barr has told me all about the game. I think my friends at the American Women of London would approve.'

'Who are they when they're at home?' roared Harold.

'We are forming a society. If we want to know how our English cousins live, what better way than a cricket match?'

'Hear, hear!' said Stokes. 'Kent are doing well this season.'

'The ambassador's daughter is one of the leaders. Shall I put your name forward, Kate?'

'Kate has better things to do.'

'Leg-before!' cried Stokes. 'That umpire needs glasses.'

The stand was no more than a bank of benches under a

primitive roof of wood. Cushions had been provided, the old newspapers wrapped around the champagne had kept it moderately cool, and, at first, Cora was able to convince herself that the day was a success.

Nobody understood the game except Stokes, who was busy entering figures on a scorecard. The men in white did a certain amount of running about, but mostly they stood still, observed by a hundred or two spectators around the edges of the field. It was soothing, like watching the stream at Ravensbrook, ripples above and stillness underneath.

Harold was restless after they had eaten. He knotted a linen napkin and killed wasps with it. He groaned at the cricket. He asked what the picnic was *for*. Did Cora have news that she was keeping quiet about, that her beloved was on the boat from Cuba? He had bones to pick with Stephen. What was he doing, leaving his consort to be preyed upon by men like that young weasel Tourbon who was sniffing around her at the Bollitts'?

When Kate begged him to stop, and put her finger on his lips, he tried to bite it.

'I think we should go now,' said Cora.

'Stokes wants to stay. Take a letter, Stokey. Use the back of that card. To Mr Stephen Crane, address unknown. "Dear Stephen, I hope you have seen lots of shooting and dying, and are coming back to write a three-volume novel about it. Your first task is to destroy that dreadful 'Monster' story you wrote, the one about the Negro who lost his face when doing some improbably heroic deed. I have spoken about this to Kate, who is an educated woman, and she agrees with me that it will not enhance your reputation. We shall have a burning ceremony at Ravensbrook." Have you got all that, Stokey?'

'Why do you so hate the story?' asked Cora.

91

'Are we to have a literary discussion? Have we come all the way to Gravesend – Gravesend! – to talk about Stephen and his lack of maturity?'

She knew it would be wiser to 'make allowances', to believe that Harold was 'not himself'. But she had a sense of Harold never having been more himself.

She said, 'I guess you wish you'd written it, but you know you couldn't have.'

Hand-clapping came from around the field, and Stokes, who had moved away to the next bench with his scorecard, murmured, 'Splendid shot, sir.'

'She is only envious,' said Kate. Her face had gone white. 'She envies us. And the children she can't have. She doesn't know if Stephen is coming back. We ought to pity her.'

Without the services of John Scott Stokes, the return journey would have been even more difficult than it was. He purchased a travelling rug and some opiates for Harold, who complained that his head was hurting. He made sure Cora had a separate compartment on the train, and found a conveyance that would take her on from Warlingham.

Kate and Cora didn't look at one another in the station yard. Secretary Stokes shook hands and said, 'We shall meet again under happier circumstances.'

As the vehicle rattled up the broken path from the main road to Ravensbrook, Stephen's absence was like a shadow over the place. Perhaps she would shut it up and go to South Kensington. She might find more peace there.

Evening light came through the trees. Mathilde was outside the house, coming towards the vehicle, and Cora knew at once there must be good news. The hips swung, the eyes flashed – you could see why she was popular with men.

'Ma, Ma!' she was saying, 'there has been a burglar!'

It wasn't good news after all. Somehow it never was. But

even a burglar was better than the rift with Kate; Kate who couldn't help herself.

'Adoni has locked him in the washroom. I was out taking Sponge for a walk. He was banging and shouting but he has given up now.'

Cora was curious. Surely burglars didn't bang and shout? No one had been sensible enough to send for the Oxted policeman, so she went with Mathilde to the scullery, down steps at the back of the house, and found the butler poring over pictures in a tattered copy of *Tit-Bits*. He had Stevie's revolver on his lap.

'You have been told not to touch that.'

'The poor boy was protecting us all,' said Mathilde. 'The man was down by the stream. He was prowling, wasn't he, Adoni? He had a telescope, looking at the house.'

'I say, "You march in front or I kill you." He say, "I am policeman" and I say, "Ha ha, you are man in brown suit."'

'Is that Mrs Crane?' said a muffled voice.

They all stared at the washroom door.

'This is Cora Crane.'

'There has been a serious misunderstanding.'

'Why, Inspector Hooper,' she said, 'how nice of you to call.'

8

The visit was by way of a private reconnaissance. Ideally there would have been a search warrant, but you couldn't (worse luck) apply to a magistrate on the evidence Fred had so far. An informal trip to the village of Oxted when he could find a free day was the answer. Work tied him down for weeks, but he had to get a move on, because his leave was due for the last week in August.

He had confided in Tom Simmons, who was impressed. 'Fred, you're a marvel,' he said. 'Do you want me to come as well? Is this lady running an establishment for rural clients, do you suppose? Gentry who don't get up to town much? Croquet on the lawn, followed by misbehaviour upstairs?'

'I keep an open mind. Thanks for your offer, but I shall go alone. I shall take a pocket telescope and find an observation point.'

'I long to hear more.'

The house, Ravensbrook, was a fair size, but not set in rolling grounds as Fred had supposed. The garden, approached with caution from a highway, was unkempt and sloped down to a stream, from which the building could be glimpsed but not properly observed.

Eventually he found a rhododendron bush that provided cover and allowed him to view most of the house through the leaves. The last train up to Victoria stopped at Oxted shortly after eleven o'clock. That gave him a long stint through dusk and into the hours of darkness, keeping an eye on the windows.

Then a madman began firing a revolver into the stream, which so alarmed Fred that he jumped up and got a twig in his eye. The pain made him stumble and he fell over. When he recovered, the madman, who wasn't English, was pointing the gun at his head.

He was two hours and eight minutes in a damp room with whitewashed walls, sitting so still that spiders ran over the back of his hand. For company he had a copper boiler and a stone sink with a disagreeable smell. Fred knew the length of his incarceration exactly, thanks to Rukes's timepiece. Until the light went he could see a vegetable patch through a tiny window. It was full of weeds, like the rest of the garden. The run-down nature of the place was another hint that Mrs Crane was not what she appeared.

'You are very cobwebby,' said Cora. She had sent the others away before unlocking the door, to spare him embarrassment, and taken him into Stephen's study.

'I propose to overlook what happened earlier,' said the detective.

'I guess policemen like prowling. I don't want to make your life any harder, but it would be nice to know what you were prowling about *for*.'

'I take a particular interest in aliens. You might say it was one of my hobbies.'

'But I'm not an alien,' said Cora. 'I'm an American.' To show there was no ill feeling she reached over and detached a filament of web that he had missed on his shoulder.

'Why did you do that, Madam?'

'Don't want you looking untidy.' She couldn't decide how seriously she ought to take him. The fact that he was there at all was discouraging. 'It's about my poor Mrs Rudy, isn't it?'

'Your Mrs Rudy may turn out to be the tip of an iceberg.'

'We all misjudge people from time to time, Inspector. There isn't a wicked bone in Mathilde's body, I promise you. She came to me when she had domestic problems and I was managing a small business. She appears to be quite worldly, but she's really a simple girl from Ohio who's terrified of cities and should never have gone wandering about London when my back was turned. Have you really come about her?'

'She tried to pervert the course of justice by seducing a police officer.'

'You are making things up,' said Cora, and hoped she sounded convincing.

'We could still charge her. She might be deported. We have enough vice of our own without importing it from America.'

Cora tried another tack. 'Suppose you were right about her, that she had an aberration in the Haymarket. Why spend all this time over one poor creature? I recall reading that you have twenty-thousand prostitutes in London.'

'The public morality societies will say anything.'

'But you see what I'm getting at.'

He saw that Cora Crane was a woman you had to be careful with. He had noted it at their first meeting, and he knew more about her now. Poise was a quality that women aspired to, in his experience, but rarely achieved unless they were rich or had married powerful men; not that his job provided many opportunties for meeting dazzlers. There was an occasional Lady Somebody whose jewels had been pinched, an occasional pretty woman on the lines of Queenie Gerald who had learned to be unruffled.

Mrs Crane was poised without having any obvious advantages. Thick fair hair with a touch of auburn gave her a good start, even if she wasn't a beauty of the kind they had drawings of in the *Daily Mail*. But the little mouth and large eyes were lively. As for the cheekbones and forehead, they were so commanding that he wouldn't have minded the opportunity to arrest her on the spot, take her back to Vine Street, and apply caliper and ruler to her bony structures, after which he could classify her in Dr Bertillon's anthropometric system.

'Yours is a strong character,' he said.

'You sound like a fortune-teller. "You will go far, but beware of the man in your garden." Or is it a tactful way of putting an American in her place? I am not as ladylike as I might be, is that it?'

'It was just a remark.' The clever woman wasn't a category Fred had much time for. Her foreignness didn't help. 'Why do you have a firearm, Mrs Crane?'

'Is it illegal?'

'Not as such. A long-barrelled Colt, I believe. Unusual to find that in an English house.'

'It belongs to my husband. He goes rat-shooting with it. The game is to draw it from a holster and fire from the hip, all in one movement, which isn't easy. He usually misses. He'd be angry if he heard me say that.'

'Is he a violent man, your husband?'

'Wouldn't harm a fly. Only rats, when he's in the mood. Why do you ask?'

'Tell me about Jacksonville. I looked it up in an atlas.'

'I lived in Florida for a while.'

'It was in Jacksonville you met Mr Crane. The November of '96.'

'It's no secret,' said Cora, but the detail was too obscure for comfort. Somebody was picking about in her life. Perhaps he wasn't a police detective at all, but a man employed privately to spy on her. She thought of Donald, who was not decisive enough to go in for such a plan, and his brother Norman, who was. Wonderful, if true. It meant the Stewarts were seeking evidence for Donald to divorce her.

She said, 'How do I know who you are? I only have your word for it.'

He showed her his warrant card and wondered why she looked disappointed. 'We were talking about November '96.'

'The town was full of journalists hoping to get into Cuba. Mr Crane was one of them. The Cuban insurrection was on the boil, against the Spanish. The insurgents were running guns there, out of Jacksonville. This is like a history lesson, isn't it?'

'Mr Crane was mixed up in it, I believe.'

'Newspapermen have a tendency to become mixed up in things. I ought to know. I've been a newspaperwoman.'

The more he picked away at a period of her life that was over, the emptier she felt. The day had been bad enough already. The last she saw of Kate, she was wiping sweat from Harold's chin with a handkerchief, and the bridge of her spectacles seemed to be growing into the flesh.

'You kept a hotel in Jacksonville,' he said. 'A sort of hotel.'

'Come to the point, Detective Hooper. You have found out about my little venture. Very well. What would you like to know? It was smart and it was popular. We had high-class visitors. I only sold it so I could travel about Europe with my husband.'

'I believe it was called the Hotel de Dream.'

'I purchased it from a woman called Ethel Dreme, D-R-E-M-E. But the other Dream kind of took over.'

Conceivably the white balconies and red flowers were still

there, the entrance shaded by a signboard in gold, piano tunes to be heard in the street, cigar-smoke from poker games to be smelt. The woman she sold it on to had no style, and it might have gone to pot by now, cream-and-lilac bedrooms and all. Cora had never bothered to inquire. But this fellow must have done. In Jacksonville the police had been her friends. She couldn't see a friend in Detective Hooper.

'It was a house of assignation,' he said. 'A disorderly house.'

Cora had always been proud of it. She still was. 'It was a house for gentlemen to relax in. We served French wines. We had a cook from New Orleans who could do marvels with a guinea-fowl and a few potatoes. We had women who'd make you stop and look if you saw them in a streetcar. It was all legitimate. I never had trouble with the police.'

'You bribed them,' he said. 'Can't do that here, Mrs Crane.'

You had to hand it to her, she didn't prevaricate or swear, as suspects did when you cornered them. She used openness as a weapon. How long her nerve would hold when she saw the inside of a cell, when she had to sit for hours on a wooden chair answering questions about her activities in England, was another matter. But that was looking ahead.

'Tell me why you came to this country.'

'Mr Crane and I like England. It's no concern of yours.'

'Blame Mrs Rudy. I expect she worked for you in Jacksonville.'

'In a housekeeping capacity. Not what you are thinking.'

'Impossible to prove either way, I suspect. But she was undoubtedly importuning in London. No good smiling and shaking your head. Besides, there is more to it than Mrs Rudy. This Mr Crane visits your establishment – I am choosing my words – and a few months later you sell up and come to England with him. You live as his wife, but in fact you are still married to a Captain Stewart. The family bought you off,

I believe. I expect that's where you had the money to start the business.'

It was eerie, hearing a stranger plod through her life, someone who had information that could make no proper sense to anyone except the person it concerned. She clung to levity as being more dignified. 'I expect Scotland Yard has a special team of policemen investigating private morals. They must have their work cut out with the English aristocracy. My life is sober by comparison. I am amazed you are so interested.'

'It isn't only you. Women who keep houses like yours have a man in the offing. Now Mr Crane has vanished. Does he often go away?'

'You are – you must be the perfect English detective,' said Cora. She felt weak with rage but unable to shut out the comical thought of Stevie as a pimp. 'Mr Crane is a writer. He is an open book. You are priceless, Detective Hooper.'

'He is pretty much the Bohemian, your Mr Crane. He spoke up for a prostitute in New York and denounced the police. In due course I look forward to meeting him. Do you have a date for his return?'

'If he was here,' she said, having run out of levity, 'he would make such fun of you that you would feel you'd been whipped. He will be here when it suits him.'

Behind the defiance he saw fear. It didn't occur to him that it could be anything else. 'For the present,' he said, 'I say only this. I would watch my step, if I were you. We are vigilant.'

He had made the best of a bad job. Annoyingly, he had lost his bowler hat in the fracas with the butler, who returned it to him on a salver in the hall as he was leaving. Crumbs of earth adhered to it. 'You can count yourself lucky, my son,' Hooper said, at which the dago pointed two fingers and a thumb and went 'Bang! Bang!, ha ha.'

Cora sent Mathilde to bed in tears. Then she took an

unpaid bill from the veterinary ('To attending Mr Crane's dog, Sponge') and used the back to scrawl a cable to Stephen, care of the *Journal* in New York, that said simply, 'I am going mad without you.'

Late at night. The Central London streets have emptied, apart from men drifting out of clubs, a few late diners leaving restaurants where the windows are still lit; a handful of tramps and beggars, harmless; a painted face here and there in the shadows, desperate. An unhealthy warmth has gathered in the alleyways where Fred, having gone from railway station to West End, leaves the Strand and walks northward, skirting the reek of fruit and cabbages from Covent Garden, emerges briefly into a still-busy thoroughfare below Seven Dials, then dives down a lane and reaches the darker, stickier seclusion of Soho. Here and there men sit on chairs they have brought from their houses, smoking and talking. Armellini's is still open. His wife is behind the counter, a large woman, bare-armed, sweating. She greets Fred, pours his coffee, talks about the heat.

'My flat is still safe?' he says.

'I only need to brush the floor and find the bedsheets.'

They have had these exchanges for years. One day he will mean it. He almost means it tonight. The little house in Wandsworth doesn't suit his mood. He would rather remain at the heart of things, plotting his next move in the business of Mrs Cora Crane. He imagines himself waking in the morning to the smell of roast coffee.

'One of these days,' he says, and goes in search of a late omnibus.

The qualifications of a Scotland Yard detective included not being surprised by anything. Villains were forever inventing new villainies, the honest were not always honest. Fred Hooper had seen a throat slashed for a pair of boots. He once arrested a woman who was lawfully wed to a trooper in the Scots Fusiliers – she was picking pockets, and the matron at Vine Street had to conduct an examination to see if she had articles concealed about her person – who aroused interest throughout the Force by turning out to be a man.

At the same time, a detective's duty was to be patient and assiduous. It said so in Standing Orders, not that words in a manual had much to do with London's streets and what went on in them. An officer wasn't supposed to pursue or arrest anyone without 'reasonable suspicion'. But he would get it in the neck if he failed to have his suspicions aroused.

Where did that leave Fred and an American brothel-keeper?

The superintendent at Vine Street, a morose ex-soldier called Oakes, to whom he mentioned the matter without giving names, yawned and said, 'Don't go looking for trouble.' Fred didn't tell him he had already gone looking for it in Oxted.

Where did an officer draw the line? Not long ago he saw his sister open her umbrella when she came home one evening, and extract rolled-up sheets of white paper. These were laid out overnight under four weights from the scales to make them flat.

He asked if the paper came from Arding & Hobbs, and she said they had stacks of it in the stationery cupboard.

So did she have permission to take it?

'Everybody takes it. The office boys use it to make paper darts with. Vi and I use it for sketching. Freddie dear? You can't be serious.'

'They used to prosecute urchins for stealing pocket handkerchiefs. Theft is theft.'

But he only cared because it was Belle. It was a tainted world. You couldn't be a criminal investigator and think otherwise. He wanted Belle to be different, that was all.

He took a more worldly view of the signed watercolours, which came later. He might not have done if they had been Belle's, but they were not, they were Miss Crumm's. Rukes took an interest in her work. 'A gem!' he would say (the latest Wandle). Or, 'I can almost hear the oompah, oompah!' (the Clapham Common bandstand). 'Go like hot cakes, they would, under the right circs.'

The lodger was becoming a fixture. His crates and packages had gone. A white-painted wardrobe contained his flashy suits. Even Belle accepted that he could stay. It was hard to fault someone who was amusing but self-effacing, who accepted gratefully if asked to join them at the table for a meal, who had trained the canary to sing (and supplied a velvet hood to make it shut up), who insisted on paying his rent and board in advance.

Violet's watercolours, he declared, were works of art. He was kind about Belle's as well, but it was her friend's he dwelt on. 'China rabbits? Hair ribbons? Patent potato-peelers? I deal with 'em in wagonloads. Works of art are different.'

Fred hadn't changed his assessment. Leonard Rukes had a touch of roguery. To see him rush about, you would think he had been in south London for years. He had established himself overnight, which he couldn't have done without artful pushing and shoving. No doubt he cut sharp bargains over the consignments he sent off to shops or other middlemen. No doubt he employed spotty youths with the gift of the gab to sell cheap goods direct to the public from street stalls without licences. No doubt he had a temper, *vide* the man he left with a broken jaw on the common, though there was no further sign of that. He had no evil in his face. Fred had him down as an informant when the time was ripe.

With Fred's approval, Rukes took Belle and Miss Crumm one Saturday to have a look at his stall in Bermondsey market.

'It was chaotic,' said Belle afterwards. 'Under a railway arch, with a sign saying "John Johnson, Established 1871." Claims he paid a hundred and fifty pounds for the business. Has a man like our lodger *got* a hundred and fifty pounds?'

'He might have. Were they busy?'

'Never stopped.' As they talked she was sketching the stall on a sheet of stolen paper. 'He was his usual self, only more so. Insisted on giving me sixpenny pearls again. Gave Vi a handsome cameo brooch. I wouldn't be surprised if he's taken a shine to her. What a lark that would be.'

'Does he mean to sell her paintings for her?'

'That's the other thing. He has offered her ten shillings each, for as many as she can do, but she has to sign them "Thos. Averton". She jumped at it, of course. It's a lot of money.'

'Who is Thomas Averton?'

'Some watercolourist he's made up, he says. I wouldn't trust Leonard Rukes very far.'

'He's a trader and a dealer. It's the way they live. I've met plenty of his kind. When they know you're on to them, butter wouldn't melt in their mouth. He knows I've got his measure. He knows that you have, too. Have a word with Violet and make sure she doesn't get led astray by his cameo brooches.'

'You mean to let him stay as long as he likes?'

'He might be useful to me one day. Don't worry, he'll move on to something grander when it suits him.'

'There you are,' said Belle, signing the sketch with a flourish, 'best I can do.'

The drawing was adequate. Not being good at living things, she had done the stall without either Rukes or his customers. A locomotive, just wheels and smoke, was running above the arch. Fred was thinking what he should say in praise of it when he saw that she had included a creature after all. A small thing with legs, presumably a dog, stood against the base of the brickwork. Even inch-long, it was lopsided. On close inspection he saw its hind leg was lifted.

'Was that necessary?' he said.

'If it was Vi's, you'd all tell her she was a genius.'

'She doesn't go in for vulgarity. I am surprised at you.'

She tore the drawing in two, then four, then eight, then sixteen.

'Happy now, I hope.'

'No need to fly off the handle.'

'I'm sorry, Freddie dear. Take no notice. I don't know what happens to me. I threw a pencil at Mr Barrington-Jones last week.'

She had moods, but what woman didn't? She was his sister, and that was enough.

9

People you met when they visited you at your home were not the same when you visited them at theirs. The Conrads in Essex had preoccupations that weren't apparent at Ravensbrook in the spring.

'Welcome to our wretched retreat,' said Joseph. He leaned on a stick ('The gout is twingeing') and let Mathilde and his wife bring Cora's luggage in.

Rain was falling on the estuary, a quarter of a mile away across fields. The house was old, with a tiled roof and gables at each end. A thick chimney ran up one side, so coated in ivy that it might have been a tree except for its pair of pots.

'Better a west wind than an east,' he said. 'With an easterly, one smells the petroleum depot.' He stuck a monocle in his eye and glared, like an actor. Was he an ageing forty? A youthful fifty? 'Ship sirens can be heard regardless of the weather, as you will discover if they wake you in the night. Like the howling of lost souls.'

'Lunch will be in five minutes,' said Jessie.

The daily timetable took priority. Borys, six months old, was fed with them at the table, ignored by his father. Cora was thanked for her box of toys, but opening it was postponed for fear the excitement might interfere with the child's afternoon sleep.

Asked when Stephen was returning, she said jokingly, 'Should I go and get him?' No need to tell them she had inquired about steamers, then dropped the idea. It was he had to come to her.

At the end of the meal, Joseph went to his study, and after an interval for disposing of Borys and dirty dishes – a village girl was employed in the kitchen – Jessie announced that this was a good time for her to take Cora down to the Thames. 'Joseph thought you would like to get your bearings,' she said.

The rain had gone over. Mathilde stayed behind. The field, where peas had been recently harvested, steamed in the warmth. Conducting them down a track, Jessie was already watching the time. They must be back by four, when the box of toys could be opened. Then their visitor might care to rest. It would be seven before Joseph reappeared, and supper would be served at a quarter past.

Cora hardly knew the Conrads. Stevie had come home late one evening, talking about the black-bearded Joseph, Captain Josef Korzeniowski from the Ukraine in his former life, whom Heinemann the publisher had asked to lunch. 'We got on,' said Stevie. 'When I sounded melancholy, he told me I wrote good books, and vice versa.' They walked about London for hours, raising one another's spirits.

How he had found and married this dark-haired little Englishwoman, who was about Cora's age, didn't emerge. 'Joseph has chosen lamb and boiled potatoes,' she said, 'with a strawberry flan in your honour.'

The path ended between blackthorn trees. A railway track ran inside a low sea-wall. Beyond were mudflats and the widening Thames, crowded with sails and smoking funnels. In the distance was the featureless Kent shore.

'Did Mr Conrad suggest which way now? Left or right?'

'You are making fun of me.'

'I didn't mean to.' But Mrs Conrad's air of domestic compliance got on Cora's nerves. 'Please forgive me,' she said. 'There is no earthly reason why Mr Conrad shouldn't decide on the menu, if that's what he wants.'

'What *should* one expect of a man? My sister puts it down to his being a foreigner. Should I tell him that running the household is my affair?'

'I'm the last person to ask. Stephen is only vaguely aware of his surroundings at home. I am no great shakes at domestics myself.'

A locomotive ran past with a glare of firebox, pressing them against the sea-wall.

'We rub along,' said Cora, 'as you must have noticed when you stayed with us. Stephen likes people dropping in. His idea of a good evening is one that lasts all night. We have had six men sleeping on the floor. Your visit was positively restful by our standards.'

'Despite Borys.'

'I like babies about the house. But that's another matter.'

If they were on the edge of intimacy, Cora avoided it. Had Jessie been more forlorn, it might have been easier to tell her a secret or two. In fact she was a bouncy creature, proud of her husband, not worried by his idiosyncrasies. And why should she be? They were proof of his presence. There he was, safe in his study, grumbling about the damp and his gout but firmly anchored in front of pen and paper; not disappeared into a void like some people.

The day jerked forward from one segment to the next. The box was opened and the child bubbled at woolly dog, woolly cat, woolly giraffe, woolly horse, woolly cow, woolly pig. He seized the pig and said 'Moo, moo', and the mooing punctured the splendour of the moment, which, Cora saw, would have been better served by a couple of plain toys rather than this ostentatious arkful.

She rested as instructed, dressed for dinner with Mathilde's help, saw the host arrive as a clock struck seven, saw lamb and potatoes arrive at 7.15 with enough steam to drive an engine; hoped for sparkling talk from Joseph, which never came. Mathilde, unhooking her out of her clothes at an early bedtime (Jessie was snuffing candles before ten, remarking that 'Joseph likes to keep country hours'), babbled about his being 'a wonderful man' and claimed to see 'sorrows in his face'. But Mathilde was unsound on men. It was probably his gout.

The farmhouse wasn't as large as it appeared, so a cot had been installed in Cora's room for Mathilde, a restless sleeper. Sure enough, Cora was woken in what felt like the middle of the night to hear the Rudy hissing in her ear, 'Ma! Ma! Burglars!'

There was a scratching sound from outside, and a man whistled. A crack of light showed at the window. It was dawn. Cora made her draw the curtains.

'Oh, Ma,' she said, 'it's two men in uniform with a ladder.'

Where did they fit into the Thursday-morning schedule? Sleep was over for the night. By the time Cora reached the window, men and ladder were disappearing around the corner of the house, but Joseph was there, in jacket and trousers that didn't match, standing with his hands behind his back.

'You can't go outside before you're dressed!' said Mathilde. 'Ma!'

'Bring my stockings and that long coat, and start brushing my hair.' Mathilde, naturally, had been hearing ships' hooters at regular intervals, and was sluggish. 'Do get a move on.'

Conrad turned his head and saw her coming. He was by the great chimney. The ladder was propped against the side of the stack, high above the roof-edge. 'You are in time to witness the slaughter of the innocents,' he said.

Birds whirled in and out of the ivy. The men were tying discs of lead to a fine black net and folding it in on itself.

'What would our Stephen make of this?' said Conrad.

'What are they doing?'

'Catching sparrows for the London market. They are sold as larks, a delicacy, but I suspect a conspiracy. The buyers very likely know they are sparrows but the sparrow sounds too commonplace. Would Stephen approve of the trade?'

'I think he would hate it.'

'Good. So do I. But it has been the custom since time immemorial, I am told, or at least since the railway came to Stanford-le-Hope.'

Cora saw the men's shabby uniforms and peaked caps.

'Porters from the station,' he said. 'I agree to it for the sake of peace and quiet. Children in the village call me a wild man as it is. If I interfere with the economy of the place, they will throw stones at my windows. I can't afford new windows.'

Conrad could help her to comprehend Stephen. The two of them had walked a second time, in the lanes around Oxted, having conversations that were broken off the minute they entered the house. According to Stevie, Conrad had become his best friend in England. That was her reason for being outside a dilapidated farmhouse as the sun came up over the mudflats, watching the unsuspecting sparrow population start another day.

'You rise early to start writing?' she asked.

'On the contrary, I rise early to shake off the torment of lying in bed not knowing whether I am going to be able to write at all. You see, I am not given to silent suffering.'

They were a porter with grinning teeth and a porter who

hopped about, checking small sacks and long poles. Grinning Porter shot up the rungs, the net sagging around his middle, his friend stopping still to hold the ladder. At roof level he stepped sideways to the stack, which had iron staples for climbing to the summit. Even at that height, the teeth still showed.

'A ship's rigging is more dangerous than chimneystacks, I promise you,' said Conrad.

'Why did you give up the sea?'

'Your Stephen asked the same question. I had delusions, is the answer. Having spent half a lifetime acquiring experience, why not spend the other half writing pretty tales for a kind-hearted public? Some hopes.'

Grinning Porter stood between the chimneypots themselves, which trickled smoke as the morning fires were lit, his arms raised against the pinky sky, ready to dive into space. He swayed as he flung the net, then knelt to secure the corners he retained, watching the lead weights carry it down, clear of the ivy. Hopping Porter bound the snare tight around the edges, and slid inside with his poles and sacks.

'Do you believe that Stephen will ever make a living from his work? A real living, I mean.'

'I told him the truth, that he stood a better chance than I. He writes about the sea as if *he* was the man who had lived with it, not me. I was horribly envious before I even met him. I told him so. I said I wanted to swear at him. Or bless him, or conceivably shoot him. "Still," I said, "I prefer to be your friend."'

Beside the chimneypots, Grinning Porter lay on his stomach, grabbing birds that tried to escape at his end, flicking them with a finger and tossing down feather-balls that plopped around Joseph and Cora. They stood well back. Wild geese flew in an arrow towards the coast.

'But will he ever secure himself? Have the same degree of confidence in his work that you have in yours?'

'I? Confidence? I annoyed him because I wouldn't take him seriously when he started praising me. It wasn't him I mistrusted, it was myself. It taints everything I do. I'd rather be a stonebreaker – I mean it, you know where you are with stones. There's a horror about every page I write. I told him that, too.'

'Did he agree?'

'He put on that low accent of his and said, "Aw, nuts, what de 'ell."'

Inside the net with the birds, Hopping Porter was stabbing the ivy with his poles, ankle deep in dead and dying sparrows, which he flung in handfuls into the sacks. They were dying of terror and exhaustion.

'When *Nigger of the Narcissus* came out last year,' said Cora, 'he put his pencil marks all over the place to say he liked things.'

'For example?' The sharp black beard came up an inch. 'The pessimist demands proof.'

'When the Nigger is dying of consumption. "Something resembling a scarlet thread hung down his chin, out of the corner of his lips." Do I have it right?'

'Word for word. He had it word for word, too. Even referred to it the first time we met.'

'That surely proves it.'

It wasn't the right time to talk about a man in Stevie's state of health, who took a morbid interest in death from tuberculosis. It touched a nerve; it confirmed a fear.

'I will concede the point,' said Joseph. 'Mr Crane finds certain passages of Mr Conrad to have literary merit. We can start thinking about our breakfast. The crime is over.'

The man came down the ladder. The other man tied his

sacks together. The survivors flew about as though nothing had happened. It was a comfort to see survivors.

A day's boating was threatened, as guests of a local landowner who liked showing visitors the delights of Essex creeks. 'You will love it,' said Jessie, surely not with malice. There would have been no escape if a telegram hadn't come – Cora had given the Oxted postmistress a few shillings and the Conrad address, so as not to miss news from abroad. This was news from Surrey, sent first thing. Harold Frederic was suddenly ill, and would she come to Kenley? Kate would be indebted.

Had a minor illness given Kate an excuse to mend the quarrel? Either way, Cora had to go. The Conrads said they would expect her back in the autumn, this time with Stephen. Joseph took them to the station, where the sparrow-sacks were waiting for the guard of the London train. Mathilde's glove was ostentatiously kissed, as opposed to Cora, who got a handshake and a wink. Well before they reached London Fenchurch Street, Mathilde had to be told to give the subject of Mr Conrad a rest.

'Find a porter, dear,' said Cora, when they were on the sooty platform.

A familiar face appeared from behind a pillar. It was Inspector Hooper, nodding and saying 'Ma'am' like an old acquaintance. He had a uniformed policeman at his elbow.

'Mathilde Rudy,' the detective announced, 'I have a warrant for your arrest for importuning in a public place, the Haymarket, on the twelfth of July last.'

'You can't do this,' said Cora. 'Ignore him, Mathilde.'

'If you try to obstruct me, I shall arrest you as well.'

'We have come rushing here because of an emergency.'

'Yes, a sudden dash from Stanford-le-Hope. Did you think no one would notice?'

'Are you having me watched?'

Mathilde had her hands clawed, ready to scratch, which didn't help.

'You have been making inquiries about steamers to America. For all I know you are planning a rapid exit from England. I have no grounds for holding you at present. But Mrs Rudy is in the bag.'

It made her sound like the sparrows. 'You must do as he tells you,' said Cora, 'and rely on me.' Though who was she to be relied on? The terrified face looked back over a shoulder as they led her away.

Mathilde would have to wait. It might even teach her a lesson. More journey, more steam, more England through greasy windows. Mrs Dependable arrives by station cart at the Frederics', where Harold very likely has no more than a gastric upset.

Young Barry, first of his adulterous children, a boy of six with silky hair and scarred knees, answers the door with a whisper. A whispering boy is a bad sign. 'Dada is asleep,' he says.

A smart dog-cart outside is explained by the presence of two doctors, who are in the living room with Kate. The women shake hands; the medical men's black clothes and superior faces inhibit kissing.

'Harold has had a slight seizure,' says Kate, adding that Mrs Crane is a close friend of the family.

There is a Dr Brown, who knows the district, and a Dr Freyberger, who has an air of distant hospitals, and speaks of 'my beds' and 'my people'. It appears that the patient's right arm is paralysed; the problem is not so slight after all.

The medical men talk airily about the brain and the heart. The condition of the blood is a source of anxiety to Dr Freyberger. Dr Brown tries to keep his end up by mentioning inflammatory rheumatism, but he is no match for hospital beds devoted to patients with dangerous blood, blood that suddenly decides to cut itself off from vital areas.

It is possible that Harold Frederic is a dying man, although no one actually says so. It is hard to conceive of his sprawling frame stranded on a bed, speaking with difficulty, bits of him gone to sleep.

Kate is in need of dependability. 'He is as strong as an ox,' says Cora, when the doctors have gone upstairs, intent on fixing a belladonna plaster, God knows what for, to the patient's leg. She wants to comfort her friend, by telling her what must be obvious anyhow, that she, Cora, will be at her side whatever happens, and that we are all at the mercy of Fate. She has a powerful desire to start talking about the sparrows and what Fate had in store for them. But she resists. She kisses Kate and says she is glad they have come together again, and Kate says, 'What a pair we are.'

What was the parallel? The point of comparison? It dawned on Cora that they were to be sisters in distress.

'You are better off than I,' said Kate. 'Stephen may be one of the roaming kind, but you can be pretty confident that he comes back in the end.'

'Certainly,' said Cora, not able to complain about such a half-hearted proposition without sounding unkind.

'We try not to think about the knife-edge we have to live on. What shall I do if Harold dies? I have sent a telegram to Hammersmith, and his daughter Ruth is coming here. Barry is old enough to ask who she is. And what happens if his wife comes?'

'She won't. "Cousin Ruth" will do for the girl. As for Harold, he'll be well in no time.'

But they had to be made to share the knife-edge. Kate spoke of how difficult it was to ensure that men looked after themselves. She roped them together, Kate and Cora, Harold and Stephen. They were 'our men' who 'needed us'; Harold with his ailing blood, Stephen ('Dear old Stevie' – the phrase was like a diagnosis) with his implicitly thin legs and weak chest. Cora could have done without that. She hoped to see shirt and trouser-legs filled to bursting with Stephen, his face browned by the sun. But all she could do was stroke Kate's hand and let her talk.

The Christian Scientists loomed up. Kate had a penchant for forces of nature; she spoke of 'Divine law' and 'curative metaphysics', and said she was sure that praying while she gave birth to Heloise halved the pain. Mind was supposed to have conquered flesh. To Cora it was second-rate magic, but now Kate meant to wheedle Harold into the experiment of turning his own mind, with all its complications, into an unstoppable force. Cora didn't like to ask what the result might be – that he would only suffer half as much? Or not at all? Be cured? Take up his bed and walk?

She said she hoped it would work.

'They mustn't ever suspect that we are not husband and wife. Living in sin isn't allowed by the healers. Christian Science operates through the Ten Commandments.'

In which case, it seemed to Cora, keeping adultery hidden from the Scientists was the least of Kate's worries. What about keeping it hidden from the Divine Principle, where the magic had its origin?

'So if it's God who is doing the healing . . .'

'I know what you are going to say. Will our not being married put us beyond His reach? Well, it would if He saw it as sin. But it isn't sin, not really. I love Harold. It can't be sin in the eyes of the Lord.'

What calamity would make Cora talk like that? She glimpsed the other Kate, the desperate woman, behind the friend with a clever brain and carnal urges. What would a desperate Cora be like?

A man cried out, whether in pain or temper was hard to tell, and Kate rushed to the stairs. The house was oppressive. A child said, 'It was only Dada having a dream,' and Cora found Barry in the hall, holding a sister by the hand.

'How would it be, young man,' said Cora, 'if you came to stay with me? And Heloise, of course, and Helen. Just till Dada is better.'

The thought of children at Ravensbrook was heaven. By the time Kate returned, Barry was being self-important about the plan; a Harold in the making.

'It is all arranged, Mama. There are brown fish in the stream that hide under stones. Adoni will show me Uncle Stephen's revolver.'

'So you see, you have no option,' said Cora. 'Mathilde will be as delighted as I am. Get their things ready and they can come back with me now.'

If there was a bulletin from upstairs, it wasn't given. The cry went unexplained. When Cora left with the children, Kate gave her a telegram for a Scientist in London, a Mrs Mills at an address off Oxford Street, and Cora sent it from Oxted Post Office on the way home.

She had the household organised in an hour. Rose Wellington, who had matured, was sent for, to help turn Cora's bedroom into a nursery, and told she would have to live in for a day or two until Mrs Rudy returned from a visit. Adoni, being from the Mediterranean, where men had feelings for children, was instructed in his duties.

What feelings did Stevie have? When the children were asleep, full of supper and bedtime stories, she sat for a long time in the study. Having them under her roof was distressing as well as sweet. She began to scribble like a schoolgirl, composing a letter that never comes, from a boy who never was. 'Dear Cora'? 'My Blessed Girl'? 'My Beloved'? She wanted authenticity, something to cling to.

'My Own Sweet Cora,' she wrote. 'I go through the world unexplained. This letter, following a silence, may look like an incomparable insolence. Who knows. Script is an infernally bad vehicle for thoughts. But if you are not angry with me, I will tell you a dream I had. Mrs Cora Crane moved like an angel among children, under the roof of a dwelling where she and Mr Stephen Crane share a new-found instinct of discovery. I saw their blonde, blazing faces. I heard their inimitable shrillings. Whence did they come? A foundling hospital? An agency for the adoption of meritorious infants by putative parents of impeccable character? Whatever, I gained one of those peculiar thrills which a man only acknowledges upon occasion. In a word: Mr Crane (he of the weak mental machinery) apologises for past errors in the child-rearing department, and says that things will be different in future. I am, believe me, your ever-loving Stevie.'

Cora had used a pencil. When she re-read this outpouring, and considered the abyss that waited for people who couldn't keep their emotions under control, she found an eraser and got rid of it.

Tom Simmons, who was in the inspectors' room, said Fred was a tough nut to go locking up the fair sex like that.

'I'm on to something big.'

'So this one works for the other one down in Surrey, is that it? You're a devil. What exactly happened at the other one's house? You didn't say.'

'A battle of wits,' said Fred. 'I decided to confront her. She's a cool customer.'

'And the one downstairs? What's the plan?'

'Let her simmer overnight. I shall grill her in the morning, put the wind up her. I've cleared it with Oakey. I'm off on leave on Sunday and I want to get a lead before then.' He took his bowler, ready to go and look for shoplifters. The hat would never be quite the same again. 'I don't intend to be made a fool of by an American brothel-keeper.'

'Is this the woman you've got locked up?'

'You've not been paying attention. I mean the master-brain. Mrs Cora Crane, alias Stewart.'

'I wouldn't like to get on the wrong side of Fred Hooper.'

'I take that as a compliment,' said Fred, and went out into the wicked city.

10

Cora was in London early, having arranged with the Barrs that Alice would spend the day at Ravensbrook, in charge of the household. At the last minute she decided to take Barry. Adoni had shown him the revolver, minus cartridges, but he woke crying in the night and in the morning his bed was wet.

'We are going to see a policeman,' said Cora, 'because my lady companion got lost in London, and I believe he has found her now.'

Barry was absorbed by the sights. He forgot about his bad knee, where he had fallen chasing the dog Sponge. Trains were being diverted to Charing Cross (runaway horses on the tracks at Clapham Junction), and his first excitement outside the station was a pavement artist in the Strand, drawing a naval battle in charcoal and red chalk. A penny had to go into his hat. An escapologist on the edge of Trafalgar Square invited him to 'wind an extra bit of chain around me legs,' raking his audience with beery breath at nine in the morning, wincing as Barry pulled harder than expected.

Did Harold keep his bastard children locked up in Surrey, a hidden family that might embarrass him if it kept

120

coming up to town? The lions at the foot of Nelson amazed the child.

At the Vine Street police station Barry sat on a bench while she asked for Inspector Hooper, and filled out a form on which she was required to state her business. She wrote 'Missing Person!' and breathed scent at a sergeant, who told a constable to hurry upstairs with it.

Barry, bored with sitting, was studying handbills of men wanted for robberies and arsons, drawn by a police artist who specialised in scowls.

'He'll be down shortly, Ma'am,' said the sergeant, and suggested she wait in an interview room.

'The boy?'

'Will be safe where he is.'

Barry was pulling down his lower lip, in imitation of a man wanted for robbery on the Portsmouth line. She told him to mind he behaved himself, and was taken along a corridor to a room with painted-over glass in the door. A wooden table had initials carved in it. An inkwell and rack of pens reminded her of a schoolroom.

The detective slipped in without a word. Pinned to his lapel was a broken-down rose, already minus a petal. The police artist could have used his scowl for a poster. When they had the desk between them he said, 'At your service, Mrs Crane.'

She told him she liked his buttonhole. His long face got longer. 'I'm fond of roses,' she went on, 'especially plain English ones from traditional stock like yours, not the fancy varieties.' Cora saw this wasn't working. 'I have come here to put things straight.'

'That was wise of you. Do you wish to make a formal statement?'

'Informal. Then you can be as formal as you like.'

Now that they had electric light in the station, subjects could be studied scientifically. Skin creamy, with faint lines running back from the eye-corners. Eyes green, nose small, lower lip prominent. Restless hands. Automatically he estimated the length of the ring finger, vital sign in Dr Bertillon's system. The ring was plain gold and unusually thick. Its yellow was brassy beside the auburn tints in the hair under the hat.

'Don't forget,' he said cheerfully, 'I know more about you than you think.'

'Let me start with Mrs Rudy. She has led a difficult life. Her husband ran off. I took her in, but she was never one of my regular girls. She was more useful to me as a housekeeper. However, she is not what you would call virtuous.'

'Pardon my asking, but are you what you would call virtuous?'

'Don't be impertinent. Strangely enough, I am. The Hotel de Dream was a business. It had nothing to do with my personal life. Which we can come to in due course. Shall I continue with Mrs Rudy?'

Fred listened patiently to her tale of lapses by a faithful servant with a weakness. It might be true. It might be smoke. Then she said, 'There was a dreadful to-do in Tallahassee,' and he paid more attention.

The faithful servant had involved herself with a politician, an episode, said Mrs Crane, that was never satisfactorily explained, but in the course of which Mrs Rudy was arrested, and her mistress tried to bribe the police.

'What happened?'

'The charge was dropped. I guess it wasn't in the senator's interests.'

Fred had never heard of Tallahassee before he read the Pinkerton report. Her story was that story. It was in her favour.

'Go on.'

Re the Haymarket episode, Mrs Rudy had been sent to the apartment to collect some correspondence. She took the chance to misbehave in the West End. It had been a mistake to let her loose in London, given her little weakness. 'You were entitled to arrest her,' said Mrs Crane. 'I was trying to protect her, that was all. I have punished her severely, docked her a month's wages. She won't do it again, not in London.'

'I believe you have reasons for wanting to keep the case dark.'

'I live quietly in England as a married woman. People accept me. My private affairs aren't their concern. Or yours, come to that. My guess is you went to Pinkerton's. You must have something against Americans.'

She threw him more bones to add to the bones he had already. Captain Stewart came on the scene in New York. After he brought her back to England and scandalised his family by marrying her, he took her on a cruise with friends in a steam-yacht down the Florida coast. After a row at Jacksonville, she went ashore and didn't return. A marriage settlement was safely in the bank, and she owned a jewel or two. The yacht sailed without her. She stayed in Jacksonville.

'Where you procured women for prostitution.'

'I bought a hotel to start with and made it stylish, though I say it myself. I've told you all this. Men brought girls there to impress them. We had more men than girls, so I ended up supplying them, that was all. It grew.'

'Why give it up? Why return to Europe?'

'Crane blew in one day. He was a newspaperman. He fancied Europe. We thought we could live in England as husband and wife without anyone noticing. It was a love affair. I washed my hands of everything else.'

It was hard to tell if she was convincing him. He played with a pen; ink ingrained in the wood came off on his fingers and he rubbed them unsuccessfully with a handkerchief. Boots clumped up and down outside. A door banged, a man shouted.

'Facts are facts,' said the detective.

'Ask Mr Conrad the novelist about me. I was coming back from the Conrads when you arrested Mrs Rudy. Ask Mr Harold Frederic, London correspondent of the *New York Times*. Ask Mr Heinemann the publisher.'

She was bluffing. Harold wouldn't let himself be drawn in. Mr Heinemann hardly knew her, and was innocent of her history. So was Mr Conrad.

Fred didn't mean to let go of her yet, but the facts were disappointing. The brothel-keeper had dissolved into a woman going on about a man she was in love with and a new life. It was the first time he had ever heard anyone use the phrase 'a love affair'.

He pulled himself together, tapped fingernails on table, said he would be interviewing the prisoner shortly. If Mrs Crane returned to the station at the end of the afternoon, he would tell her what he had decided to do.

He escorted her back to the hall. A cab-driver was at the desk, complaining that a fare had given him a foreign coin. A constable was putting up a new 'Wanted' poster. A woman with a brush and bucket, busy scrubbing the floor because the Head of Detectives was due to make a surprise visit, scrubbed a sergeant's boot by mistake. Cora couldn't see Barry.

'He was here five minutes ago,' said Sergeant O'Brien.

Fred raised his voice. 'Small boy gone missing. Anybody seen him?'

'Was a lad on the pavement outside when I come in,' said the cabman.

He wasn't there now.

'Your child, Mrs Crane?'

'Certainly not. I am looking after him. For heaven's sake, can you do something?'

Fred was more at ease with an anxious woman. He told the sergeant to find two men.

'He is only six years old,' said Mrs Crane.

'Describe him, if you please.'

In policemen's terms he became a male child, name Barry, grey shirt and short trousers, light-brown curls, nervous manner, sticking plaster on knee. 'Got that, you two?' he said to the search party.

The chance was too good to miss, a woman weakened by anxiety, who might give herself away. 'I am now officially in charge of the search,' he said. The blue backs of the constables moved ahead of them, into the crowds.

'Did he have money?' asked Hooper.

'A penny.'

Inquiries were made at every shop along Piccadilly with penny pies or cakes in the window. Alleys were darted up, a pharmacy looked into (the red and green carboys might attract a nipper), cabmen interrogated at a rank ('Keep your eyes skinned and this fair lady will reward you with a smile.'). Drivers touched their hats with their whips. 'And five shillings,' she said, imagining how she would feel if it was Stevie Crane, aged six, born out of wedlock but all the more precious for that, because more vulnerable.

Kate talked about her children the previous summer, when the Cranes and Frederics were in Ireland, at Inchgela. The men had gone fishing. Kate and Cora sat under a bank covered in fuchsias, watching Barry and his sisters at the end of the garden. Kate said, 'He'll never divorce Grace. I wish terrible things.'

'We all do.'

'It's not for me, I can manage, it's the children. They'll suffer for it when people find out, as they will. I know Grace isn't well. Every Monday when he comes back from Hammersmith, I hope he'll say she's worse. So I am as bad as a murderer.'

'You are a sweet woman. A lot sweeter than me.'

Kate wouldn't listen. 'I am wicked,' she said. 'I know exactly what the Scientists mean about cleansing the mind before they start to cure the body.'

'We can't spend our lives having pure thoughts. My first husband was a dry-goods merchant. Meant well at first but lacked fibre. I found him preposterous after a year.'

'Did you want him dead?'

'It was New York. I divorced him.'

'And your husband out in Africa?'

'You mean do I have daydreams about natives with blowpipes? Donald's skin is so thick, a poisoned dart would bounce straight off.'

She hadn't answered the question. Kate squeezed her arm and said, 'What a pair we are.'

The London dust was in Cora's throat. Vine Street had no news when they looked in. An officer who went to Trafalgar Square had come back shaking his head. Cora asked Hooper why more men weren't being employed, and was told that a child who went missing in broad daylight was not strictly a police matter at all.

'Is it not?' she said. 'I and the child wouldn't have been in the West End but for you.'

'We've had this out. Importuning is a blight on a modern city.'

'Don't be so pompous.'

'I don't make the laws, Mrs Crane.'

'You like to persecute women. Some men do.'

All the time they were peering in doorways, finding lines of sight through the crowds that led only to more thicknesses of crowd, conversing but rarely coming face to face.

They were on the edge of Piccadilly Circus. Hooper scanned the circle of glass and granite, in recent years plastered with advertisements for soap and tonics.

'I will do what I can to find the boy. If he hasn't turned up by noon, I shall have a handbill printed. There's no point in our quarrelling.'

She agreed: there was no point.

The hub of the universe was dirty, unwashed, unhosed. Boys, some of them looking not much older than Barry, darted with long shovels between the traffic, scooping up the horse mess as best they could. Cora excused herself to go into Swan and Edgar's, where they had an aquarium in the basement, advertised at street level by a wooden fish painted pink and an arrow. The child's father was a keen fisherman, she said; he might have followed the sign.

The rest room, too, was in the basement. Exigencies of womanhood, concealed from men. The attendant supplied a cotton pad and Cora put a generous threepence in the saucer. In the dull grey light of the cubicle, blood lost its brightness.

She looked in on the aquarium, a cold cellar of bubbling tanks. The only child was a girl in a summer frock, holding her mother's hand, who shivered and turned away. Muddy shapes with fins flicked sideways and vanished into weed. The water, seen through green glass, was the colour of the Atlantic at Jacksonville.

Cora rested her forehead against the tank. That winter when Stevie appeared, she thought he was a seaman. He wandered down the beach, studying the waves. He was a studier of everything. 'This town,' he told her, 'looks like soiled cardboard. You'd think lunatic babies had been playing with it.'

She had five weeks with him before he sailed off in a leaky tug-boat that was smuggling rifles into Cuba. He showed her his money-belt before he slung it from his hip-bones. Spanish coins were slotted into it like bullets, courtesy of a newspaper syndicate that didn't care how he reached Cuba, as long as he was ashore before the insurrection started.

When news came that he was dead, it was no more than she expected. He had a reluctance in his nature that dared anyone to be an optimist. Shortly before he sailed he did his Bowery imitation, joke and threat in one, and said, 'You wanna make the gods laugh? Tell 'em yer plans.' Then he clipped the gold around his waist and knelt by the bed to kiss her throat.

The tug went down in a storm off the Florida coast. There was talk of sabotage. Empty boats washed up on beaches. It was January, drowning weather. She sat in her bedroom next morning, which was a Sunday, dry-eyed, looking at the ocean without rancour because it couldn't help its nature, any more than people could help theirs, planning how she would expand the business and build Hotel de Dreams across the State, with still more beautiful girls and even rarer European dishes and wines; everything in memory of Stevie.

Except that a telegram came as the bells were clanging for morning service, informing her that Crane and others had been washed up alive on a beach to the south. No trains ran there on the Sabbath. She was arranging to hire a locomotive so he could be in Jacksonville the same day, till he reproved her by wire for throwing her money around, and she complied meekly and waited for him to take the scheduled service on Monday.

His cough could be heard all over the hotel, but he said he had never felt better. His body was whiter than before, bleached by the sea. How had he survived? Well, he drawled, he shed the money belt and gave it to the fishes pretty damn' quick.

He was prescient in saving money on the locomotive. Two months later the hotel had been sold and they were on their way to find a proper war, this time in Greece. They had thousands of dollars, which didn't last.

She ascended to street level and waited at the entrance for Hooper to find her. He had been visiting fruit and flower stalls, shouting in newsboys' ears as they bawled on corners.

'How far would his penny take him on an omnibus?' she asked.

'Miles. I have had telegrams sent to the depots, requesting information.'

She opened her mouth to thank him, and saw a shovel fly through the air. A boy fell on his side and a red object thudded into the gutter. Wooden boxes had fallen off a cart that was slewed across the road where Regent Street met the Circus, its horses steaming. Men were running between stationary vehicles.

'Come away,' said Hooper, urging her with his arm.

She wouldn't move. She wanted the strength to accept things as Stevie did, the severed foot in the dust, the boy groaning, the men tearing cloth to make bandages. Blood everywhere, inseparable from Mr novelist Crane, mocked for his red mists and scarlet threads. If he was with her at the kerbside, he would find the scene irresistible, down to the shape of the bloodstains on the cartwheel. *Even if* it had been Barry lying there, the burning eyes would have taken it in and remembered. Stevie's life was all stories, the facts and fictions muddled up together. She waited – perhaps that was it – to be incorporated in a story he hadn't yet written.

Fred got her to a stall in Coventry Street and made her drink thick coffee. He was impressed by how quickly she was calm again.

'Tell me about our missing person,' he said. 'Are you related to him?'

'Does it matter?'

'The more we know about him, the better we can help. The father's name goes on the handbill.'

'He wouldn't want his name to appear.'

'It's your child, isn't it?'

'Try to stop thinking there's more in me than meets the eye. I don't have children. I am looking after him for a friend whose husband is ill. The Mr Frederic I mentioned of the *New York Times*, if you must know. Ask your Pinkerton's about him. He is nearly as famous as Mr Crane. Little Barry has two sisters and his mother is my best friend. Can we get on?'

He led the way into Soho, down a street of cheap hotels and clothes shops. They tried a court where tailors sat out-side on steps, they inquired at red-painted stalls on wheels. Fred knocked on doors, shouted through windows, spoke to passers-by he recognised.

At Armellini's, the proprietor eyed Mrs Crane and said that if a small boy came in, he would give him a slice of panettone and send a message to Vine Street.

'I wish all the aliens were like you,' said Fred.

'My wife says you come to live upstairs very soon.'

'One of these days for sure.'

Finding the child in this ant-heap would remind Mrs Crane that he was a man to be reckoned with, that he wasn't easily deflected from the matter in hand. He left her in Armellini's while he tramped back to the station, but they had no small boys to report.

Streets shimmered with dust and sun. By the time he rejoined her he was sweating. 'We can try the parks,' he said. 'Does he like ducks?'

'He wouldn't know how to find a park.'

'He might stumble on one. There are ducks in St James's.'

'Is that the best you can do? For all I know he's never seen a duck. What about the poster? I want one printed with a ten-pound reward. Are you capable of organising that?'

Fred was pleased to inform her that he was. But he tried one more initiative, leaving her on the pavement while he entered a tenement with a reputation and found two frizzle-haired prostitutes washing clothes at a pump in the yard behind.

'Small boy gone missing,' he said, and gave a description. 'Be good citizens for once. Pass the word around. There is a five-shilling reward.'

'Bit miserly, five bob,' said the black-haired frizzler. They held a twisted skirt between them, wringing dirty water from it. 'Make it a sovereign, we might start looking, see if he's under the bed.'

Mrs Crane spoke from the shadow of the passageway. 'They can have their sovereign.'

'You women come smartly round to Vine Street, now, if you have information.'

The older frizzler, whose hair appeared to have boot-polish on the roots where they were turning grey, let go her end of the skirt. She glanced at her friend.

'Speak up, then,' said Fred.

'Keep your mouth shut,' murmured Frizzler No. 1.

'Do I have to caution you? I can make it hot for you, my girl. Hot hot hot. Let your friend say what she wants to.'

'Dickie Venables, does up old mirrors and cabinets in Brewer Street, has a lad keeps an eye open for little kids by theirselves.'

'He never harms 'em,' said her friend. 'Keeps 'em safe and hands 'em over.'

'Collects a reward, does he? Your pimp as well, is he?'

Brewer Street wasn't far. They had walked down it once

already. Far from being impressed, Mrs Crane expressed surprise that a detective was ignorant of the Venables man.

'You don't know what you're talking about,' he said, taking policeman's strides that were hard to match in a skirt. 'I can't know everything. I know the West End like the back of my hand but I get paid to keep down crime, not look for boys.'

'Isn't abduction a crime?' came from behind, where she had fallen back.

Fred walked faster still. Villainy was laid down over centuries, like dust and debris. Nobody knew London through and through. A face here, a staircase there, was the best you could hope for.

But he was lucky. Venables was in his fifties, sores on lip, black hat with a chewed brim. He came up from a cellar, gave his visitors a once-over, and declared at once that he had a great love of children, and if ever he saw a waif or stray, why, he gave it a glass of milk and set about returning it to its rightful owner; he made it sound like a parcel. He had such a boy downstairs at present. He was about to whisk him round to the p'lice.

'Would have acted sooner,' added Venables, 'but I suffer from the merc'ry poisoning on account of mirrors.' He touched the sores on his lips. 'The lad will have drunk his milk by now.'

It was a pity he was English. His mixture of subterfuge and wickedness would have suited a foreigner.

'Painstaking, that's my way,' said Fred, when the child had been plucked from the greasy mattress he was asleep on, and they were returning to Vine Street.

As far as they could gather, the child had gone looking for chained-up men on pavements, and lost his way. Trotting between them, he expected to have both his hands held. They might have been Mama and Papa, going to feed the ducks.

Mrs Crane apologised for her rudeness. The eyes looked at

him sideways, green and deep-set. 'I was distraught. You have been a tower of strength.'

They crossed the Circus, where the vehicles swept endlessly. The blood had been sluiced from the gutter. Fred's inquiry hung by a thread.

Mrs Crane said she had forgotten to visit the creature in the backyard and pay her the sovereign.

'She would only get drunk and give the game away to Venables. He might do her in for tipping me the information.'

'Is there a police fund I can give something to?'

'Our canteen has a box for contributions. Half a crown would be generous.'

She put in a sovereign when they were back at the station. Sergeant O'Brien gave the child a toffee. Fred went down to the cells and had Mathilde Rudy taken into the gaoler's room. Twenty-four hours down there had left her with a rash on her neck and a button off her dress.

'Your employer is upstairs, pleading on your behalf,' he said. 'I think she's the one who ought to be down here, don't you? Tell me about the establishment she means to open in London. Where and when? I can keep you here for weeks.'

She rocked on her chair, fingers against her temples, saying 'I swear' and 'Don't know' and 'I confess'. What she confessed to was importuning in the Haymarket. 'Help me, Jesus,' she said.

'Never mind Jesus. What is Mrs Crane planning to do?'

'Send me back to America if I do it again,' she moaned.

Fred gave up. It was hopeless. He summoned the matron so soap and a hairbrush could be provided, and had the woman released. A messenger boy was sent for a hansom.

'What happens next?' asked Mrs Crane.

'There may be further inquiries. I can make no promises.' He caught her eye, and knew that she knew there wouldn't be.

'If you are ever in Surrey arresting people, why not call and see us? Mr Crane should be back from his travels next month. You might inspire him to write a story about an English detective.'

'I don't know about that, Ma'am.'

Fred lifted the child into the hansom and gripped Mrs Crane's elbow to help her follow. He was aware of activity on the station steps. A police vehicle had come round from the stables, and someone shouted, 'Move away, cabbie!'

Those green eyes were on him. 'Strange man,' she said, and kissed him on the cheek before he swung her upwards. He could feel the mouth on his skin for days afterwards.

She waved through the grubby porthole.

When he turned, the Head of Detectives was glaring at him.

'You are Hooper, are you not?'

'Yes, sir.'

'I am very concerned for you, Hooper. You could find yourself on a disciplinary charge.'

Delighted faces behind him watched the scene.

'Her little boy was abducted, sir. I found him for her.'

'An officer must keep a sense of proportion. What would your wife think?'

'She's dead, sir. The lady must have been carried away.'

'I believe we discussed fast living at your triennial review.'

'I did obtain a canary as you suggested, sir.'

'Hardly a substitute for a wife. You must pull yourself together. I shall be keeping a close eye on you.'

In five minutes the story of Fred Hooper and the kiss was all over the station. He was stoical about the humour, explaining nothing to anyone except Tom Simmons, in whom he confided that she was the American master-mind who had been under suspicion.

'And now you've relented? You're a dark horse, Fred.'

'The case collapsed. Don't worry, I would have her like a shot if the opportunity arose.'

'So would I,' grinned Tom, but apologised when he saw that his indecency wasn't well received. 'So is it next week you're taking your leave?'

'Off Sunday morning by eight. I am hiring a Juno. Three gears and Sure-Grip handlebars. Will you be joining me for an afternoon?'

'Wish I could. But if you get as far as Kent on your last day, call in at Bromley. I lodge with my parents. Stay the night. Meet my fiancée.'

'I shall see how I go,' said Fred.

11

There was no question of Harold Frederic dying. Kate found herself changed for the better by his illness. Positive thoughts streamed through the sick-room like sunlight. For the first time since they became friends, attracted by adversity, she felt equal to Cora.

Harold was taking her advice. He had given Christian Science the benefit of the doubt. She wasn't clear if this was God's power, or Harold's bloody-mindedness, or possibly the former working through the latter. But it was Kate who got Mrs Mills to the bedside, defying the doctors and his daughter Ruth.

He was rude to the Scientist to start with. 'You walk with a limp, Madam,' he said, propped up against pillows, his mouth twisted and the words coming out slurred. 'That gives me no confidence.'

'God is a good surgeon,' she said. 'I wouldn't worry about me if I were you. He does everything for us if we reflect Him. Which we fail to do when we drink and carouse and misbehave. Would you like me to read to you about Jesus?'

'You haven't asked me yet about my complaint.'

'Oh, I ignore the body,' said Mrs Mills. 'It is the mind that counts.'

That was the crucial remark, the one that suited Harold. It was a question of the will. Mrs Mills departed with a cheque for six guineas to cover six weeks of distant healing. Kate only smiled when he said that the Scientist woman bored his head off his shoulders. Who knew what God was up to? She loved it when Harold said that he *did not intend to permit* a melancholy of the blood, a disturbance down the right side of the body, to stand in the way of his future. He, Harold Frederic, aged forty-two, wished to make that clear. If he desired a cigar or a glass of whisky, that clown Freyberger was not going to obstruct him. He put on his trousers – it took him five minutes – to prove he could do it, then pulled them off again.

There was something heroic about him, in Kate's view. She fancied she saw a resemblance to Stephen Crane, that casual defiance of the universe that Cora spoke of as though it was unique to Stephen. When the daughter, an anguished girl of twenty, put a belladonna plaster on the afflicted leg on Monday afternoon, he said, 'Ha ha! That's better!' When Kate defied her and took it off ten minutes later he shouted, 'Ha ha! That's better still!'

Illness had coarsened his manner, but even that was welcome, as proof of vitality. Secretary Stokes was sent for, to read him the foreign wires, and was told to stop muttering. After hearing a précis of the London newspapers, Harold lay back with his eyes closed and dictated a despatch for New York about General Kitchener's Army, busy slaughtering dervishes along the Nile Valley. The slurring came and went. Words kept eluding him. 'Disseminating death.' he said, 'with their . . . guns. Their . . . marine guns. Unclean guns.'

Stokes ventured, 'Machine guns?'

'Damn you, Stokey, if you knew it, why didn't you say it?'

He was hoarse when he finished. 'That'll keep 'em happy in New York,' he said. The paper was not to be informed of the illness until he recovered.

At dusk he was feverish. Kate sat with him, washing his face, telling him to rest.

'I don't want the children at Ravensbrook any longer than necessary,' he said.

'They will be having a lovely time.'

She knew what bothered him, that the Frederics were not supposed to need help. He said it wouldn't surprise him to hear one day that Cora had gone off the rails.

Kate rubbed eau-de-Cologne on his wrists. 'She is almost as devoted to Stevie as I am to you.'

'Don't compare yourself with Cora. You no more resemble her than I resemble Stephen. Dreamer Stephen, that's what I call him. Lord of the manor. What is happening about the house in Sussex?'

He was the child, wanting his fairy-tale. Kate told him that Brede Place was still being talked about, that a genealogist was still hoping to connect the American Cranes with Sir Something Crane of the seventeenth century.

The Cranes and English society were a never-ending source of entertainment. It was no use Kate calling it harmless vanity. Americans, said Harold, had no cobwebby past to look back on. That was their salvation. They demeaned themselves by sucking up to a decrepit England.

An owl hooted in the garden elms. The male nurse who had been hired was talking to Ruth downstairs. The Stokes typewriter clacked from the study.

'What about Cora and her American Women?' he said. 'Are they going to let her into their gossip-shop?'

'If they get round to starting it. Don't worry, they won't ask me. They don't know I exist.' The words slipped out.

'You have been taking lessons from Cora. Is she egging you on to join clubs and give luncheon parties and call yourself Mrs Harold Frederic? You know my social position.'

'I accept things as they are.'

'She will drive a wedge between us.'

He moved his head to find coolness, and Kate reversed the pillow for him. 'Will you try to sleep now?'

'I want to hear about Cora and the Queen again.'

Kate wished she had never told him. Another disloyal anecdote had turned into a bedtime story. But she put her head beside his. Once upon a time there was an American lady with a murky past who believed in miracles. She believed that one day she would go to the Palace and be presented to the Queen. So you are Mrs Stephen Crane, the Queen would say, I have read his books.

'Cora used those words?'

'She was laughing. Cora's no fool.'

'But she meant it.'

'I daresay she did. You'd never tell her?'

'Mustn't upset the bi-roxide blonde, must we.'

Harold was restless, wanting his feet sponged, complaining at lumps in the mattress, though Kate couldn't find them. 'You know what Stephen's trouble is?' he said. 'A soft spot for immorality. What was his first novel about? A woman of the streets. We all forget that, now he's famous for the *Red Badge*.'

His eyes were sinking deeper into the bone. 'You must sleep,' said Kate.

'Take the Leslie business in New York. Amy Leslie, the . . . tigress . . . activist . . . theatre, in plays, for God's sake.'

'Actress,' said Kate.

'Close friend of numerous gentlemen, too. All hair and teeth. She and Stephen were still *intime* in '96 when he took up with

Cora. She was after his money a year later. Said he owed it, said she needed it.'

The voice had died down. 'Court made an order last January. Attachment of earnings. Five-hundred dollars from his royalties. One reason the Cranes are so short of the ready.'

He yawned and made a contented noise in his throat. 'Imm . . . aterial boy. Immature.' Then he was asleep.

A wire arrived from Cora in the morning to say, 'Detained in London yesterday. Will come today.' The patient heard the door-knocker and wanted to know if it was the telegraph boy. Kate invented an egg man.

Presently the doctors appear, Brown with his black bag, like a servant, Freyberger sinister in morning coat and striped trousers. White hands are busy over the bed. Stethoscopes are applied to arteries. Kate, who was once a schoolteacher, would dearly like to ask them if sick blood makes a different noise to healthy blood, but fears a rebuff.

Freyberger raises and bends the left knee, in order to tap it with a silvery hammer. The leg trembles but doesn't jerk. Freyberger shakes his head.

The prognosis is not mentioned in so many words. But the orders are unequivocal: absolute rest and four pints of Jersey milk a day. There is a discussion about whether a local farmer can be found to bring a cow over every morning and milk it on the lawn, so that the first glassful will be hot from the udder.

Kate catches Harold's eye. She smiles encouragingly but it's too late.

'I have never in my life,' growls the patient, 'heard such poppycock from professional men. Doctors are like, like . . . parsnips, like . . .' – an artery pulses in his neck, but he triumphs – 'like *parsons*, they don't keep up with the times. You wouldn't know a germ if you saw one.'

He may be on shaky ground, but Kate is proud of him. Not so Ruth, who is apologising to the striped trousers and begging her father to see reason. He ignores her, having a wonderful time, declaring that he has an intellectual contempt for milk whether hot or cold. He adds that self-respecting authors do not go in for cows on lawns.

The medical men try to look dignified as they leave. Kate is entrusted with powerful sedatives, and Freyberger tells the nurse to use force if necessary to administer them. This doesn't happen because Kate forbids it. The sedatives are left in their ribbed bottles with red labels, and she has to hope that Harold will fall asleep naturally and not hear Cora arrive.

She came soon after eleven, bringing two presents for Harold, hothouse grapes from her and a crayoned drawing from Barry of omnibuses and figures in helmets, apparently policemen. Cora had taken him up to London the previous day and lost him briefly, before a policeman returned him. A trivial matter – Cora swept it aside. How was the patient?

'I have had a time of it,' said Kate. 'But we have all survived better than expected. The Mrs Mills you sent the wire to has begun her healing. The effects are visible already.'

How splendid it would be, thought Kate, if the Cora who had no time for miracles was converted into a Cora who took God the Scientist to her heart. Stranger things had happened. Lives could change in a flash. Kate had a vision of tomorrow's Cranes and Frederics united by this bond that no one referred to but was always there. In that mysterious future, when divorce or death had done their stuff, and they were proper wives at last.

'As soon as Harold is on the mend, you must try and have some outings,' said Cora. 'We could go down to Brede Place again. I shall be having a conservatory built for my roses and peaches. I need to talk to the builders.' She glared at Kate. 'You are laughing.'

'Certainly not.'

'You think I see England through rose-coloured specta-cles.'

'I wasn't being unkind.'

'According to Mrs Mack, Brede Place has a ghost. I shall put you and Harold in its bedroom. It goes back to the sixteenth century—'

Noises from upstairs cut her off, confused shouts and thuds. They hurried into the hall, a wide space with a broad uncarpeted staircase. Harold in his scarlet bathrobe was sitting at the top, arms locked around a banister, shouting abuse at the nurse and his daughter.

'Lift his legs, Miss Lyon!' called Ruth. Her heavy features were red with anger. She looked a bit like her father. 'We don't want to hurt the legs.'

'I intend to greet my friend Mrs Crane like a normal being,' said the patient.

Kate went up a few steps and froze. Bare feet at the end of striped pyjamas stretched towards her, asking to be saved. But the power to act or think had gone.

'Let the man come down, if it's what he wants,' said Cora. 'Hello, Harold.'

'How dare you interfere!' screamed Ruth.

The nurse, broad and fortyish, had embraced the patient from behind, and was trying to ease him back without doing damage. 'Be a good man, sir, be a good man.'

Harold swung his head, and skull met nose.

The attendant recoiled, knocking an alabaster figure of Mercury from a ledge, which broke. The pieces whirled past Kate. Close behind came Harold, bumping on his seat, robe fluttering around his knees. She had to jump back or he would have knocked her over. Upstairs, the nurse dripped blood, and Ruth sat with her head in her hands.

'Good-day, Cora,' said Harold.

Having prompted the scene, Cora took charge of it, telling the nurse to get himself downstairs and help them carry Mr Frederic into the drawing room. She gave no sign of being embarrassed by his condition. She treated him as she always did, with scepticism.

When he demanded a glass of whisky and a Corona, and appealed to her as a woman of the world who knew what idiots doctors were, she declined to give an opinion on a matter that, she said, Kate must decide. 'You wouldn't wish to cause dissension between us, would you now?' she smiled.

Best of all, Cora was deft in her handling of Harold on the subject of the missing man, the absent friend.

'Still no sign of him, then?' he said. 'He is probably suffering from melancholia, induced by not having any more ballads . . . bullets to dodge. They say he has been back to New York again.'

'I hear rumours.'

'I hope you are being astute about it, Cora.' He had his whisky by this time. Ruth had rushed to the post office to send a telegram recalling Dr Freyberger. 'You know how much I admire Stephen. But he is a quirky fellow. Do you know what he said once? "I can't help vanishing and disappearing and dissolving. It is my foremost trait." It's intolerable, leaving you in the dark. I only hope he decides to come back.'

Kate murmured to him to stop.

'Cora's my friend. Aren't I allowed to express an opinion?'

'Ask your newspaper if they have any private information,' said Cora. 'I know you're fond of him, even when he writes stories like "The Monster" that offend you. There must be correspondents who've seen Stephen. Will you do that for me?'

'I shall get Stokey to stir them up.'

'I shall always be your friend,' she said.

It was the mixture of grace and expediency that struck Kate. A skill like that was beyond her. But she knew it when she saw it.

Mathilde was waving a Western Union cable when Cora returned. The news was good, as far as it went. Crane was all in one piece. The time-stamp indicated that a few minutes before 3.23 the previous afternoon, local time, he had been leaning on the counter in the Key West cable office, filling out a form to assure Mrs Cora Crane that he is well, that he has been recently in New York, and that presently he may be in Havana. This extensive intelligence is signed 'Crane', but whether to save thirty cents on 'Stephen', or because the Western Union operative has omitted the given name in error, or because Stephen intended the plain masculinity of his surname, isn't clear.

'Do you know what I hoped for in my innocence?' wrote Cora, when she had heaved the private volume into his study, and shut herself up there with a pot of dark brown ink. 'I thought you wanted one more war to prove yourself in, and when it was over you would shoot back across the Atlantic as fast as triple-expansion engines could carry you. Some hopes. I can even find a text in the *Red Badge*, last page, where your soldier finds redemption. (I copy out the words so as to hear your voice.) "He saw that the world was a world for him . . . He had rid himself of the red sickness of battle . . . He had been an animal blistered and sweating in the heat and pain of war. He turned now with a lover's thirst to images of tranquil skies, fresh meadows, cool brooks – an existence of soft and eternal peace."

'Hooray for cool brooks! I paddled in ours with Kate. Mud

144

between the toes is exquisite. But not hooray for a lover's thirst and a homecoming, not yet, anyway.

'Speculating on the movements of a lover is demeaning. It is part of the fatal espionage of suspicion. It defeats the object of the exercise. You have been in New York. Have you been there only once, or is a revisit implied? I refuse to go into particularities. You were or you weren't. You saw Amy or you didn't. It is not that I am indifferent, simply that it is less painful to pretend to be.

'I have found some verse in a drawer of the desk. I put my hand in for a piece of blotting paper, and out came half a poem. You don't bury secrets, or if you do, you bury them inside your head. Once a thing is written down it becomes our common property. This is the basis on which I make entries in this book, that you can see my thoughts whenever you choose. It is like a mutual readiness to be seen naked.

'The poem disturbs me. If the subject is me – and who can it be if it isn't? – then you are less tolerant of the past than I've supposed. What should I make of it?

> Thou art my love
> And thou art the ashes of other men's love,
> And I bury my face in these ashes,
> And I love them—
> Woe is me.

'Am I being too anxious in trying to calibrate the feelings of someone like Stephen Crane? Or is that in itself a fallacy, to imagine that "someone like Stephen Crane" can avoid the mundane any more than the rest of us? If I am susceptible to jealousy, why shouldn't you be?

'If you were here . . . I would not be writing this. I fancy myself as a writer but the idea doesn't possess me, and I have learned from you that it is the possession that matters. I am under-employed, that's the trouble. I see people from time to time. Kate, to whom I feel closer than ever. Harold, who has been ill. The Conrads, in Essex. A strange police detective called Fred Hooper, whom I encountered when the Rudy got into one of her scrapes. He is like a beanpole and gets very cross, and you could write about him if you wrote satirical stories about the English. Except you like broader horizons.

'You would have found me unsatisfactory if I had been running an establishment for sea-bathing enthusiasts and businessmen with their wives in tow. But I fitted in with your scheme of things. I recall you walking in the first time and making yourself at home – you were leaning against a piano, dressed like a hobo, telling one of the girls that the opera house in New Orleans reminded you of gloomy cities in Europe. She said, "Gee, I would like to go to Europe," and you said, "Gee, so would I. But I know what to expect before I go there." I have a shrewd suspicion you had never been to New Orleans either.

'I have been consulting your calendar. You left Oxted on April the 11th. It is now August the 25th. You have been away one-hundred-and-thirty-six days. Sponge looks for you in the shrubbery some mornings and barks. I tell him: Keep looking.'

Calamities were to be expected in a cold-hearted country such as England, and Mathilde added her night locked up in a vile cell with a bucket to the list of things that Europe had to answer for.

Adoni, the boy-man, told her to 'look on the bright sides' and gave her a finger-ring that he said was silver, and came from Thessaloniki, but was obviously tin and came from somewhere a lot nearer. His manner had changed.

'Here is a magazine that has interesting stories,' she said, fitting in a reading lesson after breakfast. 'See? Follow my finger. "Mai-sie ven-tured on the hearth-rug and pulled the span-iel's tail."'

'Rose is comb-ing hair of Bar-ry,' said Adoni, who was looking out of the window. His solemn, burnt-skin features were heartbreakingly beautiful. 'Rose is pret-ty per-son, yes?'

'Do you want to be educated or do you mean to be a clodhopper all your life? It is no skin off my nose.'

'Pardon me?'

'I wash my hands of you.'

'Adoni must wash nose?'

It struck her that the vain monkey was poking fun, and she sent him out to get the borrowed pony ready for the children, who had been promised a morning's riding in a field. Dismayingly, Ma left him behind when they set off. She decided the brass and silver needed cleaning, and Adoni was told to put on his butler's apron and make the place shine. This left him alone with Rose Wellington, who had to stay and do the washing because the laundrywoman was owed money. Mathilde took the precaution of leaving behind the milk and home-made cookies. When the children were hungry she said 'Fancy Auntie Mattie forgetting!' and slipped back to Ravensbrook, a quarter of a mile away across the stiles.

The copper was bubbling in the washroom but there was no Rose. She began to search the house. Cutlery and brass lamps were assembled on a green cloth in the kitchen, which was empty. She looked in Adoni's boxroom. Empty, smelling of the pomade he put on his hair. She was in Ma's bedroom – empty – when a banging on the front door made her jump. Two men in bowler hats were outside, one of them carrying documents. Behind them a horse and van were approaching.

'Sheriff's representatives, Ma'am,' the man with papers called up to her. 'In pursuit of an order of the court, relating to a Broadwood Pianoforte, property of Whiteley & Co., I am here to seize the aforementioned.'

'The owner isn't here.'

'Irrelevant, Ma'am. Please to open the door. There is a police officer with the carter,' and Mathilde saw him walking beside the van.

'She isn't far. I will have her sent for.'

Mathilde had good lungs. She shouted for Adoni. When she got downstairs, he was in the door of the study, the revolver in his hand. He was grinning.

'Bad men is coming?' he said. 'I tell them, keep the trap shut or look sharp!'

'Give me the gun at once.'

'I shoot bullets to give them frights.'

He waved the Colt above his head, out of her reach. Mathilde wrenched his arm down and sent him off to get his mistress back from the field. 'Dirty lout!' she called after him.

The cellar door had not been closed properly; she had forgotten the cellar. Rose was in the washroom, looking contented and stirring clothes with a stick. Mathilde wanted to smack her, but it would have to wait.

Ma put her usual face on things, offered sherry to the men in bowler hats, said airily that she was glad to see the back of the instrument because no one had ever been able to tune it properly. But she lost her temper with Sponge for chewing a rug that he had been chewing unhindered all summer.

The piano would be missed. Men that Mr Crane brought down from London, journalists and the like, who emptied the larder and filled the house with smoke, used to knock out tunes on it. Their songs made the dog howl. Ma, who knew some music she claimed to have learned as a well-brought-up child in Boston, did better than that. When she played, late at night, Mathilde could hear it from her room, lying with her eyes closed, pretending they were at the Hotel de Dream again, and it was Jimmie, light-boned Jimmie, who might have married her, playing in the salon.

They were safe in Jacksonville. What was bought and sold there might have been flowers and wine and piano-music and pretty conversation, since that was the air the place had. Everyone was proud to work there, to be smiled at by Ma. There were picnics by the St Johns river, taking a few girls, who sat ladylike under the oaks along the bank, like pupils of an academy, giggling and saying 'Yes, Miss Cora' and 'No, Miss Cora'.

Bitterness came over Mathilde when she thought what they had been reduced to. Why couldn't they go back and start again? Why did they have to stay in this vile England?

It was no use Ma saying that Jacksonville left a lot to be desired. Mathilde was shocked to be asked by her once if she wasn't glad to be rid of the stable of little whores whose welfare she looked after.

'Did you enjoy supervising their hygiene?' Ma demanded. 'Did you never wonder about human depravity when they confided in you what some Sunday School superintendent wanted to have done to them? Did you never regard their bites and bruises with alarm?'

But all that Mathilde cared to remember was the tranquillity, and the dollar bills piling up in the safe at the back of Ma's office. And the piano keys that Jimmie swept with his long fingers, glancing her way and smiling.

12

Fred in the backyard, greasing the chain on the hired Juno, didn't want any fuss. A week's leave was what police officers were granted, and he took it because it was there. Mrs Monge had made his breakfast. He moved on from chain to tyres, giving them a touch of pump.

Suddenly the place was full of people. Belle came downstairs in her bare feet, and Miss Crumm arrived at the front door with an armful of clothes, ready to spend the week at the house. It was barely eight o'clock.

'We want to give you a good send-off, Freddie dear,' said his sister. 'I have packed you a Cornish pasty as a surprise. It's with your socks in the saddlebag. Also a small tin of liver-salts, just in case. I have sewn back the loose bits of your cycling map. It might last the week.'

'And I saw this on a stall the other day,' said Violet Crumm, producing a book called *The Cyclist's Compendium*. 'May I make you a present of it, Mr Hooper?'

'Most kind.'

'You see? Each page has a stretch of road on it. It shows gradients, landmarks and distances.'

'You shouldn't have.'

'It only cost tuppence. I bought it at Mr Rukes's stall in Bermondsey.'

Behind her friend's back, Belle pursed her lips in a silent 'Oo?', with raised eyebrows and a satirical nodding of the head.

'Shan't have any excuse for not doing my forty-five miles a day.'

He turned to Belle, gave her a peck on the lips, told her he would aim to be back the following Sunday afternoon. She looked slight and fragile, especially beside her friend, who talked excitedly about the Thomas Avertons she was going to paint during the week for Mr Rukes.

'I am going to be allowed to do some of the easy bits,' said Belle. 'Help with the sky. Do a dead dog if I'm lucky.'

Fred had one of his pangs for her. One day he might forgo the bicycle and take her to the seaside for a week, except that there was something not quite right about going on holiday with your sister.

As he wheeled the machine through the house, Rukes came downstairs and presented him with a tin box inscribed 'Schnitgler's Patent Puncture Remedy'.

'Imported from Germany. One tin will last you a thousand miles.'

'Is there anything you *don't* deal in?'

'I draw the line at stolen goods. Also articles that can't be mentioned in polite society. Otherwise, I'm your man.'

He insisted on shaking hands, on remarking how separations only served to bring families closer together, on shouting 'Bon voyage!' as Fred sailed down the street.

Half-dark tunnels could be seen through houses, connecting open doors at front and back. A man without a collar was sitting on the edge of a horse-trough in Wandsworth High

Street, reading a newspaper. Flies circled over slab-cake in a window. As Fred got into his stride on the Mitcham Road, the sun was already burning through his cycling cap, making the baldness prickle.

Fred took his holidays seriously, set himself goals of so many miles a day, dependent on sight-seeing. This time his route took him south and west as far as Guildford, with daily detours. At a place called Shalford, where he stopped to buy an orange, he found an ancient set of stocks outside the churchyard, and dozed in them. The man who kept the beerhouse where he put up for a night said the mills that made gunpowder for the fleet at Trafalgar were just down the road. Fred found them in ruins. As he was leaving, a bird-dropping landed on his cap. This was supposed to be lucky. Fred wasn't feeling lucky. He liked things cut and dried, and at the back of his mind the American woman was bothering him.

Another night he was at a railwayman's cottage. You saw more poverty here than in Wandsworth. Anyone would give you a cot, a blanket and a slice of bread and butter for ninepence. The blanket smelt sour and he caught a flea, but discomfort was only to be expected. Leg-muscles ached at first, then settled down.

In mid-week he thought to have a quiet day at Leith Hill, a beauty spot. 'Track only,' said the *Compendium*. '965 feet, highest point in south-east England.' He pushed his way up the hill, which possessed all the correct features, ascending layers of greenness, cooling shadows from belts of trees, air full of butterflies.

Near the summit he passed a party of naturalists in a wood; he assumed they were naturalists because one of them, a young female, was pursuing butterflies with a net, but they were larking about as well, and he could still hear them in the distance when he had climbed the staircase outside the tower at the top.

By the time he had enjoyed the view, they were at the base of the tower, and as he was going down, they were coming up. He had to squeeze past four or five young men, City clerks at a guess, and three women in turbulent hats. 'Make way for grandad!' ordered a man in black-and-lemon chequered trousers. A whiff of scent and he was past them. 'He trod on my foot,' squealed a female, and the joker said, 'Failing eyesight, poor old bloke.'

A butterfly net and a hamper were at the foot of the tower. Fred wheeled his bike a hundred yards to a gully and sat down for a pull of the ginger beer in his saddlebag. Forty winks after a restless night (he had had to use a piece of soap to catch the flea) seemed in order. Bees, targeting flowery bushes beside him, droned restfully. The buzzing faded.

A blow on the head made him sit up. An alarming wetness ran over his ear. His finger came away with a substance like jelly that could have been brains but had a meaty smell. Fred picked flakes of pastry from his scalp, and the remains of a pork pie. Getting to his feet, he saw them across the gully.

They claimed not to have known he was there. The men clung to one another, hysterical. The women, all bare-armed, with their hats and jackets on the ground beside them, rolled their eyes at him and giggled. The joker in check trousers held out a spoon and said, 'I say, old chap, may we have our pie back?' A sallow youth said he had 'chucked it at young Matthews here' to defend a maiden's honour, and missed. Young Matthews knelt behind a female in a green blouse and said, 'What, this one? She likes a bit of tickling, Doris does.'

'I think an apology would be in order,' said Fred.

'Doris will give you a kiss,' said Matthews. 'Doris will give anybody a kiss.'

'Cheeky monkey!'

'Fair's fair,' said the comedian. 'A great big kiss from Doris and you can keep the pie as well. That do you, grandad?'

Fred asked them if they knew that the wilful throwing of objects to the prejudice of public order and public safety was a punishable offence. More hilarity greeted this.

Funny-trousers said, 'Excuse me,' to Matthews, and stooped over Doris, who was reclining on her elbows. 'Here's a real treat, grandad. Better than a mutoscope on a pier. Ta-ra!' He took the hem of the woman's skirt and flicked it above her knees.

There was a flash of legs, stockings, plumpness and ribbons before Doris screamed, 'Ooh what a liberty!' and covered herself up.

'That do you?' said the comedian.

Fred sighed. Florence, who abhorred nakedness, had been almost as strict about her underwear. Complicated performances used to go on behind the bedroom screen. Belle was less careful, could be seen wandering about upstairs in her petticoat until the lodger came. To be reminded of these private matters by a hussy at a beauty-spot was intolerable.

'This do you?' he said. He stepped up to the comedian and punched him in the mouth, a good straight knock that put him on the ground, spitting blood and a tooth. Not quite in the Rukes league, but still, a satisfactory punishment.

'Nobble him!' shouted Matthews, but Fred held his warrant card in the air, warning them that he was a police officer, and if they didn't want to go to prison for affray, they had better keep very quiet.

He left them looking sullen and pedalled hard down the bumpy track, his knuckle bleeding, the day under a cloud. A companion might have raised his spirits, Tom Simmons or

154

Belle. Only the other day the *Daily Mail* showed a man and woman scorching past on a tandem bicycle, waving dangerously at the artist.

Without warning he had a vision of Mrs Cora Crane sitting behind him on a tandem, skirt billowing, pedalling as furiously as a man, the brim of a cheeky cap touching him between the shoulder blades as she leaned forward on the pedals and said, 'Golly, this is fast.' Fred didn't go in for flights of fancy. He thought it must be his liver.

Slackening speed as the path levelled out, between fields of wheat as brown as toast, he was injudicious with the brake. He ended up in the hedge with scratched face and hands. The lapse grieved him; he was a careful rider, as he was a careful everything else. He urinated into the thorns, disenchanted with the glories of Surrey.

A spoke had gone in the front wheel and the machine was developing a wobble. He had to push it for miles, and it was late afternoon before he found a blacksmith, with the usual three or four villagers hanging about, helping with advice. It was a fancy bike, they concluded, running dirty fingers over the tyres. A youth with no socks said that properly speaking he ought to have a new wheel.

The smith ignored them. He pushed his goggles up his forehead and began tapping and wrenching. A man whose head seemed to grow out of his shoulders said that steam omnibuses were starting soon on the Brighton Road from London, going one behind the other, hundreds of 'em, mark his words. Bicycles were finished and so were railway trains.

'One shilling,' said the smith. 'He should hold, but don't give him a rough time.'

What with his fleabites, his torn knuckle and his liver, Fred decided an early night was appropriate. He sought advice. The smith thought the Swan over at Melham was the place. No, said someone, there was Mrs Job by the bakery. No, she had chickens in the spare room.

'Tell you what,' said the sockless man. 'Luke here has a sister over at Crow Turn'll give you a clean bed, very reas'n'ble. Throws in a lovely slice o' pie.' He wiggled his eyebrows. 'All soft an' creamy.'

'You shut your mouth,' said Luke, but not angrily. He was the one lacking a neck.

The man without socks took Fred's arm. 'Hey, fine woman, lost her 'usband in a railway smash. Go straight up the road from here, finger-post to Leckham, mile and a half, over the railway bridge, first cottage after that, by the crossroads. Got a tin roof.'

Fred pedalled slowly, the golden light behind him, tree-shadows starting to lengthen. His progress tomorrow would continue to the east, across the broad middle of Surrey towards Kent and Tom Simmons, and then straight home through the suburbs, his leave over for another year.

Turning at the Leckham finger-post, he calculated that now was the half-way point. He could still pause and change his plans, returning by some other route. In the morning he was free to veer north-west into Berkshire, where he had never been. The dusty roads would be the same. Ninepence would still buy a bed. Any variation from the quiet dullness of this and every other trip was accidental, like the business on Leith Hill.

In Oxfordshire once, cycling by a deserted canal, he came level with a sloping field, unfenced to the water, where a man and woman were misbehaving. He was past them in seconds, but in his memory it still ranked as an incident. In Norfolk, still further back in time, he stopped at a fishing village near Yarmouth. It was an evening in September. On the beach after dark, men were shovelling mounds of dead herring into carts.

He had been told it was a sight worth seeing. The fish gave off a cold phosphorescence, like the blue of gaslight.

A young woman broke away from a group of friends and walked with him, asking who he was and what he was doing there. His rank was sergeant then. Florence had been dead a couple of years. 'You can take my arm,' she said. 'My name's Florence.'

He fled to his lodgings. What if she had said her name was Polly or Victoria? What if he had been as bold with women as he was with villains?

Malformation of the wheel made a noise at each revolution, like a clock ticking. From the hump of the railway bridge he saw the tin roof of the cottage. There was no sign of life but the door was open.

It was as good a place to stop as any. Luke's sister would appear wiping her hands on an apron, a plain woman if her brother was anything to go by. Not that Fred had any time for suggestive conversations like the one at the smithy. But as he tick-ticked along the road, he couldn't stop another fancy getting into his head, that the woman would look like Florence did when they were courting, neat hair and small teeth, a bosom that he avoided looking at directly, and a swaying walk that she never seemed able to control.

At the last minute, as he slowed, he had an impression of a person, but not its face, in the room beyond the door, and stood on the pedals to escape.

His liver was getting beyond a joke. He found his way to the Swan at Melham, and for one shilling and sixpence had clean sheets and two fresh candles.

Fred's progress continued eastward, as planned, for the rest of the week. He visited churches in varying states of disrepair. He saw the last of the harvest coming in. He bought a tiny cat made of glass for Belle and a brass-rubbing of a plaque for Miss Crumm. He mended a couple of punctures with Rukes's remedy and got glue on his trousers. His face and hands grew healthily sunburnt.

If anything was wrong with him, it lay beyond the power of liver salts, whose fizzing bitterness he gulped down every morning. He went cycling to feel the fresh air on his face, not to be assailed by impropriety in the shape of that woman – five foot five, goldish hair, greenish eyes, sitting behind him on the tandem bicycle, which was a figment of the imagination, or kissing him in the street, small mouth, lower lip prominent, which wasn't.

She made him angry. He had made no promise as such to abandon the case. It would do no harm to remind her that Fred Hooper, like Pinkerton's, never slept. On Friday morning he arranged to be cycling through Oxted.

Ravensbrook was raw-red in the sun. The rascal who answered his knock, the Greek, tried to shut the door in his face, but toe of boot stopped that. The Greek shouted, 'Meesis Cora! Help!'

Fred spoke quietly through the crack. 'Tell your mistress who it is.'

An eye peered at him. 'Meesis Cora not at home. Please to leave the visiting card.'

'The butler should think of that first,' Fred heard her say. 'Now open the door quietly and let's see who it is.'

She wore a plain dress, and her hair, free of hat, was revealed as a heap of curls, gripped untidily by combs. He couldn't remember if she was hatless the night the Greek had the gun. If so, it hadn't registered. His blood must have warmed up today because the fleabites began itching.

He was the last person Cora expected to see. She had forgotten about Detective Hooper. In the Dream days there were police officers who kept coming back for a free drink or occasionally a free girl, but this was England, with no mutual interests needing to be served.

With his bicycle and jolly cap she would hardly have recognised him. He 'happened to be passing through.' The day was close. His face was perspiring. It crossed her mind that he was ill. She asked him to come inside.

'So am I still on your list of suspicious characters?' she asked, when he had removed the clips from his baggy tweed trousers and followed her to the drawing room.

'Not unless I find fresh evidence.'

'Well, that's a relief.'

The man cleared his throat. 'I saw your roses as I came up to the house. You said you were fond of them.'

'Did I?' The conversation began to trouble Cora. 'Yes, I remember, you had a rose in your buttonhole. I could snip one of mine for you. Would that be good for a detective's disguise or bad?'

'I doubt if it matters either way. Have you lived here long?'

'Upwards of a year. It isn't permanent. We shall be moving down to Sussex when Mr Crane returns. Brede Place, near Rye, if you want to make a note of it.'

'Always on the move.'

Was he interrogating her or making conversation? 'Believe me,' she said, 'I want nothing more than to settle down permanently.'

The bay windows were open and the detective was sitting close to one, but he appeared to be getting hotter, not cooler.

'Cycling in this weather must be hard work,' she suggested. It was then she remembered having given him a vague invitation to call, and apologised for being so inhospitable. Rose was sent to the cellar for a jug of lemonade. He drank two glassfuls and said he mustn't keep her.

Barry burst into the room.

'Knock,' she said. 'Remember?'

'Sorry, Aunt Cora.'

'This is Inspector Hooper, who rescued you. He has come to make sure you haven't disappeared again.'

'I've drawn the piano the men stole. Aunt Mattie said I could show it to you.'

What looked like a ship's boiler on legs had been rendered on the slate in red and yellow chalks. Hooper gave the child a halfpenny. 'And close the door as you go out,' said Cora.

'A piano?' asked the detective, as if the point of the visit had been reached at last. 'Stolen?'

'It's of no consequence.'

'Forgive me, but theft is increasing in the Home Counties. Bands of thieves select isolated houses.'

She watched him prowl about the room.

'Stood here, didn't it?' he said, examining leg-dents in the carpet. 'Was the house empty at the time?'

'At least I know why you're in the area. Don't worry, I shan't give your secret away. You have come to look for bands of burglars, haven't you? To be honest, I can't imagine you on a holiday.'

'With respect, Mrs Crane, you don't know anything about me.'

'That's true.' She wouldn't have seen him as a touchy man. 'You know far more about me. There is a Mrs Hooper, I take it? Some little Hoopers?'

'My wife died years ago. We had no children.'

'And you've never remarried?'

'It isn't a matter I care to discuss.'

'Why ever not? You make it sound like an ailment. You're not old. There are women galore. It's no way to live, by yourself.'

He stared at her. 'I have a younger sister and we share the house.'

'Very convenient. Doesn't she want to get married either?'

'I wouldn't go worrying about my sister if I were you.'

'You keep being offended.' She couldn't resist teasing him. 'You are the one who came asking about me. Why shouldn't I be curious about you?'

'I am a police officer, pure and simple.'

'Stuff!'

He gave her a blank, official look. There was probably as much passion in him as in anyone else, if it ever came to the surface. She had intuitions about men, even cops. But Sponge barked, Heloise cried, the detective thanked her for the lemonade, and then they were shaking hands on the doorstep. She was still uncertain why he had called.

Fred came away smarting, furious at being questioned about little Hoopers. He should never have gone near the place. Holiday moods were the problem. You pedalled through miles of nowhere and your mind succumbed to thoughts that it normally had no time for.

He had seen enough holiday till next summer. After another night with his legs over the end of a mattress, he decided to go home a day early, via a brief visit to the Simmons establishment in Bromley. It was the middle of the afternoon when he arived. Tom had just returned for his Saturday dinner. 'This is the man who collared one of the Greenwich anarchists in '94,' he told his parents, and insisted on singing a ditty that circulated at the time:

161

It's a B.O.M.B bomb!
It's a B.O.M.B bomb!
They say it's very hard on Scotland Yard,
It's a B.O.M.B bomb!

Hettie, Tom's fiancée, a tall girl with a tiny mouth, was brought round, and blushed a lot.

Before Fred left, he and Tom went for a stroll, along a stream behind a brickworks, to talk shop. He enjoyed hearing his colleague rattle on about Vine Street. The world of crime was where a man could be happy. Rumour said that Wilk the forger was back in business. 'I know he's top of your list,' said Tom.

Fred wanted the details. But they were only rumours. The man might be in Hoxton. There might be a printer. 'We can talk on Monday,' said Tom. 'You're still on holiday. Have you gone far?'

'Far enough.'

'I heard you telling Hettie the places you'd seen. Half Surrey, it sounded like.'

'Leith Hill is a corker.'

'You looked in at Oxted.'

'Pretty village. The Greenwich meridian runs through the High Street.'

'Didn't you say that Mrs Crane lives there, the American woman?'

'Very smart and detective-like of you to remember. The word has gone round. Fred Hooper spent all day helping a female find a small boy.'

'I was only pulling your leg. But I'm curious. Did you call on her? No reason why you shouldn't.'

'None at all. Only I'm not answering any questions on the subject. Not even yours, and I know you're a friend. Let's just say that the next time a woman gives me a kiss in a public place, I shall arrest her for indecent assault.'

'Now you're pulling mine,' said Tom. But he let the matter drop.

The journey home through Crystal Palace and Streatham took longer than Fred expected. The southern suburbs were crowded and he had another puncture. By the time he reached Wandsworth and returned the cycle to the shop, where they grumbled about the wheel, it was getting late.

The house was empty, windows shut, stale with heat. After killing slugs he found corned beef and made a sandwich. Belle, no doubt, was at Violet's, and since he wasn't expected till the next day, they might be spending the night there instead of here.

Silence was what you needed in a bedroom, but it was unusually intense as he lay sweating under a sheet, trying to sleep. The holiday came back to bother him. Hedges and telegraph poles went by in his head. He had his vision of a tandem, the peak of a cap bouncing against his spine with the rhythm of the cyclist. His liver still hadn't settled. Any minute now he would hear a voice in his ear saying, 'Golly, this is fast.' To keep his mind off it, he kept running through the ditty about the Greenwich outrage, 'It's a B.O.M.B bomb! It's a B.O.M.B bomb!'

To crown everything, his sister and her friend returned. He heard their voices, and then a laugh that sounded like the lodger. Fred pulled on trousers and shirt, and went downstairs. Miss Crumm, who was the first to see him, nearly fainted.

'We weren't expecting you till tomorrow,' said Belle. 'Was your holiday not all right?'

'I did two-hundred-and-seventy-one miles.'

'Puncture kit up to scratch, I trust,' said Rukes. 'You will be wondering where we've been.'

'I expect someone will tell me.'

'You'll never guess,' said Belle.

The lodger had taken them to a music-hall in Ealing.

'They were in safe hands,' said Rukes. 'We went in the fourpenny gallery so they could see a bit of life as she is.'

'And if I hadn't come back tonight, I suppose I would have heard nothing about it.'

'Not true,' said Belle. 'I couldn't not have told you. It was fun. Girls with bare legs pretending they were soldiers, a wandering violinist who kept falling off the stage. A girl in a pink dress sang – what was it, Vi?'

'Something about no one had ever kissed her.'

'And the men kept calling, "Give us 'arf a chance"'.

'It was a bit vulgar,' said Miss Crumm, and added it was time she left.

Rukes was penitent. 'I feel I have let you down, Mr Hooper. I saw it as harmless fun, educational, almost. But if I have overstepped the mark, I shall leave in the morning.'

'An undertaking not to let it happen again will be enough.'

'Done!' said Rukes, and stood for a moment with his eyes closed and hands folded, as if in prayer.

Alone with his sister, Fred asked her what on earth she had been thinking of.

'It made a change. Anything to get away from all this.'

'All what?'

'Arding & Hobbs, for a start. I'm considering handing in my notice.'

'And then?'

'Emigrate to America and be a telephone girl? Anything except *this*,' and she gestured at the coal stove and the dark uncurtained window, implying that Disraeli Street was as bad as her office.

He could interrogate suspects but hardly his sister. 'You

know you can always rely on me,' was the best he could manage. 'Whatever happens.'

'Well, let's hope it doesn't,' said Belle, and went to bed, leaving him mystified. Women again.

13

If it hadn't been for Brede Place, Cora might have managed her money. 'In that case why are you going there?' said Kate. 'It's seventy miles from London and you can't afford it. *And* it's like a medieval castle. *And* I like having you five villages away. Stay where you are.'

'Stephen needs somewhere to be himself.'

'He's the kind who makes himself at home wherever he is.'

It saddened Cora that no one understood. He was so fond of plains and deserts, of his 'great honest West,' that the least she could do was find him a substitute, a place to retreat to. Since it was England, a castle was what he needed.

'Be honest,' said Kate. 'You fancy living in a house with a history.'

'Maybe I do. But I wouldn't do it if it weren't for Stevie. He doesn't really want gangs of journalists and hangers-on descending at all hours, keeping him from his work. Just close friends like you and Harold, blazing fires, dogs asleep on the floor . . .'

It was painfully simple, Crane in the room above the entrance, writing and writing. But would it ever happen?

Almost enough to cover the lease, if she didn't pay the back-rent at Ravensbrook, had been in a linen bag in Stevie's desk, behind the drawer where he kept his pens. The Brede Place money was due soon, at the next quarter-day, September 29. On top of that, essential repairs to the roof were to be paid for by the Cranes. She thought about tarpaulins and buckets to catch the drops. They could live with buckets as long as they had roses.

Then the piano was seized, and Cora had to nibble at the treasure to keep local tradesmen happy. Word of a distraint went round like an infectious disease. Butcher Figg and the rest thought they smelt bankruptcy or eviction or both. Swift distribution of gold pieces was needed to make them retreat behind their counters, bowing and scraping.

Kate tried to give her money for having fed the children, who were at home again because Harold insisted, but Cora wouldn't hear of it. She knew the Frederic finances were in chaos. Mrs Mills the healer was still doing her long-distance praying, and the patient was still confined to the house.

Harold had made a will but refused to let Kate see it. 'I thought it meant his wife would get everything,' she told Cora, 'till I found a draft on Stokey's desk. It says I am to have this house, but it's mortgaged. Not that it matters because I know he is going to get better. But his American copyrights are mortgaged, too. Grace will get the London house, and she's no better off.' She took off the wire frames and massaged her eyelids. 'Where has it gone? Not that it matters.'

If Kate dreaded poverty, Cora was angered by it. She had the habit of money. She went to see a lawyer to try and have Crane's frozen royalties released, but the old boy she spoke to took fright at her tale of New York actresses and writs. Then she thought of Sarah Bollitt at Cranleigh Hall, and wrote to ask if her husband would supply a formal introduction to the proprietors of Tourbon's Bank. A week later came a friendly letter to say that Mr Bollitt had spoken to their Mr Philip Tourbon, who would be pleased to receive Mrs Crane by appointment. This wasn't the boy Tourbon who had ogled her during the unfortunate weekend. Cora had hopes.

Anything could come of anything. 'I have been to see an attorney,' Cora wrote in her locked book, in a dream-letter that might be transmuted one day into a volume of Dream Letters to an Unknown Lover, by Imogene Carter. 'I got tired of waiting for a hundred dollars (might as well say five hundred while I'm at it) to come in via your agent Reynolds, whom I wrote to in New York *sans* response. I went to see an attorney but he was useless. He kept saying, "We are in England, Mrs Crane, not America."

'And then I saw a banker.'

Skeletal entries gave themselves away by their brevity. If Crane ever read it, he would say, 'And what else?' Nothing else, she would smile. Or, if not in a smiling mood, she might say, 'I heard you were in Havana but I had no address to write to, even if I defied you and sent a letter. People said you were writing despatches about the price of bread and what the inhabitants thought of American soldiers, but no one sent me them because they assumed you were telling me all there was to tell in your letters. I should have said, What letters? You cut me off. What was I supposed to do? Eat grass? Not pay the rent at Ravensbrook and risk eviction? Not sign the lease to Brede Place? Not get the builders in and have to spend the winter catching water in buckets? I went to see a banker. Whatever I did, it was only for my mouse.'

The bank, up an alley behind a fish and vegetable market, failed to produce Mr Philip Tourbon for their appointment.

He had been summoned to Paris at short notice. Men in black coats gave her the bad news and parked her in a closet where a discouraging character called Wrench came to look after her, which he did by showing great interest in the absent Mr Crane and very little in her. He was the general manager. Cora got the feeling that he had never discussed money with a woman, except possibly dress bills with his wife.

Various things about Mr Crane could be seen perturbing him. These included his absence in Cuba and the fact that his income arose from the writing of novels. He was not familiar with the name, although he threw Charles Dickens into the conversation to show that he knew what a novel was.

'May I inquire,' he said, 'what sum of money Mr Crane will be depositing with the bank?'

'You have it the wrong way round. I am here about a loan. I am relying on an introduction from Mr Bollitt.'

'Dear me,' said Wrench.

He dwelt on property. No doubt her husband owned freehold property in England, and deeds to that effect could be produced? Disappointed, he ran out of steam. To be America's foremost writer was all very well, he would take her word for it. 'But you see, my dear lady,' he said, 'we have to be realists in the City of London. Let me give you an example. Say a person wishes to make a substantial borrowing. Let us say fifty pounds. The bank will look for what we call *security*.'

'I once owned an hotel in America,' said Cora, 'so I think I know what bankers mean by security. We are wasting one another's time.'

An attendant came to show her out. The corridors had carpets that silenced footsteps. But as they rounded a corner, a door opened and a man said, 'Mrs Crane, what a pleasure! I knew you were in the bank.'

It was Charles Tourbon, his eyes wandering across her as they did before. 'Please,' he said. 'In here. My modest quarters. How charming you look.'

They sat on gilt chairs in a room decorated with engravings of Paris and a painting in oils of a Tourbon. There were preliminaries. He talked and Cora listened. The painting showed his late father. The missing Philip was his uncle. Bank protocol had directed her to old Wrench. Charles hoped it had been a satisfactory meeting. And how was Mr Crane? Was he still globe-trotting? Did she have more of those riveting travellers' tales?

'I expect him back shortly.'

'In the meantime, is there anything we can do?'

Cora said she had hardly come to Tourbon's to admire the furniture. But Mr Wrench had not been helpful.

'He isn't the final arbiter. He is an employee. The Tourbons are the bank.'

'So what do the Tourbons say to a loan of two-hundred-and-fifty pounds secured against unpaid earnings from books?'

'That's a tall order.'

'Of course it is. But I have been introduced as a friend of the Bollitts.'

'As a friend of mine, come to that. I personally would write out a cheque this minute, if I were permitted. But you know what banks are, protocol and all that. I would find it necessary to talk to Mr Philip. He is a prudent chap. I fear I know what he'd say.'

'So the answer is no.'

'Before we go any further, why don't you call me Charles and why don't I call you Cora?'

'Because that would suggest a friendship that doesn't exist.'

'Here am I, trying to make things easy, and you keep snubbing me like mad. What have you got to lose?'

'I leave that to your imagination, which I fancy is working overtime.'

'You see, you keep doing it. I have never had a conversation like this with a woman. One minute you tell me we are strangers with nothing in common, the next you are making indelicate remarks.'

'By referring to the imagination?'

He extended his legs towards her and drew them back. 'I refuse to go on discussing your loan, or whatever it is we are discussing, on these premises. Let us meet in a tea-shop or Kensington Gardens or anywhere you choose, and establish ourselves on a friendly basis. We might eat dinner at a respectable restaurant.'

'So we might, if Mr Crane was present as well.'

'You're a stone wall. I have to confess, I like women who are stone walls.' He stretched his arms over his head. 'I will see what I can do. I can make no promises. You are in no great hurry?'

'No more of a hurry than you.'

'We will both have to be patient,' he said, and rang for one of the black-coats to show her out.

Drawn game so far, she thought. It was after this that she wrote in her book, 'And then I saw a banker.'

From the City she went to Milborne Grove, to be greeted by a dozen letters, most of them bills. The only one she opened had a red seal with an eagle imprinted. Miss Hay was writing to her from Carlton House Terrace.

'Our hopes for a Society of American Women are nearing fulfilment,' read Cora, 'and this note is by way of a "progress report" for those who have expressed interest in our ambitious project. We hope that an executive committee will emerge as a result of a meeting here next Thursday, after which plans for the inauguration can be set in motion. We are desirous of this taking place early in 1899.'

The letter was dated the previous Friday. Today was Thursday, and the dress she had worn to visit the bank would do. Cora didn't hesitate to see the letter as an invitation. Never mind the small matter of what time the meeting was to be. If the wife of the finest living American novelist didn't deserve special treatment, who did?

Miss Hay, the ambassador's daughter, hadn't bargained for such a powerful urge among her compatriots to set up a feminine outpost in London. The English mania for clubs and societies was catching. No respectable female with American connections was to be left out. A Mrs Griffin, in at the start, a large person who made every remark sound like a command, was keen on 'women of substance'. 'Defer to her,' said Miss Hay's father, who was careful not to get involved beyond cordial endorsements, 'for she is mighty. She is a Regent of the Daughters of the American Revolution.'

Helen Hay deferred to them all, without taking them too seriously, except for one or two who were so eminent that they alarmed her. Lady Randolph Churchill, the former Jennie Jerome of Brooklyn, made a brief call, glittering from every pore, and before she left gave the ambassador's butler a recipe for a cocktail she had invented. The Duchess of Manchester, who was born in Cuba, showed her face and told a mildly improper story about a horse, which Mrs Griffin forced herself to swallow. Rank was a funny thing.

The only woman Helen took to was a Mrs Craigie, who had been married to a businessman, and now wrote novels under a pseudonym about witty people entangled in bad marriages. Pearl Craigie was young and shrewd, interested in the world

but unworldly in her manner. Like Helen, she was drawn into
the scheme without caring much for it.

After the Thursday meeting at which 'our brave little ship,'
as Mrs Griffin expressed it, 'has been finally launched,' Pearl
stayed behind to chat. She was still there when a servant came
to say that Mrs Stephen Crane was in the waiting room.

'*The* Stephen Crane?' said Pearl. 'I am curious.'

'She won't be what you expect. But here goes.'

The visitor bustled in, pulling off violet gloves like plucking
feathers from a chicken, and remarking that evidently she was
either too early for the committee or too late.

'Mrs Craigie and I have decided we never want to see a
committee again in our lives,' said Helen. 'Let me introduce
you. You will know Mrs Craigie by the pen name she uses for
her novels, John Oliver Hobbes.'

'*A School of Saints*,' Cora said promptly, misplacing a word
or two. 'And do you sell many copies?'

'A fair number.'

'Mrs Craigie has a play opening in the West End shortly.'

'I shall try and see it,' said the dauntless Mrs Crane. 'I write
myself, you know. I use the name Imogene Carter.'

'If I were in your place,' said Pearl, 'I would be tempted to
make no bones about it – say I was Cora Crane, and cash in
on the connection.'

'Surely Crane soars above the rest of us?' said Cora. She
described a recent visit to the home of Mr Joseph Conrad, who
had apparently confirmed that her husband was a genius, and
made him want to blow his brains out – whether Mr Conrad's
or Mr Crane's wasn't clear.

After more along these lines, Pearl looked at the clock and
said she must go.

'So are we three the committee?' asked Cora.

Miss Hay treated this as a pleasantry, and said that she

guessed Lady Randolph Churchill and the Duchess of Manchester would have been glad to stand aside if they knew there were so many candidates.

'You mean they were here today?'

'Fleeting visits. The important thing is that they lend their names.'

'I would have lent you mine. You only had to ask.'

Was that a preposterous thing to say? Or was the wife of the man who wrote *The Red Badge of Courage* entitled to feel slighted? Democracy was the sweetest word in the language, and all that. Miss Hay was stumped. 'It never occurred to me,' she said. 'Please don't be offended.'

But Mrs Crane was glowing. 'Now then, you two,' she said, 'I will give your society something to look forward to. By next summer Mr Crane and I will be established in our mansion in Sussex, which is being got ready. It is very historic, and I think should be better known. We have a ghost, a dungeon, a ballroom, beds galore, conservatories of flowers, big lawns, big gardens, gravel paths and stone monuments, and a lake for rowing on and woods filled with bluebells. It is called Brede Place, and it is one of the most glorious situations in England. I invite you all there for a summer fete. The entire society and its menfolk.'

'Good gracious,' said Mrs Craigie, who was stuck halfway between the fireplace and the door, where a maid was waiting with her wrap.

'There will be hoopla, coconuts, a steam merry-go-round and a fortune-teller. It's the least I can do for you. I shall run a special train down from London, with wagonettes from Rye. Who would the society like to meet there? Mr Kipling lives in the neighbourhood. So does Mr Henry James. Mr H.G. Wells is no further than Folkestone.'

Miss Hay didn't know what to make of it. Cora said

she hoped that 'Jennie Churchill' would be able to come, not to mention the Duchess. As she worked herself up, the occasion mutated into a ball or a banquet, or perhaps both. A chef from the Trocadero would be hired to supervise the roasting of sheep and the boiling of fowls. There would be tents and a band, and a string orchestra would play in the ballroom. It seemed to be winter now. Flags of the nations hung from the gallery. Light from lanterns and fires gleamed on women's jewels.

Miss Hay would not have been surprised to hear crowned heads of European dynasties listed among the guests. Pearl took her wrap and left. Cora stopped in the middle of a sentence and said, 'I got carried away. But I did mean every word.'

Saving Brede Place was simple. All Cora had to do was flatter a man. Flowers began to arrive, sent indiscriminately to Milborne Grove and Ravensbrook. She ignored them. Sooner or later there would be an invitation, and then the fun would start. She tried to see him as Crane would, a figure in a story. The pearl pin in the absurd cravat, the tight trousers that revealed the knee-cap, the shining silk hat that crowned his suave little features, would be the foil for a Wild West hero in down-at-heel shoes. But Tourbon worried her, too, waiting in the wings, his plans predicated on sexual intercourse, giving her those explicit looks.

Cora liked a bit of subtlety. It was what her customers used to like about the Dream, which supplied their needs without being too obvious. Behind the scenes there had to be practical management, naturally – such-and-such number of girls, special requests to be notified in advance, discreet medical advice on call. But the place ran on illusion. Gentlemen dropped in for the evening to read newspapers and dine and play cards and discuss real estate and railroads. As an afterthought they slept with pretty women.

Even Stevie, who said he had no time for illusions, had been happy to walk in from the street – at first she was dubious about this shabby figure, lounging with its hands in its pockets. He chatted to the girls, asking them about their lives. 'All in the course of duty,' he told Cora, grinning, later on, the first time he was in her private drawing-room, before they were lovers, before she was in love with him.

He gave her a copy of a story he had written years earlier about a girl of the streets called Maggie who came to a bad end. Did Cora know Manhattan? Well enough, she told him. 'But not Chatham Square, I'll bet,' he said. 'I lived in a twenty-five-cent lodging house in '92. Plenty of Maggies down there, below Canal Street.'

Tough men in a tough world appealed to him, in spite of his unhealthy look, or because of it. When he came back from the dead, spewed up by the sea on Daytona Beach, and she was watching him recover in a bed full of hot-water bottles, he revelled in what he had seen, men *in extremis*, the elements bent on destroying them. 'Brutality laid bare, that's the thing,' he said.

As far as she could tell, he saw no poetry in sexual intercourse. On the other hand, who did? Stevie, she suspected, saw violence in the act, a weakness in human nature that was laid bare by it. But was his furious hard-headedness itself an illusion? Was there another Stevie, one she didn't know about? She would have to ask him. If she ever saw him.

These unpromising thoughts got worse when Tourbon moved on to invitations. 'I *must* see you,' he wrote. 'I suggest the theatre. Being a literary woman, I am sure you have a play in mind.'

She sent a note to say that an interesting work was having

its first night at the St James's. A few days later they were taking their seats in the stalls to see something called *The Ambassador*.

A hard evening's work lay ahead.

'Are you aware,' said Tourbon, 'that the chappie who wrote this play calls himself John Oliver Hobbes, but he's really a woman called Craigie?'

'How amazing!'

'I read it somewhere. You ought to have known that. You live with a fellow who writes books. Or *did* you know it, and pretended not to?'

He had more brain than she had given him credit for.

'The English expect women to keep their knowledge to themselves.'

'You are American, you can do anything,' said Tourbon.

His shoulder rubbed hers. Lights dimmed and the colours of gowns faded into a gloom where the men's blacks and whites were more striking. The play was about love in London high society. Witticisms that made Cora smile had young Tourbon falling off his seat. The ambassador, who liked women, was chided for a five-day courtship. 'I believe the *world* was created in six,' he said. Tourbon slapped his leg and howled like a dog.

True society hovered at the edges of the fiction on the stage. Cora might have been part of it herself, if she had put up with Captain Stewart and got him to go into politics, say, and become a Member of Parliament.

'The incomparable Mrs Stewart, whose supper-parties are the talk of the town, is married to Mr Donald Stewart, MP, who is tipped as the next Secretary for War, and is the daughter-in-law of Field Marshal Sir Donald Stewart, hero of the Indian Mutiny. Diplomats, explorers and members of the peerage throng her soirées, but she has a soft spot for those of artistic bent, especially for writers.'

Especially for Mr Stephen Crane, who has nothing to do with the above. Cora was hot and bored, her thoughts in Cuba. She was unsure about the place. Lush green? Baked dust? At times she was vague about Crane, whose moustache and cowboy boots and crooked smile hung in the air like spare parts, waiting to be put together again.

During the interval she and the boy ate dishes of ice-cream with a hundred others in a gilt-and-gaslight tunnel. He was anxious to know which of the witticisms appealed to her most. She couldn't remember any.

'Come along,' he said, 'what about, "I never go where I'm not invited – but then, I'm peculiar"?'

'Side-splitting.'

She endured the last act. The worrying part was what would happen afterwards. Cora longed to go backstage in search of Mrs Craigie and be invited to stay and drink champagne. Miss Hay and her father must be there somewhere, perhaps in the best box, where jewels and a white shoulder could easily be Lady Randolph Churchill.

Applause and cheering exploded. When the cast had finished bobbing up and down, people began shouting 'Author!' and Mrs Craigie appeared, a small figure in white against the curtain.

'Would you like to meet her?' Cora said in Tourbon's ear.

'You mean, is she my type. That sounds like another of your indelicate questions.'

The moment passed. Reluctantly, she saw the wisdom of sticking to the job in hand.

It was raining but her new friend ran into the street and procured a cab in seconds. Supper loomed up, hors d'oeuvres with a hint of lechery, meat coursing with blood. The boy was already in fingery mode, brushing her arm with the tips. Presently it would be knee.

'Nothing wrong with supper,' she said, 'but why don't we go exploring? Do you know Limehouse?' It came out on the spur of the moment.

'You amaze me. Who goes down there at night?'

'You'd be surprised. You might find it amusing.'

He slid the roof-flap and gave the instruction.

Crane was there once, with Conrad, who walked them around the docksides he had known when he was in the merchant service, and down Limehouse Causeway, where there were more Chinese than Englishmen. Crane brought home strips of dried fish and pickled eggs, which she threw in the trash can, and told her Limehouse stories when they were in bed.

Cora had no plan, but as the cab ran east, she could see that Tourbon's curiosity about the adventure was getting in the way of his seductive tendencies. It was better than a West End restaurant where he would try and persuade her to eat supper in a private room, and sulk when she refused.

'What does Cora Crane propose we do when we get there?'

'Tell the cab to wait, leave your silly hat inside, and go into one of the Chinese houses in the street. They have blue lamps over the door. They don't like Westerners but they like their money.'

'And what do we Westerners get for it?'

'Tea and a dish of noodle? Whatever you want, really.'

They were beyond Fleet Street and the City, sliding into a thicker darkness. Gas-jets struggled against looming warehouses.

'What are the attractions?'

'They say a gambling game called fan-tan is addictive once you get the hang of it. Or there's opium. A few daring souls try the pipe.'

'My dear Mrs Crane,' he said, and his arm tried to get round

179

her waist. 'You love to sound a mystery woman. Opium, indeed!'

She got rid of the arm and said it was simpler than people supposed, as long as you visited a den with a proper layout and a cook who knew his business. 'He rolls the pill in his fingers, sticks it on a kind of darning needle, heats it up on the lamp, and pops it in the pipe. One deep breath, that's all you take. Then you curl up on a mattress in a dream. Afterwards you're exceedingly thirsty.'

'Are you saying you've done it?'

She didn't answer. If Tourbon was looking for the exotic, she was ready to supply it, as long as she wasn't called on to supply anything else.

They crossed the neck of a basin crammed with barges, lit by lamps strung between poles. The Thames was through a cut on the other side, foaming against dark walls. 'I like to go slumming once in a while,' she said.

'You and your Mr Crane.'

Limehouse Causeway was a long street, dirty-looking, not especially sinister, with men passing under lamps in two and threes. Tourbon chose a blue shade at random and left his hat behind, looking pleased with himself at this drastic act. A sovereign held between thumb and finger got them inside. Cora gave herself up to the experience. It was what Crane was always doing.

She enjoyed it, as she used to enjoy the Dream when clients were spending money and looking happy. Limehouse was a clever choice. From the moment that the customers in their sloppy blue clothes scuttled away through a curtain of sacks, leaving them in a room as narrow as a railway compartment to be served fish and rice, she was optimistic about Tourbon. His obvious sense of superiority to the surroundings (conqueror in boiled shirt, consort in red velvet), softened his manner.

Tai-Ling's premises – it sounded like Tai-Ling in the whistling tones of the proprietor – weren't much use to a seducer. She would have a clear run at the loan.

'Where did they go, those men who were in here?' he wondered.

'Out through the back?'

'This place is a rabbit-warren. I keep hearing noises. And the sweetish smell that I get a whiff of, now and again – what does Cora Crane think it is?'

'A dessert of some kind? They have a fruit called lychee.'

'I believe it could be the opium that you know all about.'

He teased her with it, pursuing the mystery-woman idea. 'Well, perhaps I am one,' she said. 'Or have been in my time. But, you know, I have to be practical these days. I have to think of pounds, shillings and pence.'

'All in due course.'

'A lease must be signed. Pay attention. You are a friend now. Friends have obligations.'

'Which will be met, as soon as the niceties are settled – bank procedures, very tedious.'

Before she could go on, the boy was being masterful again. He summoned the boss and they spoke by the sacks in whispers. Tai-Ling shook his head, a white banknote for five pounds floated under his nose, the head-shaking stopped. Tourbon took her arm and said that the proprietor would make an exception for a beautiful Western woman. They were invited to Tai-Ling's private quarters.

If half her reason for agreeing was to keep on the right side of him, the other half was Crane and his mania for 'experience'. Not that she expected brutality laid bare or anything so interesting. But it pleased her to be doing what Crane did, to observe everyday things for their own sake. For Crane's sake.

Another narrow room and its watchful Chinese sailors had to be negotiated, a broken staircase, a corridor reeking of aromatics ('Velly nice lychees,' Charles said in her ear), where the clink of coins came from behind another screen of sacks, then more stairs, and finally a square room with dirty linoleum on the floor, and mattresses she didn't like the look of.

An oil lamp burned with a pinkish light. The proprietor showed how to recline against a pillow, turned to one side. He fiddled with a little round tin, drew out a sticky plume of what looked like molasses, and worked it in his fingers till he could fix a pellet to the end of a darning needle.

'Is this how you remember it?' said Tourbon.

'You mustn't talk.'

The speared opium was thrust at the lamp, bubbling in the flame. The fingers twirled the boiling capsule, too nimble for pain. They whisked it into a bamboo pipe with its bowl halfway along the stem.

Tai-Ling held the pipe in both hands. He passed the bowl above the flame to make the opium fry, before presenting the mouthpiece to Tourbon, who drew deeply a couple of times and lay back gasping like a fish.

The procedure was repeated, but Cora only touched the mouthpiece with her lips to absorb a spoonful of smoke before handing it back. Even that was enough to make something tilt inside her head and cause the flame to dilate.

The two lay like travellers beside a camp fire. The proprietor had vanished. She saw Stevie clear, his blue eyes, his dusty shoes. Heard him say, 'Yes, I sail in the morning.' The flame flattened and spread into an ocean of glass, burning in the sun.

Then she was back in the room, in time to hear Tourbon groan and rush into the passageway. There was a sound of retching. Feet came running, buckets were rattled. Later she smelt boiling tea.

182

'Where am I?' she said, when he appeared in the doorway looking at her. 'Where have you been?'

'I was bored. It had little or no effect on me, I am sorry to say. But it has been a novelty.'

'I am not as brave as I thought. I had such dreams.'

The charade worked, as it usually did, stricken woman dependent on powerful man. Frightfully cold-blooded of me, thought Cora, but cold-blooded of him as well. The most she would be prepared to countenance on the journey back, she decided, was a little pawing of the upper areas. 'Dear Stevie, A man stroked my bosom yesterday and gave me a cheque for £250.'

Black river and black streets streamed past. She waited to see how things would develop, curious, wanting to laugh at herself, bobbing up and down over cobblestones, facing a pale little man bobbing to the same rhythm in the corner opposite. He asked if he might lower the window to admit some air, and kept his handkerchief pressed to his mouth. She realised that nothing was going to happen tonight *re* bosoms. Or *re* bank loans either.

'Must see you again,' he muttered, when they were back in the land of bright lights and silk hats. He apologised and left the cab hurriedly near Admiralty Arch to spend the night at his club, and sent the driver on to Milborne Grove.

Mathilde was sitting up for her.

'A pleasant evening, Ma?'

'I don't much care for the theatre. I would like you to brush my hair. It will calm my nerves.'

'I shan't ask why they need calming.'

'Very sensible of you.'

Cora saw herself naked in the mirror before the nightdress descended. She heard the dream voice again, 'Yes, I sail in the morning.' Out loud, she said, 'Liar.'

14

The kiss became famous. The *Police Review* printed a paragraph to say that 'A romantic incident involving a well-known detective is being treated as a case of mistaken identity.' Fred brushed it aside. 'Don't you lot have anything better to talk about?' he said. 'Poxy magistrates for one. Stingy boot allowances. When do we start to use fingerprinting? Now shut up and let me get on with my work.'

Tom Simmons didn't join in the leg-pulling. He and Fred were looking for Wilk. The rumour that he was in Hoxton persisted. Tom tried to locate a printer with a criminal past, the kind the engraver would need to recruit.

The beautiful thing about crime was its never-endingness. It gratified Fred to know that the sons and daughters of the trade were always there, just out of sight, that they were spawning their descendants in grimy tenements, as they had been spawned, back and back for generations, ready for the forces of law and order to prove themselves against. After his week's leave, Fred always came back like a stick of dynamite.

As well as the Wilk inquiry, he nobbled a burglar who hid in shops and broke out after dark instead of breaking in.

He went to see Mrs Crane and found her at home in South Kensington.

The bad side of being there, renewing acquaintance with five foot five, green eyes, was also the good side.

'Not still on your holiday?' she said.

'No, Ma'am. I am here on official business.'

'You look very smart.'

So he should. He was wearing his stiffest collar, and a dark red handkerchief was stuck in the breast-pocket of the jacket, which Mrs Monge had sponged for him.

'I hope you aren't thinking of arresting me,' she said. 'I have an appointment with a dentist at eleven o'clock.'

Hands small, shapely fingernails, resting in lap, which was covered by dress made of light fabric, which contained the legs, which emerged from black boots.

'It's about Venables, who kept the child. I want to make an example of him. I need your assistance.'

Fred made it sound as serious as possible – the abduction of children, the association with prostitutes, the possibility of murder.

'Murder?'

'You never know with a man like Venables.'

The woman had the knack of driving him to say things he hadn't meant to say, as well as thinking things he hadn't meant to think.

'Murder may be overstating the case. But he's a bad lot.'

Her boots made him think of the bicycle pedals they might rest on, which had inevitable consequences, leading him from boots to knees, and upwards through shadowy bones and sockets to the hips, which left him in the dark, like a man in a bedroom where a wife is doing things with her clothes behind a screen.

'Inspector Hooper?'

'Yes, Ma'am. You were saying?'

'I am waiting to hear what you want from me.'

Fred pulled himself together. 'To begin with, a full statement from you about the child. How he was lost, how he was found, your recollections of the basement where he was being held. I can come back tomorrow or whenever is convenient. We shall work on the statement together.'

'But I can't,' said Mrs Crane. 'It would cause the most awful ructions if it got into the newspapers. I told you who the father was, a well-known American journalist. His wife is my friend. Only, you see, she isn't exactly his wife. He has two wives. Or he has one wife, who is English, and then the other lady, who is my friend, who is American, who he isn't married to. She's Barry's mother. Do you follow?'

'More or less. But duty is duty.'

'Of course,' she said, her boots stirring, ankle speaking to knee, knee to hip, 'and if it was your Jack the Ripper, I might be willing to ruin Mr and Mrs Frederic's life. But not for that toad in the basement. Please, my dear Mr Hooper. Will you not force me?'

'I can make no promises,' he said sternly. 'I may need to interview you again.'

'Look in when you're passing. Like you did at Ravensbrook.' There was a parting of lips. 'We shall be friends if we go on like this.'

Walking away from the house, he turned right instead of left, and came to the dead-end of Milborne Grove. Retracing his steps, he saw her at a window. She gave him a wave. Hours later he could still see the smile.

Crime went on as usual. A burglar who was one of Fred's informants fell off a roof and broke his neck. Tom Simmons went around low pubs in Hoxton, pretending to look for a printer who would handle indecent material from the Continent, carrying a packet of pictures to make his inquiries seem authentic. He showed them to Fred, who wasn't amused.

'Where'd you get this stuff?'

'Oakey had it in his safe. Some of it's from Queenie Gerald's. Look at these postures. I rather like the Wheelbarrow, but you'd need to be a contortionist.'

'Put them away. Stuff like that can corrupt a man.'

But the pictures did the trick. A carter on his second glass of rum told Tom about a Mr Cape who would print anything, and Fred, digging into his memory, recalled a villain he sent down years ago, a Czech printer called Kapek who stole banknote paper from Waterlow's, and was thought to have changed his name. Kapek was very stout, a bladder of lard, and so was Cape. Fred's long shot hit the mark. They put a watch on premises in Shepherdess Walk, near the canal.

Fred left most of the work to Tom, who welcomed the chance of sharing in the glory if Wilk was caught. There was always plenty for Fred to do. He caught a cheque-smasher after spending hours in the inspectors' room with compass and ruler, measuring signatures to sift the real from the forged. He sat patiently in Marlborough Street police court while the bad-tempered magistrate knocked papers on the floor and mixed up one case with another. When Fred wasn't working he was thinking about the woman he didn't want to think about.

A pickpocket gave him the slip in the Piccadilly Arcade. That wasn't like Fred. Mrs Armellini insisted he drink a raw egg in milk, he looked so seedy when he went in for his cup of coffee. 'You have things on the mind,' she said. 'It is time you take the room upstairs. I look after you like your Mama.'

He was having a bad time with Belle, who went about

stony-faced because Rukes the lodger wanted to take them all out for supper to celebrate Miss Crumm's birthday.

'What's it to do with him?' she said. 'I don't think I shall go. Vi keeps quiet about her age, but we all know what it is, all except Rukes. I wouldn't want to be reminded I was thirty. I shall be thirty myself in December. I hope you are listening, Freddie dear. I hope nobody plans a celebration for *my* thirtieth birthday.'

'I shall try not to.'

He did what he could to console her. They would have a shock in the inspectors' room if they could see him fussing over a pale-faced sister who thought life was passing her by.

What Rukes proposed was to take them 'up West' for 'a slap-up supper' at a place called Merano's behind Piccadilly Circus. 'I think we have to accept the man's offer,' said Fred. 'It's very generous of him. I have never eaten a meal at a smart restaurant and nor have you, but so what? He sees us as his family.'

'He wants Sidney there as well. I keep forgetting Sidney exists.'

'Try and be more charitable. Just make sure he doesn't bring his cushion.'

On the day of Rukes's treat, the Cape inquiry showed signs of life. Coloured inks were delivered to Shepherdess Walk. The shutters were put up in the afternoon. No one resembling Wilk had been seen, and since it was unlikely that he had been on the premises all along, Simmons posted extra men out of sight to watch for him. Even if the plates were ready, they wouldn't print without the engraver. The moment he appeared, a message would be sent, alerting Hooper.

They knew at Vine Street where he was to be found, but the supper got under way without interruption. Rukes insisted on champagne at eight shillings a bottle, and asked Belle to open it with a 'Ladies Patent De-Corker' that he had in his pocket. 'With your permission, Mr Hooper.'

'Granted,' said Fred.

The game entertained him, his lodger up against a menu in French and a tablecloth covered in cutlery, making no secret of his ignorance and so outmanoeuvring the waiters.

'Are these cutlets or is it a pie? We need enlightenment. With your permission, Mr Hooper?'

'You are the host.'

'Gar-son, you speak English? Hurry up and translate this lot and I shall write it in pencil alongside.'

Fred watched passers-by as he ate, now and then glimpsing a hat or a cheek that reminded him of Mrs Crane. It was like an illness. Presently he would make an excuse and leave them. Belle was bearing up. She was short with Sidney, who drank too much and spilt gravy, but she livened up when the manager brought a prearranged cake, saying it was his *plezhair* to present *zis gatto*. A single candle burned on it, a tactful gesture.

Everyone clapped except Sidney. Miss Crumm, who was next to Fred, whispered, 'I am glad you are here. I was dreading this evening. You being here makes people behave better.'

It was an odd thing to say. 'Who do you have in mind?' he asked.

'I have spoken out of turn again.'

By now the restaurant was noisy, but not noisy enough to pursue the conversation. Rukes was showing Belle a trick with matches. Sidney was stuffing cake.

'I have to slip back to the station,' he told them. 'I hope to return shortly, but if I don't, I can rely on you, Mr Rukes?'

'Everything will be taken care of. We shall go home in a hansom.'

'Do come back,' said Belle, and Miss Crumm added a 'Yes, please do.'

Outside, he forgot them at once. Steadfast, sober, Fred moved across familiar territory, through the noise and sharp electric-light shadows of the Circus, into the quiet of Vine Street, up the steps of the station, and down again five minutes later when he had established that no word was in from Hoxton, or likely to be at this hour.

Only when he was in Milborne Grove, watching the apartment, did peace descend. She wasn't there. No one was there. The uncurtained glass in the windows reflected his eye looking in. He made no secret of his presence. If she returned, she would find him in the road, or the long garden at the back, or even inside the house – he knew about locks – with the news that burglaries had been reported in the area, and he had made it his business to warn her because they were, after all, friends. The word was hers, not his.

Around midnight he ventured in, using the back door. He found a candle and matches in the scullery, and toured the apartment.

Unopened letters covered the hall table. Carnations had been thrust into a vase, a card still attached to them by wire, inscribed 'From your philosophic C.T.' A room upstairs had a silk dress laid out on the bed. A madness came over him. He held it to his face, breathing her scent.

The West End was empty when Fred returned. It was nearly one a.m. A last call at the station seemed politic. 'Ah,' said the desk sergeant, 'a PC brought your message in a cab, Mr Hooper. We whizzed it round to Merano's, but you weren't to be found. Came about eleven.'

Scrawled on a page from a notebook was 'HE'S HERE.'

The police cab made his bones rattle, he told the driver to go so fast. If they lost a wheel it could be the end of them. It felt like the end of Fred anyway.

Tom Simmons and his men were still clearing up.

'Did you get him?'

'He's upstairs, double-cuffed and guarded. Hope it was all right, me going in. I didn't want to wait too long.'

'You did the right thing.'

'Pity you missed it though.'

They were in the cellar, by the press. The machinery was still warm. Roubles were stacked on a ledge. Some of the rust-red paper had been knocked into an oil-bath, where it floated like leaves.

'Arrived on a Post Office bicycle, cheeky devil. Little blue hat and all. He must have had a special knock. He was inside in seconds, and his bike.'

Both the inspectors were brisk and congratulatory, each insisting he wouldn't have got anywhere without the other. Simmons didn't ask where Hooper had been – why should he, the way things had turned out? Even if he was told the truth, he wouldn't believe it. Fred hardly believed it himself.

He heard what he had missed. An iron bar behind the door had slowed down their entry. They caught Cape at the back, still in his printer's apron, leaving via a window. His wife was upstairs, squashed into a wardrobe. Wilk had vanished.

'I told the woman she'd go down for as long as her husband if she didn't help us. She said, "Look behind the wardrobe." There was a hole knocked into the house next door.'

'Why didn't they all go through it?'

'Too fat. Wilk's only a small chap. They didn't realise till it was too late.'

'And you caught him next door?'

'He had spare clothes there. He was doing himself up to look like a bargee off the canal.'

It was a famous case already. A commendation came down in the morning from the Head of Detectives. It was addressed to the two of them. Inspector Simmons was praised for 'leading a raid that has captured one of London's leading criminals.' Inspector Hooper had played 'an important part' in supplying information. Fred was an afterthought.

When he asked Belle what happened after he left, she said, 'Let me see. Vi got sulky – she was quite upset after you went. Mr Rukes tried to interest the manager in buying a dozen patent de-corkers. I had a headache. Sidney was ill on the way home, and we had to stop the cab and let him go behind a fence to recover. That was about all.'

'I was sorry I had to leave.'

'A policeman rushed in looking for you later on. Said you were nowhere to be found.'

'Detective work is like that,' said Fred. 'I was on a big raid over at Hoxton.'

'And there was I, thinking you were slipping off to see a lady-friend.'

He was startled. 'What sort of talk is that?'

'When they came looking for you, I thought, "Freddie, you scheming old thing." I worked out you had an assignation at Armellini's. Put it down to women's intuition.'

'You wouldn't make much of a detective,' he said.

It brought him back to his senses. It was a warning. If this didn't cure him of the American woman, nothing would.

15

Kate was proud of saving Harold by strength of character. He walked, he talked, he ceased to grope for words. Fourteen miles away as the crow flew, Mrs Athalie Mills of Seymour Street, London W., sent prayers shooting up into the sky because Kate had ordained that it should be so, and the sky sent them shooting back into the person of Harold Frederic.

For a while Cora wasn't encouraged to visit, due to her lack of sympathy with the supernatural.

'I do hope all is well with you,' wrote Kate. 'H. has no specific news of Stephen, except that he was seen in New York a month ago. Now prepare yourself for a surprise. Harold is cured. There was nothing wrong in the first place, because there is no such thing as disease. People might call it a Miracle, but as Mrs Mills points out, it is only Science.

'I do believe that THIS AMAZING NEWS will reach your soul, as it has reached mine and transformed it. He has this minute gone into the garden and is smoking a cigar and urging Heloise to climb a tree. He is insisting we all go for another outing to Redhill where we went once before. Are you in Kensington? Have you heard from Stephen? Is your heart still set on your castle?'

Cora replied in the form of roses sent special delivery, and a note to say how happy she was about Harold's deliverance. This avoided the need to answer questions, asked or implied, and admit that since they last met she had pawned the revolver and her diamond ring, borrowed four pounds from the Conrads by post, written deviously to the owners of Brede Place, who were abroad, travelled down to the house, given a builder a few sovereigns to get on with the roof, asked Mr and Mrs Mack to please get the goats out of the hall, and in general had done what any woman had to do in a crisis, be as self-reliant as a man.

'I have no intention of blaming you,' Cora wrote in her book. 'Nor of blaming myself. We are all what we are, and what you are is a man who can't keep his hands off a war. I had to smile when I saw one of your despatches in the summer, after you had been at Guantanomo, saying you were "a child who jumped into a vat of war in a fit of ignorance." You made it sound like you were in Cuba by accident. The same sort of accident that sent you to Greece? That made you write the *Red Badge* in the first place?

'I can tell you, Imogene Carter is near the end of her tether. There are the debts and there is the loneliness. It would be one thing if Crane was dead. Since he is merely disinclined to write, it tempts her to take a different view of love.

'She makes no apology for having met a young pipsqueak called Charles, who happens to be a banker. (Please refer to above remark about debts.) As pipsqueaks go, this one is about average, but his persistence is impressive. He has taken her to the theatre, once. They were in Limehouse, once. At present he is sending her letters and bouquets and she is not responding to them.

'There are moments when Imogene desires squalor. Thoughts that usually sit in Kensington go slumming. You may have guessed this already – you are in the business of studying such matters. Your strong suit is heroics, men wrestling with others but primarily with themselves in order to survive as creatures with a streak of nobility, or at the very least decency. Still, I believe that in secret, you are as fascinated by the grubbiness of human behaviour as I am.' Cora crossed out 'I am' and substituted 'Imogene is.'

'Why else would you be so interested in *fallen women*? We have never spoken about this. Everyone is capable of moral lapses. I suspect you are. I know I am. I wish I could believe, like you, that it is heroics and not squalor that decide the course of what we do, what we are.'

The mood lasted. What Cora wrote merged into what Cora did. She had Charles Tourbon invited to the day out at Redhill, explaining to Kate that she was borrowing money from his bank, and a spot of social intercourse would do no harm.

Cora's non-committal invitation to him ('We shall make an amusing party') was accepted by return. Charles would be at Ravensbrook as instructed on Saturday morning. She thought to have the house gleaming, with Adoni doing his English-butler act in the hall, but guessed that young Tourbon would be more susceptible to Bohemian goings-on. When he arrived, Mathilde was to show him into Crane's study and leave him in the easy chair with the buttoned back, where he couldn't miss the Mexican blanket and spurs.

The revolver was still at the pawnshop, but she found a cartridge belt half-filled with bullets in the cupboard and slung it over a corner of the bookcase. Old galley-proofs from the drawers were taken out and pinned up like donkeys' tails to add presence to the room. She even left the mysterious half-a-poem, 'Thou art my love, And thou art the ashes of other men's loves,' on the edge of the writing desk, where the visitor couldn't miss it.

Reminders of an absent man, having adventures of his own far away, were more likely to encourage young Tourbon than put him off. As long as they didn't encourage him too much.

The house was full of last-ditch flowers – dahlias, roses that looked as if they could do with a coat of paint, bleached hydrangeas. By the spring the stockbroker's villa would have new tenants – a stockbroker, maybe. Her desire for spring in Brede Place was so fierce that whenever she thought of it, she could see the concentrated yellow of daffodils poured over the ridge, reaching to the white lake in the valley.

Sitting upstairs, she watched Adoni come careering up the drive with his passenger, in the station trap that she had borrowed. The Greek was in his shirt-sleeves and made lunges with his whip, like a man swatting flies. The passenger jumped down, even lankier at an angle as he flipped a coin and passed out of vision to be admitted by Mathilde.

She thought of him seeing the photograph of her and Crane by the fake boulders in Athens. In the end, the Frederics were so late, Charles would have had time to read the galley-proofs. They were supposed to be coming from Kenley in a landau, hired for the purpose by Kate because its hood could be raised to protect Harold from the weather. Instead, they turned up in a farmer's cart. A wheel had come off in Oxted High Street when the landau hit a stone, the axle broke, they nearly overturned, the driver was bleeding, the day was ruined.

'You remember Charles Tourbon,' said Cora. 'He looks after my financial affairs. Don't you, Charles?'

'I don't know which is worse,' snarled Harold, 'English roads or English drivers.'

The day turned out not to be ruined. Tourbon was even more

enterprising than she thought. A friend of his at the Surrey Motor Club called Roberts kept two vehicles. A telegram to Godstone, he had no doubt, would produce one of them, with luck the Daimler Wagonette, inside an hour. Ignoring Harold's sarcasm about miracles of locomotion, Cora had the telegram sent off.

She took Kate for a stroll in the garden. They had not been there since the day they paddled in the stream. Sponge ran ahead of them, barking at the water.

'I have never seen you flirt with a man,' said Kate. 'Wicked Cora.'

'You mean practical. Don't be cross with me, there's a dear. If you were a man, I would flirt with you.'

'What a strange—'

'Don't say it. We are not a strange pair, we are perfectly normal. The only strange thing about us is the men we live with, the men we let into our beds. I don't mean the banker either.'

A form moved between the trees.

'He is coming after us,' said Kate.

'He has money to burn. I shall convince him that he is helping to patronise the arts.'

'So this is where you escape to,' said Tourbon. 'A gloomy spot to find a pair of Nereids in.'

'Were they not creatures of the sea?' Kate sounded like the schoolmistress she used to be. 'I believe that rivers had Naiads.'

Her disapproval was like cold air. Cora countered with the yarn about the Roman legionaries who saw the ravens come to drink. She lied to make it more interesting, claiming to have found a Roman coin in the backwater – 'there, where the branch sticks out over the pool. Mrs Frederic was with me, weren't you, darling?'

'We have had lovely summer days here,' said Kate, and wandered off.

'There is a legend that on a moonlit night, if you watch your reflection in the pool, you see the face of a Roman looking over your shoulder.'

The spirit of Crane brooded over the place. Sponge appeared, barking at the boy-wonder.

'I am privileged to be here,' he said. 'With your friends. At your house. The study was amusing. What were the bullets, a warning?'

'Mr Crane is a student of the American West. They are memorabilia.' Kate was between trees, nearly at the house. 'If we go this way, I can show you the grave of the dog before this one.'

'You can show me Julius Caesar in a toga for all I care. Allow me to do one thing. Allow me to call you Cora.'

'Let me think about it.'

'It's easier to say, "Cora, I am in love with you," than "Mrs Crane, I am in love with you."'

'I've thought about it. Stick to "Mrs Crane".'

Cora whisked him back to the house, to light refreshments, and the search for wraps and shawls, and Harold's sarcasm about motor cars. Her only concern was to bring about the 'jolly party'. Love wasn't on the list.

The arrival of the motor gave a respite from all that. The amazing creation was late. It was a miracle it was there at all. They heard shouts from the road before it appeared, four red cart-wheels grinding up the drive, with a crowd behind, pressing in past the gates.

'God help us,' said Harold, 'it's a threshing machine.'

A loop of chain at the side connected rear axle to engine, a casing of black iron slung below the vehicle that made Harold shake his head. The upperworks were like an open hearse with benches. Perched high at the front was the undertaker, clothed in leather coat and goggles, guiding his progress over the gravel by means of a tiller in front of his chest. When it stopped, blue smoke gushed out. Harold told him he was on fire.

Tourbon wrong-footed Cora again, this time by his restraint. Having conjured up the smelly beast, he made no defence of its awkward progress towards Redhill. It banged and shook, stopping to be fed with petroleum from cans under the seats, or to have its chain lubricated, or to let the engine cool. Cyclists overtook them. Kate kept trying to wrap extra clothes around Harold's legs and shoulders. He flung them aside, insisting he had never felt better. On the incline at Bletchingley, he asked would it help if they got out and pushed.

'It has taken longer than I thought,' said Tourbon, when the Bull's chimneys came in sight. 'I am famished and I expect everyone else is. Luncheon is on me.'

But even with a white tablecloth and steaming dishes, the occasion refused to become jolly. Harold picked at his food. When the women were together in the cloakroom, Cora said, 'What can I do to make amends? I should never have let us in for that journey. Is he really all right?'

'He knows himself cured. The knowledge is the cure.' Kate dried her hands. 'Cora dear, what concerns me is you and your banker.'

'I expect I shall manage.'

'You seem determined to go off the rails.'

They watched one another in the mirror, powdering a nose, rescuing a curl.

'I don't think he and I are going anywhere in particular,' said Cora. 'Even if we are, it's less important than Harold. What do the doctors say?'

'I banned them from the house. Ruth went back to

Hammersmith so she wasn't there to interfere. Can you see what it means to me? Harold has recovered so it follows that his heart must be pure enough to satisfy God. Even you can't argue with the logic of that. Harold and I may not live perfect lives, but they are evidently good enough for the Supreme Being.'

She sounded more desperate than happy. Cora hoped that the Supreme Being had better things to do, but refreshing thoughts like that would have to wait till Stevie came back and made her sane again.

She put an arm around Kate's waist, which didn't give an inch, all whalebone. 'Shall we go to Ireland again, the four of us, as Harold suggested? In the spring perhaps. Stevie and I will be settled into Brede Place by then. The men can row round and round Dunmanus Bay, and come back with a pitiful plate of mackerel like they did last time. You and I will be asleep in our bedrooms. Remember the white curtains, always swaying in the breeze?'

'It will be lovely.' Kate softened, pressing her hand on Cora's.

'Fast asleep so as to annoy them. Lying naked on the beds and brushing them away like bees. "Go away, you horrid men." When we are all at supper, they will wonder what we are smiling at.'

'You are a secular woman, Cora Crane. You may even be wicked as well. I shouldn't be as fond of you as I am.'

'You should be fonder.'

Whalebone reasserted itself. 'Come along. They will be waiting by the car.'

There had been developments. The Daimler Wagonette was leaking petrol, and Charles was negotiating with the Bull for a coach to take them back. Fatigue had caught up with Harold, who lay on a sofa in the smoking-room, eyes closed. Kate was frantic, giving him sips of brandy, refusing to let a doctor be called. The outing unravelled. When Charles insisted he must pay for the coach, Kate snapped, 'Out of the question.'

'Your friends haven't enjoyed themselves,' he said to Cora, when he caught her alone in the empty hallway.

'You aren't seeing them at their best.'

'I am seeing you, is what matters. I have a suggestion.'

'No.'

'How do you know what it is?'

'Because I am possessed of average powers of intellect. I shall return to Kenley with my friends, and no doubt you will find a train to take you to London.'

'Might stay the night with the Robertses at Godstone. I think you'd like them. They would certainly like you. You could be Mrs Cora Crane, wife of noted author and adventurer, the whole shebang. Or if it suited, Mrs Nobody, woman of mystery.'

'Pull yourself together. You are my banker.'

Voices and the noise of wheels came from the yard. Harold, helped by the manager and Kate, emerged from the smoking-room.

'Come with me,' said Tourbon.

'Nothing doing.'

'Please, Cora Crane.'

'What about my loan?'

'On Monday I shall put the matter in hand. I'm mad for you.'

'One gets over it.'

Then came the slog of going home and pretending there was nothing wrong with Harold that a good night's sleep wouldn't cure. Cora kept returning to the boy Tourbon. Had she been too dismissive, or not dismissive enough? They

rattled through the autumn evening, nothing solved for anybody.

At Kenley the coachman had to be enlisted because of the
legs, which had temporarily stopped working. What strength
Harold possessed went into ordering people to leave him in the
drawing room, but the order came out as a croak. 'There's a
good chap,' said Secretary Stokes. They edged him to the stairs.
'Not that bloody sickroom,' said Harold, rage in his voice. His
shoes dragged across the floor.

Cora waited downstairs. Dahlias filled the grate; it was
almost time for fires. The hall at Brede Place swam in front
of her, dogs and Stevie dozing by the flames. Whatever compassion one had for a friend and her troubles, the mind went
on peering jealously down the avenues of its own future.

John Stokes's face came round the door. 'All under control,'
he said. Mrs Frederic was at the bedside, and a telegram was
going off to Mrs Mills. But he would like a private word.

'If it concerns sending for a proper physician, I think you
should.'

But it was about Crane.

'New York knows he is a friend of Mr Frederic. The
overnight wires include some information. I have it here.'

'Gratifying to know he still exists.'

The secretary showed her a passage underlined in red.
Florida newspapers were full of reports that the writer Crane
had disappeared. One minute he was in Havana, the next he
was nowhere to be found.

'That's Stephen for you,' she said.

The war was over but the peace wasn't signed. He was
playing at intrepid journalists, off looking for wounded heroes
or drinking with the Spanish commanders who lost the war,
who would tell him what defeat felt like.

She asked where his despatches were coming from.

'Nowhere,' said Stokes, and waved more red marks at her. 'That's the point. He has stopped filing. Apparently he was staying at the Grand Hotel in Havana but he left there three weeks ago.'

No despatches for three weeks didn't sound like Crane. 'So what are the authorities doing about finding him?' she said.

'It is being suggested' – further red squiggles – 'that his presence in Havana was technically illegal in the first place. Havana itself was never occupied. Apparently Mr Crane got in by pretending to be a tobacco buyer. He could have been arrested. It is all rather complicated.'

'On the contrary, it's very simple,' said Cora. Danger clarified her feelings. 'I shall stir things up. He has to be found.'

16

The forgery trial was fitted in smartly at the Old Bailey. They all went to prison, especially Wilk, who wouldn't be seen for many years, as befitted a man with a funny foreign name. The judge commended Inspector Simmons for the arrests, adding that his colleague was to be commended, too, and made them a grant of five pounds each from public funds.

'I wanted to get up and say you were the driving force,' said Tom, when they were outside on the pavement, where rain was starting to fall.

'Think no more of it.'

Fred, though, thought of it continually. He had been forced to make up a yarn to cover his visit to Milborne Grove, alleging that he sighted the dipper, the one who had given gave him the slip in the Piccadilly Arcade, and chased him all over the West End, only to lose him again. Either version, the lie or the truth, left him looking a fool.

'We may get our names in the *Daily Mail* yet,' said Tom, and left to go to Smithfield market where a butcher was passing off horse-meat as beef.

'Hello, Mr Hooper,' said a woman under an umbrella. 'I was in the public gallery.'

It was Violet Crumm, her cheeks looking as though the rain would make the colour run if it got at them. Fred didn't know what to do with her, except explain he was heading for Ludgate Circus and a bus to the West End.

'I'll come with you, if that's allowed. It was jolly interesting. I should have brought a sketch book.'

'You'd have been arrested.'

'It was awful when the woman cried. I suppose you're hardened to it.'

They walked down Seacoal Lane. Fred remarked that it was a long way for her to come. She said that Belle had told her about the trial, and she was curious. 'Anyway,' she said, 'I like to get about London. I often take an omnibus and look for scenes I could paint.'

'By yourself? Hold on, here's one for Piccadilly.'

They crammed into a dry seat downstairs, and she was off again. 'I have decided to be more ambitious. I went to a wharf last week and sketched a ship unloading timber. Yesterday I went to Bermondsey Market. Have you ever been there, Mr Hooper?'

He smiled at the idea that there were places he hadn't been to.

'Where Mr Rukes has his pitch, except the name on top is "John Johnson". Do you know what, it's gone. Closed down. Disappeared.'

'No he hasn't. He was at home last night.'

'I find him a strange man.'

'I thought you got on with him.'

'He makes me nervous.'

Fred gave her his speech about knowing young Rukes's sort, men who sailed near the wind but had kindly natures.

'In twenty years I wouldn't be surprised he'll have a handsome office in the City and be a highly regarded merchant. He will remember the name of Violet Crumm and get you to paint him in his top hat and tails.'

'I hope I'd say no. I would like to be so successful I could decline commissions I didn't want. Not that it will ever happen. Bandstands and River Wandles are more my level.'

She was agreeable enough as someone to sit next to on a bus. It was unfortunate that women like her got stuck in spinsterhood. Women like Belle.

'I alight here,' he said. 'I have enjoyed your company.'

'Me, too.'

Fred thought no more of her until the evening, when he remembered to ask Rukes about Bermondsey Market.

'My word, news gets around,' said the lodger. 'I see better opportunities at the Elephant. As I was on the point of telling you, I am going in for change all round. I am spying out a regular berth, where I can live above the shop.'

Fred said there was no hurry.

'Can't stand still in business.' Rukes ran up to his room and came back with a silvery object on a cord. 'Parting gift, result of transferring stock to new premises. Allow me to present you with a superior quality policeman's whistle I found a gross of that I didn't know I had. As used by the German state police. Next time you are pursuing a Charlie Peace or whoever it might be, give the alarm with this and think of Leonard Rukes.'

He had livened up the place. Fred would be sorry to see him go.

When the front desk claimed to have a personal letter for Inspector Hooper, which had been handed in by 'a female person who kept a handkerchief over her face,' Fred suspected a leg-pull. Humour in the Met was predictable. Someone thought there was still mileage in that kiss.

He didn't open the letter till late in the afternoon, when no one was about. It was cheap paper but educated writing, purporting to be from a woman who signed herself 'B'. It didn't seem to be a joke.

'I am the person that you helped,' she wrote. 'I had an accident to my wrists when you were at a certain house. I must see you. It is police business. I will be at Jackson's Tea Rooms at 5 p.m. today, Wednesday. Or leave message for me at cash-desk. This is a sincere letter.'

Arm's-length was the rule with tarts, even when it was the girl called Blanche he had taken pity on because of a passing resemblance to Belle. Resemblance was nothing. Fred once fished a corpse from the river, wearing a suit with a shrivelled carnation still in the buttonhole, that bore an uncanny resemblance to the Prince of Wales, of whom one heard stories. It turned out to be a member of the Worshipful Company of Fruiterers, seriously in debt. Everyone looked like someone else.

All the same, he went. With Queenie Gerald in prison, the girls would be like lost sheep. This one might want to earn money as an informant.

It was past the time she proposed. Waiters watched the dwindling clientele leave for the suburbs, and Blanche, sitting with a pot of tea gone cold and half a bun, would have passed for a respectable female with her shopping under the table. Her only jewellery was a wedding ring.

Soft-soap or tears were to be expected. Anger wasn't on the agenda, but it flamed at him, hot in the face.

'I want you to tell me straight out,' she said. 'Do I have my rights? Am I just dirt? Does my word count for anything?'

Grievances, that was another thing about tarts.

'You know the law as well as I do. You're still a subject of the Queen. But you've been declared a common prostitute. Your word doesn't carry the same weight.'

'So if I make a complaint about a policeman, nobody's going to believe me?'

'It would be your word against his. I'll give you some free advice. Keep your mouth shut. Find a job in a laundry or a milliner's.'

'You helped me before,' she said, hunched over the table in the brown coat and hat that she would change for something showier before she went man-catching. Curls were not in evidence, except for one that had escaped the hat and lay by an ear, quivering like a steel spring. 'Please.'

'I'm soft-hearted, that's my trouble. Get to the point.'

'He makes me have relations with him.' She spoke in a fierce whisper, staring at the bun. 'He says if I don't, he will see to it that my husband gets to hear.'

Wherever Hooper went, impropriety haunted him these days. What had he done to deserve it? The woman was telling him the story of her life. Her husband was a purser on a steamship in the China trade. She was lonely and short of money . . .

'A heart-rending tale,' said Hooper. 'What station is the detective from?'

'Vine Street. He was at the raid on Mrs Gerald's.'

He recalled the noise the young PCs made, laughing over the pictures.

'Tell me the constable's name.'

'It isn't a constable. It's Inspector Simmons. I read about him catching the gang. Doing well for himself. Dirty devil.'

He definitely shouldn't be there.

'I could have you sent to prison,' he said. 'I could make your life a misery.'

'You were the only copper's ever shown me a kindness.'

'It hasn't done you much good.'

'I'm working again, I don't deny it. I only want to make him stop. I won't be treated like dirt.'

'I'm going,' said Hooper, but he didn't go. It was the anger he couldn't account for. He listened to her recite locations, a mews here, behind a stables there, an alley off Half Moon Street. Prostitutes knew the geography better than detectives. They were all liars. He would have been happy to believe in fabrication if it wasn't for the anger.

'Be glad I'm not charging you with perjury,' he said.

'You're all the same.'

In the end the prostitute was the one who went. Fred watched her pay her sixpence at the desk and disappear into a swirl of hats and faces. He ate the bun and drank the cold tea. He liked to finish things off.

The Head of Detectives had them in for an official commendation. It wasn't all that different from a reprimand. The head clerk pointed his pen at them and then at a padded door. They stood to attention facing H.o.D., who had the canary on his thumb.

'We meet under happier circumstances this time, Hooper,' he said. 'I trust there has been no more misbehaving in the street?'

'Absolutely not, sir.'

'And the situation at home is satisfactory?'

'Very much so, sir.'

'You still have that canary?'

'It doesn't sing much, sir, but my sister is working on it.'

'Look how alert this little fellow is,' and H.o.D. waggled his thumb, causing the bird to fly to the sill, where it stood looking at the Thames. 'I understand you were not at the scene with

209

your colleague because you were pursuing a man elsewhere. You do seem unlucky, Hooper. It's a great pity.'

'I entirely agree, sir.'

'As for you, Simmons, you have made a brilliant start to your career with the Metropolitan Police. This has nothing to do with the fact that the Commissioner knows your uncle. You have stood on your own two feet. Well done.'

He shook canary-droppings from a sheet of paper and read what was on it. 'The Commissioner wishes me to say that you both have upheld the reputation of the CID in a most commendable fashion, and it will be duly noted on your records. On a personal note, I see the judge made you both a pecuniary award. I expect you want the Benevolent Fund to benefit.'

'If that's possible, sir,' said Fred.

'Leave it with me.'

The Embankment felt autumnal when they emerged. Tom was laughing. 'Benevolent Fund, my arse. He'll buy a new cage for his canary. I'm sorry he spoke like that to you, Fred. I don't think he's quite right in the head.'

The air was full of gulls. A waterman was sculling out to a string of barges.

'We need to have a chat,' said Fred. 'Down by the river.'

'I was going to Shepherd's Market—'

'It can wait.'

They dodged traffic to reach the river wall, where Tom lodged his hips against the stonework.

'You recall the Blanche girl,' said Fred.

Tom, picking the band off a cigar, said, 'The one who cut herself at Queenie's.' After the trial he bought a box of small Coronas and handed them round the inspectors' room, boasting that he intended to smoke nothing else from now on. 'I'd have arrested her but you told me not to. What's up?'

The sculler had let the tide pull him under the bow of the foremost barge, where he grabbed a chain.

'She wrote me a letter. We had a meeting.'

'Dangerous woman.' Tom turned and put his elbows on the wall, holding the Corona awkwardly between thumb and finger, as if he needed practice with a cigar. The little moustache was still at the experimental stage. He looked more boyish than ever. 'I hear she fancies doing a Queenie and setting up an establishment of her own. But you tell me, Fred. I'm still the novice.'

'She has a story about being hard done by. Sees me as a soft touch, I daresay.' They were both staring at the Thames. The waterman was moving about the deck of the barge. 'Says a police officer is blackmailing her.'

'Oh, very nice, very congenial,' said Tom, and took his eyes off the river. 'I don't put much faith in whores myself. Nobody does.'

'All I want to hear is that it isn't true.'

'How should I know? I don't bother myself with rumours. It doesn't pay. We all hear stories. Some Yankee piece blabs to the custody sergeant. Says the officer who nicked her went back to her digs and said he'd drop the case if she was nice to him. Nobody asked him if it was true. We all assumed it wasn't.'

A flying rivet caught Hooper in the stomach once, when he had a burglar cornered in a yard. It felt like that. All he could find to say was, 'Tom, what are you thinking of?'

'And what about that other Yankee piece, the one you go and see at her country house, the one you committed the disciplinary offence with outside the station? We don't want to see that gone into either. No chap in his right mind wants to see things gone into.'

'I need to know if it's true.'

'So you can spoil my chances of making Chief Inspector and then Super and then Chief Super and then Head of Detectives.'

'So I can talk you out of misbehaviour. Make you see sense. Some bad coppers get away with it but some don't.'

'You're envious of me.'

'I looked on you as a friend. Like a son.'

'I can't stand here all day.'

A tug had come up-river. Brown foam bubbled around the stern as the screw held her against the tide. The waterman flung a rope, which they used to haul the towing line across. Engines thundered and the air above the funnel trembled with heat. The barges began to move.

Tom was away, striding towards Westminster Bridge. Nobody wanted to see things gone into.

When he arrived home that evening, Fred was carrying a sugar mouse that he had purchased at Armellini's for his sister, in case she needed cheering up. He had taken the thing from its paper bag and put it ready on the palm of his hand, when a uniformed police inspector came out of the parlour and said, 'Is that for me?'

It wasn't funny. An officer returns from work to find another lot of officers searching his house, while his sister, paler than ever, whispers in his ear, 'It's not your fault, Freddie dear.'

They had come looking for the lodger. Fred opened his mouth to say, 'There must be a mistake,' but he had heard that said too often by the wicked and the misled. He kept quiet and listened.

They were an Inspector Watkins and two constables from 'M' division, based at Southwark, acting on information received from the Birmingham Constabulary. 'Leonard Rukes' wasn't the name they had, but they knew he was the right man, five foot seven, gift of the gab, scar below left ear. On the arrest warrant he was down as 'Arthur Grimshaw'. They knew about Grimshaw in the Midlands, my word yes. Up to his ears in fraud. Ran a long-firm once and got away with hundreds of pounds. A receiver of stolen property.

'What a cheek,' said Watkins, 'lodging with a Scotland Yard detective.' He was trying not to laugh.

In the background Belle was comforting Mrs Monge, who said she never dreamt and would she have to go to gaol?

Birmingham had been seeking Grimshaw for months. At first they thought he had gone abroad, but that must have been a deception. An antiques dealer facing charges tipped them off about Bermondsey to save his bacon, and they asked the Met for assistance. 'M' division was a day late at the market. After searching the locked-up sheds without success they went back for a second look, and found a scrap of paper pushed in through a shutter. On it was written 'Try Rukes, 37 Disraeli Street, S.W.' Somebody wanted him caught.

That was around midday. It had taken hours of telegrams to and from the chief constable in Birmingham, who wanted to send his own men to mount the raid, and had to be told he couldn't. Now here they were, confident they were only one step behind their man.

No one knew when Rukes alias Grimshaw had flown. He was there at breakfast-time; gone when Belle returned from work. His fancy waistcoats and curly-brimmed hats had been taken. Left in his room were a few alarm clocks and German police whistles. Watkins and his men carted the stuff away as evidence. Monjy went home weeping.

The fire had been lit in the parlour. Fred sat there with his sister.

'I shall be the laughing-stock of the Met,' he said.

'Rukes had a way with him. Even I could see that.'

'You didn't want him here in the first place.'

'Clever me.' She came to kneel by his chair and stroked the strands of hair across his baldness. 'I never know what I want anyway. I'm a trial to you, aren't I?'

He was taken by the charitable way she steered the subject away from Rukes. 'Hardly,' he said.

'I am your hopeless sister who dreams about foreign parts and never goes farther than Arding & Hobbs, which she's so fed up with she could die. Why don't you go off and live in that flat over Armellini's? Then I can emigrate.'

'I'd try California if I were you,' he said.

'I have been saving up. I shall soon have enough for a steamship ticket and clothes.'

'Or Argentina. It's full of English engineers. I expect they all need typewriting ladies. I shall miss you.'

'I daresay there's a plump Italian daughter at the café got her eye on you already.'

'You are the second woman this year has pulled my leg about getting married.'

'Who was it?' She prodded his waistcoat. 'Tell your sister.'

'I was interrogating her. She was trying to flirt with me.'

'Sure she wasn't a lady-friend?'

'Quite sure.'

Belle pretended to be disappointed. She nibbled the sugar mouse in between stroking his hair, calling him 'Freddie dear', chattering away; like ointment on a wound.

17

Once she knew that Crane was missing, Cora's crossness became excitement and furious activity. A silent lover got on her nerves, whatever excuses she made for him, for example, that plain fighting-men of the kind he admired were not given to long complicated letters. (So why not write short uncomplicated ones? 'Dear Cora, I saw two battles yesterday and gave a dying man some water. Wrote 800 words and cabled it to New York. Well, dear, hope you are in good health. Your pal Stevie. PS, send soap and tobacco.')

Now things had changed. Cora sent Mathilde to help look after Kate's children, until such time as Harold's blood was working properly, and based herself in Milborne Grove, where she let rip with a one-woman campaign. Mr Alger, US Secretary of War, one of Stevie's gallery of stuffed shirts, was sent a message with stirring phrases, 'our most distinguished author' and 'literary world deeply alarmed'. Crane's last known address was the Grand Hotel, Havana, and the undersigned was alone in London, in despair. Signed, Cora Crane.

The New York *Journal* was sent a cable demanding to be told what Mr Hearst was doing about his correspondent, who might be a prisoner of the Spanish forces and suffering unspeakable hardships for all they knew. 'I am his wife,' she wrote, 'I have to know.'

Laying it on thick came naturally. She tracked down Mr Heinemann in his office and asked him to write a letter to the London *Times* deploring the lack of official action to help find his missing author. Mr Heinemann made placatory noises; her husband would be back in England in no time. In that case, said Cora, whose cunning was unlimited when it came to money, the publisher would have no difficulty in advancing ten pounds to keep her going. But, like Mr Pawling before him, Mr Heinemann didn't seem to hear.

The American Women were worth trying, if only on account of their husbands, but the power behind them, Mrs Griffin, was out of the country, and it was impossible to find anyone who could promise anything until she returned. Helen Hay invited Cora round to the Embassy, where they talked cosily in a tiny drawing room while the noise of traffic came down the chimney.

'My father asks me to assure you that Washington will be given all the facts,' said Miss Hay.

'Can't they make the Spanish tell them where he is?'

'He says the situation in Havana is chaotic. What an awful time it must be for you.'

'No worse than it is for soldiers' wives.'

'You are being very strong about it.'

'I get mad with people. It takes my mind off things.'

She had got mad with the *Journal*, who told her that Crane was no longer on their staff, and they could take no responsibility for a freelancer. She had even got mad with Crane, despite the fact that his life was in danger. Or, it was with the endangered Crane that she got especially mad, due to her suspicion that whatever danger he was in, he had encouraged it in the first place. One of the impenetrable mysteries of affection was how you could grieve about someone till it nearly broke your heart, and at the same instant want to slap the someone's face for making your life a misery. Both sensations were true, and neither excluded the other.

How long had they been married, Miss Hay wanted to know.

'Since the spring of last year. We were in Greece, both of us war correspondents.'

'That's what I call romantic. You met on the battlefield, so to speak.'

'I could pretend, but I'd be lying. We were already acquainted in America.'

Cora knew that most of the time, people were taken at their face value. Life became too complicated otherwise. Mr Alger wasn't going to demand her wedding certificate. She was never sure who knew her true marital status, or lack of it. Did Conrad? Did Charles Tourbon? She and Stevie used to dissect the bourgeois ethics of marriage in the Dream days, when Jacksonville seemed a heathen enclave where conventions didn't count. The rules changed when they went north, in the unreal interlude between the Florida they left behind and the Europe they were making for.

'Excuse me while I get us some tea,' said Miss Hay, and gave instructions down a tube. 'So are you from New York originally?'

'Neither of us is. I'm from Boston. Mr Crane's family is old stock from New Jersey. He was named for his forbear Stephen Crane, who signed the Declaration.'

Their ship was the *Etruria*, Cunard Line, New York to Liverpool. Stevie had never been to Europe, or sailed in anything but tugboats and US Army transports. The day he bought the tickets she was inspired to tell him about the

Atlantic at night, the blaze of light from the piled-up decks that travelled on the water with the ship.

'Saloons full of men in boiled shirts,' said Crane.

'You and I in our cabin, hearing the ocean go by.'

'Aw, nuts, de lady's gone all lit'ry on me.'

He booked a double cabin and a single because Mathilde was coming with them. What he didn't tell Cora till the last minute was that she and Mathilde were sharing the double. He was a bad sailor, apt to be ill, he explained, and besides, he needed solitude to work at a story during the voyage.

She was upset? Why was that? What was there to be upset about? They were going to Europe to start a new life together, ain't that a fact? A few nights sliding about in the same cabin (it was March, equinoctial gales would tear at the *Etruria*) were of no consequence. So. He pulled the cigarette off his lip and kissed her. There y'are, old girl, look on the bright side.

This foolery with an edge on it was hard to stomach. Embarking was worse. She and Mathilde were sent ahead, with their luggage. 'Half the passengers will be American,' he said. 'Best to lie low right now. Society's a brute. When I come on board, if I'm with a man seeing me off, four-square fellow, ignore me, will you do that? One of my brothers. I can't stop him.'

Cora watched them come up the gangway together, having posted herself near the ship's officer whose tedious duty was to salute each arrival. The brother was older and bulkier than Stephen, with a sombre hat and square spectacles. She watched them amble along the deck, the brother gesticulating and Stephen nodding, before retiring to the cabin, where she snapped at Mathilde to stop admiring herself in the mirror and get the trunk unpacked.

'Do have something,' said the ambassador's daughter, and Cora set aside the *Etruria* as the cake-stand came towards her.

Helen Hay held her fingers spread on the trolley. A circle of diamonds had to be remarked on. He was English, she smiled, they would marry in the spring, but her family was bigger than his (did she mean more powerful?) and the ceremony would be at White Plains in New York State.

'It's strange,' she said, 'I almost wish Ronald and I could sail away and get hitched without having our families crowding round. Was yours upset when you married in Greece?'

'My people washed their hands of me years ago.' That much was true. 'The Cranes pretended to be cross with Stephen, but only because they go back for generations in the same place, preachers and lawyers and so on, and it would have been the proper thing to do. To marry me at Port Jervis, I mean.'

It made a presentable story. Truth, anyway, was out of the question. Would Mr Alger bestir himself if he thought it was a mistress beseeching him, not a wife? Would Ambassador Hay?

Crane spent much of the voyage playing poker in the steerage. One afternoon she found him with three men in his cabin and dollar bills on the bunk. Between times he wrote like a maniac, spilling sheets of manuscript paper on the floor, not bothering to go for dinner but getting the steward to bring him a bowl of soup. Cora wandered the decks by herself, wondering what England would be like after eight years.

He had a habit of joining her late at night, when few passengers were about. Once he took her down to the engine room, where he had befriended a junior officer, who showed them the stokers shovelling like demons.

Mostly he talked about the war in Greece, next stop after England. He had never been to a war! He was a writer about wars but he had not smelt powder or seen blood on a battlefield! 'Between you and me,' he confided, 'I am a fraud,' and waited for her contradiction. His needs were simple: one revolver, one pair soft leather boots, one hip-flask for whisky, one wide-brimmed hat. His only fear was of losing his nerve under fire. When Cora teased him with sounding like a soldier, he saluted and said, 'Yes, Ma'am.'

One night she got him to talk about his brothers. They were in the observation saloon, spray bursting on half an inch of glass. The man who saw him off was Edmund, he said, a fine individual. Then there was William, also a fine individual. When the time came ('When will that be, Stevie?'), which of them should be the first to hear? He did some head-clutching with mock groans. Should it be old William, the judge? Or old Edmund, the farmer and district postmaster at Hartwood, N.J.? He was damned if he knew.

'Send them each a postcard,' said Cora. '*I have arrived in Europe with a woman not my wife. Select a preference from the following – I am pleased. I am resigned. I am disgusted.*'

'Bitterness doesn't suit you.'

'I'm not bitter. I have made my bed. I merely object to finding fresh thorns in it.'

'We marry the minute Captain Stewart gives you a divorce.' He brushed his nose against hers, a gesture that made her think of cats.

'Darling Stevie,' she said, and he licked her ear – the saloon was empty, dim-lit by blue electric bulbs – and whispered, 'Me old pal, Cora,' making it sound the height of endearment.

'We must meet again before too long,' said Miss Hay, as Cora was leaving. 'When Mrs Griffin returns, we shall be summoned to a luncheon to launch the Yankee Women of England or whatever we are calling ourselves.'

'I am as keen as ever. I haven't forgotten what I promised about Brede Place.'

Charles Tourbon made a nuisance of himself with flowers

and notes, none of which contained money. Carnations from abroad came cradled in tissue-paper and faded within hours of being exposed to an English fall. 'You are evidently not at Ravensbrook,' he wrote. 'May I visit you in Kensington in furtherance of our business discussions?'

Cora burned the notes, not having a plan for him at the moment, now that she was trying to save Crane from being ignored by the world.

On one occasion the boy Charles appeared to have sent the entire contents of the florist's. They arrived when Cora was out, and Carrie had distributed them throughout the apartment, using milk bottles when she ran out of vases.

'Restrain yourself,' said Cora. 'They are not from Mr Crane. They are from a madman who may well arrive at the door one day, asking for me. He will be wearing a cloak and a silk hat which makes his face look the size of a monkey's, and his name is Mr Tourbon. Do not let him in on any account.'

Carrie wept when she was told to find a cab, and given sixpence for the driver to take the lot away and present them to a hospital. All this weeping by a creature who liked to feel that romance was floating about the apartment made Cora aware that her own behaviour consisted chiefly of furious activity, with feelings for Crane kept to a minumum.

It was sensible to keep the mind off love and stop it getting the upper hand, but she would have enjoyed a period of sitting still and howling about him a little; except that this wasn't a wise thing to do by oneself, and the only candidate for the role of listener was Kate, who was otherwise engaged.

A letter from Mr Conrad came as a relief. She liked him because Crane liked him. They had moved to a distant part of Kent, he informed her, several miles from the sea, so as not to be pestered with sea-fogs and ship-sirens.

However hard he tried to present himself as a plain sea-captain who had made the mistake of going in for authorship, Cora found him a scrupulous figure whom she trusted because he spoke, and in this instance wrote, of Crane with such tenderness: 'You must miss him dreadfully, but he will repay your patience with his matchless stories.'

Conrad had a practical side, too. He had been talking to Mr Blackwood, of *Blackwood's* magazine, about a scheme for raising money. Would Cora like to know more? Would she care to meet him on his next visit to London? He suggested Victoria Station in two days' time. She sent a telegram, accepting.

They met in the refreshment room, a cavern of hissing urns and a sub-human chatter of voices and cutlery.

'No news?' he said, lowering himself with his stick for support.

'None.'

'What does he say in his letters?'

'He doesn't write.'

'I rarely sent letters when I was at sea. I was occupying one world. It was unnatural to be communicating with another.'

'I have written to Reynolds, but if he knew anything I'm sure he would have told me already. The man has vanished. I have contemplated going to Havana, but how do I know if that's where he is? Let alone have the money to do it.'

'Let me tell you about *Blackwood's*. I have put a scheme to them. They advance you a substantial sum, seventy-five pounds was mentioned, against short works of fiction that Stephen will write for them when he returns. Should the works fail to materialise, I will give them stories of my own.'

He rapped the point of his stick on the black-and-white tiles for emphasis, and people looked at him. He was like a magician, with his pointed beard and flashing eyes.

'Wonderfully kind,' said Cora, 'but out of the question. You would be mortgaging yourself. What if Stephen won't produce the stories?'

'You mean dereliction of duty? Not when it comes to his work. I say to Jessie, never trust a writer. He faces a lifetime of those blank pages stretching ahead of him, into infinity. They subordinate normal civilised behaviour to their demands. But a true artist like Stephen knows he has to obey. Unlike myself. I shall wake up one morning and say: "Enough, I intend to grow vegetables and read other men's books." But Stephen will write till he drops.'

'You and Crane are a mutual admiration society. What does Jessie think?'

'She is too busy knitting a coat for Borys or seeing how many meals she can make out of three lamb chops.'

'And?'

'Having married a demented sea-captain who's left the sea and keeps lamenting his efforts to do what God plainly never intended him to do, she thinks all writers are weak in the head.'

'You're prevaricating. She thinks Crane is a lost cause, doesn't she? I could tell it in her manner in the summer. She shudders at the thought of someone as irregular as Crane. Or me, come to that. I don't blame her in the slightest.'

'She wants your happiness. As I do. You must cheer up. I am melancholy by nature. It's a common weakness where I come from. But you and Stephen are children of the New World.'

When it came to kindliness, Conrad was in the top class. Greatness, too, for all she knew. The fine sentences rolled out, a shade too remote from her level. Two tables away a naval rating was arguing with his wife, waving his finger in her face. She understood that better.

'Did you know we weren't married?' she said.

He rapped the stick again, impatiently.

'So?'

'I have a British husband in government service. They are a distinguished family. I walked past their house in Kensington only last week. My career has been chequered to say the least.'

'As a novelist I am fascinated. As your friend and Stephen's, it has no significance.'

Cora felt she was falling, deeper and deeper into an emptiness where it ceased to matter what she said. She told Conrad how she feared that her fractured life before she met Stephen might have to be atoned for. Happiness was too much to expect; Stephen would never return.

They were fears too deep for her journal; too deep to tell anyone, except that here she was, telling the magician.

'Stop tormenting yourself,' he said. 'Stephen will come home and write his books and have you with him, because nothing else makes sense. And then you will come and stay with us in Kent, and we shall all tell one another our secrets, which will divert us but change nothing.'

The assurance was so comprehensive, the brilliant eye so full of encouragement, that Cora was calmed for the first time in weeks. The sailor stopped jabbing his finger and the wife cheered up.

Cora even convinced herself that when she returned to Milborne Grove, she would be greeted with good news. But when she did, there was only another box of softening carnations.

Cora tried to occupy herself by reviving her Imogene Carter newsletters for a newspaper syndicate – anything to take her mind off Cuba. The London office of Bachellers was lukewarm, reducing the fee from four dollars to three, with no guarantee of payment if an article failed to sell. She spent hours in the public library at Kensington, preparing an account of the coming motor-car craze in England. She told the story of a 'typical outing' in a Daimler Wagonette, with 'gentlemen and ladies dressed in the height of fashion' being conveyed across Surrey to 'a sumptuous lunch in a hostelry,' where 'time has stood still, and the horses in the yard looked on in amazement at this throbbing engine of tomorrow.'

It was rubbish; Cora knew it was rubbish. Never mind, it filled the hours. She paid a fortune for more cables to more officials, knowing she would soon be written off as a crank, or already had been written off. The Barrs wrote to her saying they were sure Stephen was alive, which only had the effect of reminding her that he might be dead.

All this had happened before, when he was with the gun-runners, and she sat in her window at the Dream, watching the January sea, telling herself that hope in such circumstances only meant more torment. So she stopped hoping, and immediately he came walking through the surf at Daytona with his pockets full of sand. How could she recreate the miracle? By giving up hope as she did before? But it was harder this time. Calm contemplation of a world without Crane wasn't possible any more.

The day the news reached Milborne Grove, Cora had been up before dawn, helping Carrie cover the drawing-room furniture and clear away books and ornaments, ready for the sweep. The man was there by seven, barging in with the self-important air of the trade, slippers on his feet, top hat on his head, and the teeth grinning in his black face to remind the household that sweeps brought good luck, and had to be treated with respect.

He was hardly in the apartment before a telegraph boy was hammering at the door. Cora sat on the stairs to read the cable.

A corner caught on the envelope as she tore it open, and in her hurry she ripped the message-sheet, and had to reassemble the pieces. She saw the words 'HAVE TO TELL YOU'. Her hands shook as she pressed the torn edges together on her knee. Then the message came into focus and he wasn't dead after all.

It was from the New York *Journal*, and said that Crane had been located in Havana at a Mrs Horan's lodging house. General Wade of the US Army had put the word about in the city, at the request of the authorities in Washington, and eventually out popped the missing man, in sound health, declaring that he was sorry if he had caused any trouble, but he had been living quietly and writing. General Wade was reported as saying, 'I do not know his business or why he has not corresponded with his family.'

'He says he can't get the brush up, Ma'am,' reported Carrie. 'Says there's loose bricks up there.'

'Tell him he ought to know about bricks if he's a proper sweep.'

Mrs Horan's lodging house was the last straw. It sounded like low comedy. Crane had never humiliated her before, or at least she had never felt the humiliation.

Carrie was in the hall again. 'He says he isn't a builder, Ma'am.'

'Tell him either sweep the chimney or pack up his brushes and go.'

Anger brought relief, of a sort. It got rid of the sweep and left the chimney half swept, it drove her to spend four guineas of the almost-gone Brede Place money on a long grey coat, it had her composing cutting letters to Crane in her head. After twenty-four hours of this, she was beginning to calm herself when agent Reynolds replied at last, and her anger began all over again, worse than ever.

The letter, which had been weeks in transit, was brisk and

condescending. Had he but known, he assured her, he could have set her fears at rest at an earlier stage. (In that case, why hadn't he cabled? He wrote on expensive stationery, with his grandiloquent name on the top embossed in black: 'Paul Revere Reynolds'. A six-dollar cable wouldn't have ruined him.)

Mr Crane, wrote the agent, was as busy as a bee. He had moved to a lodging house as an economy. Short stories and poems were pouring from his pen. A peach of a tale about a murder at a snowbound hotel was as good as sold to *Harper's*. Havana must be good for his creative juices! There was absolutely no cause for concern!

Had a woman ever been treated with such contempt? The answer to that was obviously yes. She had been on the receiving end of it in the Harrington Gardens days. But they were Stewarts and this was Stevie. The rage was more comprehensive than before. Buying clothes or being rude to people had their uses, but not this time.

Cora sent a card round to Tourbon's Bank by messenger. She would be 'At Home' on Wednesday at six p.m. Carrie was got rid of for the evening.

A plain dress left Cora's arms bare. Hair: loosely pinned. Complexion: flushed. 'Dear Stevie,' she might have written, if she hadn't decided that action was better than words, 'Promises made at times of affection require a better memory than most people possess. I have no claim on you that is going to govern your instincts and make you something you are not. Be as "bad" as you like. Run after all the whores in Cuba as long as you shut up about it. What I refuse to accept is indifference. You are in touch with your precious Reynolds on a daily basis as far as I can gather. I will not be put on one side like that, like something at the back of a cupboard. I warn you – I mean it—'

Hard raps on the knocker announced the coming of the

guest, who greeted her in his sardonic way and stood in the hall expecting someone to take his hat and coat.

'Leave them on the chair,' said Cora. 'It's the maid's night off. This is how the poor live. Come into the drawing room.'

'I seem to be the first.'

'Or the last. You might as well sit down. You will notice the fire is smoking. This is due to circumstances beyond my control. I had better warn you, there isn't much in the way of refreshments. I could find you a glass of whisky. There are Southern hot cookies, home baked.'

'I think if you said anything normal like "Hello Charles, how nice to see you," I would fall off the chair with astonishment. I expect to be offered nothing. I expect to be told to keep my compliments to myself. I am that unspeakable fellow who wants to call you Cora, who even made a remark about love.'

'I was flattered. Only don't do it again.'

'You see? You have this habit of saying yes and no in the same breath. You like to be flattered. You refuse to be flattered. You are a mystery to me. I have no idea what goes on inside your head.'

'I wish to go to bed with you,' said Cora, and then it was done, or rather it wasn't done, but the essential step was taken; was almost sufficient in itself.

The visitor didn't move. A tongue of green smoke came at him from the grate. He did some coughing and said, 'No fire without smoke, ha ha. What an astonishing woman. It is due to your being an American.' His shoulders went up and down. He was pretending to laugh. 'I am sorry to disappoint you, Cora Crane, but the English aren't so easily shocked. I am impressed by your boldness. Amused, perhaps.' The smoke was in his throat again. 'You amuse me and I amuse you.'

'Stop babbling. Yes or no?'

'So you're serious,' he said.

The way it worked at the Dream was for the man to install himself under the sheets, where the woman would join him five minutes later. Fumblings in public were frowned on. Upstairs the doors and walls were padded, so that no sound escaped the bedrooms except an occasional cry that could have been a voice raised in anger. When she was first in the business, Cora made sure that the beds themselves were as silent as possible, until she discovered that men as a rule liked to hear their own bedsprings singing. Perhaps they thought it enhanced their virility.

The springs at Milborne Grove were well-behaved. Not a jingle escaped them. She joined Tourbon in the dark, as she had stipulated, and the flesh got on with it. His warmth slid between her fingers and she whispered to him not to bite her breasts so hard. Altogether it was roughly what she expected. His pleasure worked its way back to her, and gave her half a minute of it herself, palms resting on the Tourbon buttocks as they bounced between her knees.

Afterwards was another matter. Carnal beds could be lingered in without harm under the right circumstances ('We are like little pigs in clover,' she remarked to Crane on their first night together), but this one had to be escaped from.

Cora was in the bathroom, struggling with a recalcitrant gas-geyser, when she heard the front-door knocker. As she hurried along the corridor, wrapping herself in a robe, the banker asked quietly whom it might be.

'Mr Crane with his six-shooter?'

Another bicycle, another boy in a pillbox hat, handing her a yellow envelope. 'REGRET INFORM YOU', and her stomach churned again, 'MR FREDERIC PASSED AWAY 6 P.M. SUGGEST YOU COME TO KENLEY. MATHILDE RUDY.'

The boy Charles understood; his time was up; he extracted an embrace, a hand lingered on her behind, and he was gone, black overcoat and silk hat making for The Boltons and a cab. It was too late for Kenley. Cora waited till the morning, when Carrie arrived to do the fires. She left instructions for readdressing messages, and was with Kate in Surrey by nine o'clock.

18

Cora arrived to find the house full of draughts and whispers. Ruth was upstairs, dealing with the undertakers' men. Secretary Stokes was going through papers in Harold's study, now and then burning a letter in the grate.

The children had gone with Mathilde to spend the day at the zoo, leaving Kate to be strong and dignified, the grieving widow whose job it was to tell people, as widows did, that his end was peaceful and she was glad his suffering was over. The problem was that the real widow was in Hammersmith.

'What do you call a mistress who has lost the man she lived with?' she asked.

'He adored you,' said Cora (that well-known authority on love and men). 'Everyone who knows you, knows that.'

'Yes, but what *am* I? I shall become Kate Lyon again, go back to America and find a school to teach in, and pretend to everyone that I did have a husband once but unfortunately he's dead. Everyone will feel sorry for me, and I shall hate that more than anything.'

'I shall be too busy feeling sorry for myself.'

'I can't believe that,' said Kate. But she sounded more in

control already. 'I heard about Stephen. He's safe, is he not?'

'It was a misunderstanding.'

'Men go in for those, don't they. Thank goodness we have each other.'

They were more sisters-in-adversity than ever. They walked in lanes thick with leaves, they sat in cold bedrooms talking about the last days of Harold. Victory was almost won, said Kate. Mrs Mills had assured her that he was at the crucial stage of something called chemicalisation. The mortal mind and body had moved from a material to a spiritual basis. 'I thought my darling was going to live,' said Kate, 'but in the end neither of us was strong enough. Or pure enough.'

Cora kept her thoughts to herself. She heard how the women had fought over him, Ruth demanding doctors, Kate standing firm with a Bible clasped to her chest, Mrs Mills at the foot of the bed, eyes closed and lips moving; Harold sticking his tongue out at her. In the middle of it all a lawyer's clerk appeared outside the house, and flung divorce papers, served by the real Mrs Frederic, through the kitchen window and straight into a butter dish.

It was a descent into chaos. Cora was chilled by it, to see lives close to hers running out of control. The doctors returned. Ruth invited them in. Kate said, 'Over my dead body.' Dr Freyberger warned of legal consequences if death occurred without medical attendance, and they got in through the back door. Harold waved a white handkerchief when they appeared in his room. Was that a signal of surrender?

The doctors announced it was too late, and he died that evening.

At the interment they stood on the edge of the group, out of the way of Mrs Frederic, a large woman in a veil like a visor, supported by her daughter.

A hen had got into the cemetery and was pecking between the graves. 'Life goes on,' said Cora. The earth had been scattered. People were turning away. 'You have the children. You will always have Stephen and me.'

'Mind you stick by Stephen. Don't ever let him go.'

'There is something I should tell you.' Other people's love-lives were always a diversion, so in a way she was being kind to Kate by telling her. But she was being kind to herself as well, having a need to explain how badly she felt about Crane, who had driven her to such desperation. 'I have had a little lapse with a man.'

In the distance Mrs Frederic was being helped into a carriage. Kate said, 'Oh, Cora!' and took her arm as they moved off. 'I could see it coming. I think I know who it is.'

'Was, not is.'

Which was the greater infidelity, she asked Kate, her spending half an hour in bed with the boy Tourbon, or Stephen doing his vanishing act – silent, heartless, indifferent?

'You can't compare unkindness with fornication,' said Kate.

'I agree. Unkindness is worse.'

'I don't know anything any more. You'll stay with me a few days, won't you?'

'As long as you like.'

On one of her brief visits to Ravensbrook, Cora found mail forwarded from Milborne Grove. Among it was a package containing one orchid, the worse for wear, and a puzzled letter which said that the writer, who didn't sign his name, would visit her again if convenient, and enclosed a small present that she might think appropriate. Cora gave the orchid to Mathilde, burned the five-pound note on a shovel and posted the ashes back to the bank. She felt no ill will; the boy Tourbon had behaved no worse than she had. It was even possible that when he said he was in love with her, he had been telling the truth.

*   *   *

Kate's sorrows weren't over. Because of Christian Science and the angry doctors, an inquest was called for. Cora was dismayed to realise that the coroner, a man with a forked beard, was going to pick her friend's character to pieces in public, to see if she and Mrs Mills between them had harmed Harold.

Everything was made to seem different. Events became unnatural when described out loud, on oath. The venue was an ill-lit public hall. Since Kate was the woman who cohabited with the deceased, she was naturally under grave moral suspicion from the start. After giving her initial evidence (they kept recalling her for more), she returned to sit next to Cora, whose hand she bruised by squeezing it so hard.

When it came to the treatments that had been on offer, Cora had little sympathy with either camp. Mrs Mills, who wore a black hat with plumes and looked like someone from a circus, spoke earnestly about the power of Christ, but it seemed to Cora, as it had from the beginning, that what Christ cured (if anything) was souls, not bodies. The medical men were not much better, implying that if only Mr Frederic had drunk gallons of milk and stopped smoking cigars, and possibly had more belladonna plasters on his leg, he would soon have been leaping out of bed.

To their credit, a few witnesses did suggest that Harold in life was a strong-minded man who liked alcohol and tobacco, and didn't suffer fools gladly; fools being a category that included both the medical profession and women like Mrs Mills. This was good news for Kate, because it made it unlikely that someone as domineering as the deceased could have been bamboozled into having anyone attend him against his wishes. It was also bad news for Kate, because Mrs Mills had undoubtedly sat at the foot of his bed, reading the Bible and praying, so perhaps he had been bamboozled after all.

The seats in front of Cora were full of newspaper reporters with sharp pencils, who, she guessed, were going to be less interested in the finer points of bamboozlement than in how many guineas Mrs Mills charged for her services, and how outraged the doctors were, and how long the dead man had been cohabiting with Miss Lyon. All these matters duly appeared in the London newspapers.

Kate was numbed by the proceedings, which went on for a second day, and told Cora overnight that she was indifferent to whatever conclusions the coroner and his jury came to. This seemed unwise to Cora, who noticed policemen at the back of the hall.

Forkbeard delivered a bad-tempered summing-up in which he said that Christian Science was abhorrent and medical men were wonderful. After this he gave the jury a list of questions they had to answer, none of which mattered except the last two – was anyone criminally responsible for the death, and if so, was it Miss Lyon or Mrs Mills, or the two of them together?

Unsurprisingly, the jury of middle-aged house-owners came back after half an hour and declared through their foreman that Mills and Lyon had committed manslaughter. The foreman looked as if he wanted to put on a black cap and say, 'And may God have mercy on your souls.'

The coroner did what he had to do, issue a warrant for their arrest, after which policemen led by an Inspector Blake came from the back of the court and carted the women off to Croydon police station, followed by Cora and Stokes in one carriage and supporters of Mrs Mills in another.

They were prisoners, but Inspector Blake had intimated that bail would be available. Cora waited in the carriage while Stokes was inside, arranging it for Kate in the sum of forty pounds, a figure that reflected the gravity of the offence. In the eyes of the coroner's jury she was a man-killer. If a criminal jury agreed with them, she could be locked up for years.

Then Cora would rear the children, Stephen would be their Dada, and everything would be truly wonderful, except that while this wonderfulness is going on, Kate is languishing in gaol. It was a wicked day dream but it lingered until Kate emerged from the police station looking changed, as if flesh as well as colour had been sucked from her face.

That night, doing what she could to comfort Kate at the empty house in Kenley – the children were at Ravensbrook – Cora decided to take the only possible step, and visit her friend the detective, who must be well up in killings and that sort of thing. 'Friend' was overdoing it. But she thought she could make him listen.

19

A painful interview with the Head of Detectives left Fred Hooper enraged at being reprimanded for not knowing he had a criminal as a lodger. The cage on the desk was canary-less. Perhaps that explained his superior's ill humour. Fred controlled his temper but only just.

'With respect, sir,' he said, 'the man came with a family recommendation, paid his rent promptly and behaved in a gentlemanly fashion.'

'Detectives should have a sixth sense, Hooper.'

'I don't recall seeing any reference to it in Standing Orders, sir.'

'I had a little bird who thought he was clever,' said H.o.D. He rattled a pencil across the wires of the cage. 'He got out through the window and a sparrowhawk ate him. One more slip and you're for it.'

On his way home Fred cuffed a boy who was committing a nuisance in an alley, and told him in future to use the new urinal in Wandsworth High Street. The sanitary fish-fryer caught his eye as soon as he entered the kitchen, and he took it outside and threw it in the dustbin.

'Don't be alarmed,' he called to Belle, who must be upstairs. 'I am throwing out rubbish we can do without.'

Metal cutlery ('Made in Brussels, lasts a lifetime') went in with a crash, followed by a device for stretching boots and the Patent Puncture Remedy. The birdcage would have gone, too, but it still had the bird in it.

His Birmingham watch made him hesitate. As a matter of principle it had to join the rest, but he had grown up in a family where possessions were rare – they were pretty thin on the ground in Disraeli Street – and a solemn act like throwing away a timepiece that was still ticking needed a witness.

Fred disentangled it from his waistcoat and laid it on the kitchen table. It was then he saw the envelope with 'Fred' written on it in Belle's handwriting.

'Dearest Freddie,' he read, on stolen paper, 'I have gone to the seaside! They are stocktaking at A&H and a week's holiday is due to me. I have not been to the seaside since we were children. I shall find a clean boarding house and decide whether I am going to emigrate. Canada might be nice. My plan is to do drawings and watercolours of the pier, beach, Channel etc., if the rain holds off. Vi is so grand these days with her Thomas Avertons that she painted for Mr Rukes before he did a bunk that I feel quite eclipsed by her, and it will be a relief not to have her looking over my shoulder and complaining about dead dogs, etc. I am not a true artist but it is nice to pretend! Monjy will leave your tea every day and is anxious to show willing over buttons that need sewing on etc., due to her feeling guilty about having wished Mr Rukes on us. I shall miss you, dear old Freddie! Your loving sister, Belle.' The signature filled half a page, a vast 'B', a corkscrewing of ink at the end.

It was rum. His sister was rum. She always had been, and at thirty (nearly thirty) it was no use expecting her to change.

She must have planned it in advance. A typewriting lady couldn't simply say she was off to Brighton in the morning – he thought it was probably Brighton, though it could be Hastings or Eastbourne. Anywhere on the English Channel.

Even by Belle's standards it was a particular rumness. It made him uneasy. Quarrels with Miss Crumm, to whom she was attached – he saw them setting up house together one day, as ageing spinsters did – had upset her in the past. That might be it. Later he would stroll round to the Crumms' and see what Violet had to say.

His immediate task was to get on with the slug wars by the light of a police lantern. When someone knocked at the door he thought it was probably Miss Crumm in person, and didn't bother to respond, because having announced herself she would walk in. But whoever was there continued to knock.

'Keep your hair on,' he said, before he wrenched open the door, which was inclined to stick in wet weather, and saw a silhouette against a cab-lamp that spoke to him and said it hoped this wasn't an unsuitable hour.

That was hardly the word. As far as he was capable of it, a line had been drawn under Mrs Crane. Silk stocking from ankle-bone to knee-bone thence thigh-bone and so on no longer had the power to invade dreams, or if it did sneak in – and sleep was a funny thing – he woke himself up and drank a glass of water and walked about on the linoleum, by an open window, waiting for the dream to die down.

'So is it all right if I come in? I have told the driver to wait.'

Just this once, he thought, and then it was too late. The woman he had got rid of reasserted herself. He beckoned her in and lit the gas in the parlour, remarking, because something had to be remarked on to help him uncork his powers of speech, that he hoped she hadn't mislaid another boy.

'Worse,' said the voice he had meant never to hear again. 'The last time we met, you asked for my help, and I refused. If it's of any use, I will be happy to testify about the child-snatcher.'

The last time they met, Fred was wearing a newly sponged jacket with his best handkerchief in the pocket. Now he was sporting a shirt without a collar and dingy braces.

'How did you find out where I lived?'

'I gave a young sergeant at Vine Street half a crown. Said I was your cousin from New York and I'd lost your address.'

'Very enterprising,' he said gloomily. It would be all over the station, Fred Hooper and his American beauty. 'It wouldn't be your Mrs Rudy, I suppose?'

'I wish it was. It's like this. A man I'm acquainted with died of an illness. They held an inquest, and for reasons I can explain they decided he had been killed unlawfully. I have been so worried. Then I thought, Inspector Hooper will know what to do.'

'Make a clean breast of it, Ma'am,' he said, seeing everything solved in one go, his improper thoughts finally succumbing to the knowledge that she was a dangerous criminal, that his initial suspicion of her being up to something had been confirmed in a roundabout way. He had time to wonder if he was on to a sensation, such as her poisoning a blackmailer, before she smiled at his pleasantry, as she must have interpreted the remark about clean breasts, and told a different story altogether.

The mistake lay in not stopping her before she got going. By the time Fred had the hang of the case, he had found a stub of pencil and written 'Kate Lyon, common-law wife' and '£40 bail' on the back of Belle's note, and given the woman hope. Instead of saying that events in Croydon would have to take their course, he spoke of 'finding out what's going on' and 'having words in ears'.

Nothing had changed. Her proximity was as powerful as before. The visions were no less distracting.

It wasn't as though he was being asked to pervert the course of justice. He could easily pop down to Croydon and see how things stood. Then he would visit her in Kensington and report progress.

'I shall leave you in peace,' she said. 'I won't ask where your sister is. Ironing your shirts somewhere?'

'She is away on a holiday.'

'I'm only teasing you. There you are, we have ended up friends after all.'

He had half a mind to go to Croydon that night, but stopped himself because it was impractical at such short notice. The fact that he was more willing than ever to rush about on behalf of a woman who used to run a brothel disconcerted him without it having any effect on his behaviour. No laws were being broken. Friendship had arisen between him and five foot five, sea-green eyes, without encouragement on his part.

Romance as such didn't come into it. Romance meant courtship, holding hands, pecks on the cheek, wedding ring and bells, and at last the performance behind the bedroom screen, preceding the performance in the bed, the rumpled nightgown and the briefly lowered pyjamas.

Beyond romance there was passion, of course, which could lead to criminal behaviour. Women were regularly strangled with scarves and bootlaces because of it. Men were got rid of with poison by adulterous wives. Detectives were well-informed about such things.

Passion was against the law. Viewed optimistically, did rubbing a silk dress on your face count as passion? He hoped not.

Croydon wasn't a town that meant anything to Fred. Suburban bricks and mortar were spreading towards it but farmland still

241

intervened. On his ancient *Metropolitan Police Map Showing Environs* it was represented by a church spire and a 'T' for telegraph office. The joints of the London and Brighton line connected it to London.

The risks involved didn't worry him. If anyone asked, he was following up information about stolen property supplied by an informant. A couple of hours should be enough. By tomorrow he would be visiting Mrs Crane again. He sat back and enjoyed the view from the train, mainly dark fields containing beasts beneath dark skies. It was late afternoon.

As a preliminary he had been to see the lady in Seymour Street who was charged alongside Miss Lyon, on the pretence of checking points of evidence. The case had been in the papers, so he equipped himself with facts from copies of the *Daily Mail*, and made up some questions. But Mrs Athalie Mills, having answered them, proved to be a sharp old bird. A constable from Croydon had already called on her and visited the local station, to make sure the bail conditions were being met. Why hadn't they sent her a more senior policeman like him in the first place?

'Muddle, Ma'am. And which constable did they send?'

'His name was Jones.' She had noted his number, a habit her father had taught her. It was 997.

'Very satisfactory,' he said, and closed his notebook.

Arriving at West Croydon station, Fred felt a surge of youthfulness, as if he was a young detective again. Florence used to see him off at the front door and say, 'Now you be careful, I don't want them bringing you home on a stretcher.' The memory came back, of a woman who cared about him, whose life was mixed up with his. You could hardly compare Florence with Mrs Crane, but in the years between, there had been no one else.

It was getting dark, and the place was busier than he

expected. Road wagons were being loaded at the sidings. Flames escaped from a foundry. He passed shops, some lit by paraffin lamps but most by gas, and a Methodist chapel cut from the same raw brick, not yet weathered. The police station was large and newly extended, and it was possible to identify the structure at the rear as the station-house by the objects that were just visible on upstairs windowsills – socks laid out to dry, no doubt in direct contravention of orders.

Fred loitered by the entrance till a pair of uniformed constables came out, and asked them if he would find 997 Jones inside.

'Dormitory number two, sir.'

Carbolic on the stairs and someone whistling took him back to his station-house days. He looked around the door with '2' on it. Men in their braces were playing cards on one of the cots. Others were asleep. A youth with large ears was crouched at an iron-legged table, braces dangling from his trousers, carving a lump of wood with a penknife.

'I am looking for P.C. Jones.'

'That's me, sir.'

It was jug-ears. Fred beckoned him into the corridor. They ended up in a whitewashed cubicle for mops and buckets. The warrant card was flashed, long enough for Jones to recognise it but not to see the name because Fred kept his thumb on it. The only illumination came from the corridor.

'I am here from Scotland Yard,' he said.

The whistler was still at it. Boots clattered down a staircase and a door banged.

'We are looking for smart lads with initiative who know how to keep a secret. Are you up to it, Jones?'

'Will do my very best, sir.'

'This unlawful killing case. It has some puzzling aspects.'

'Sir?'

'The ladies are very clever when it comes to killing. We detectives see it all the time. Spoonful of arsenic in the tea and Bob's your uncle. These particular ladies went in for foreign practices and they may have killed off a man in the process. Or they may be blameless. I can't be sure. Neither can you. The question is, are the charges going to be dropped? You're a lad with his wits about him. What's being said?'

'There's an inspector thinks they need making an example of.'

'And he's called?'

'Mr Blake, sir. He had the doctors in again to question them. But I heard the Super wasn't keen. Sir, can you help me be a detective in London?'

'One thing at a time.'

A heavy tread separated itself from the other sounds. A voice called, '997 Jones?'

Fred put a finger to his lips and drew them into the shadows. His shin knocked a bucket over. Even then he thought he could carry it off.

'What are you doing in there, Jones? Come out here, lad. And you, sir.'

It was a uniformed sergeant with a boxer's face and beer on his breath.

'No need for alarm, sergeant,' said Fred. 'I work for a detective agency. I am looking for stolen property.'

'And I'm Charlie Peace. I am arresting you for importuning a police officer for immoral purposes. We have had a man hanging about here before. Pull your braces up, lad. I shall deal with you later.'

'I had better speak to your Super,' said Fred. Mrs Crane had done for him, but even now, being marched out of the building with his arm gripped, he was looking forward to

244

informing her that the Croydon police were in two minds about the case.

First he had to deal with the sergeant.

A man with beer inside him would be that fraction slower. As they crossed the yard, under a glow of foundry-light crimson on the clouds, Fred noted the cobbles, slippery with rain. He stumbled and said 'Whoops!' then swung round to give the sergeant a sharp punch in the belly, kick his heels from under him, and tear his arm free.

By the time whistles were sounding he was in the street. He had an anxious few minutes when alleys led away from the railway station, before he managed to double back and reach the tracks a hundred yards to the south, then walk back to the end of the Up platform.

They would put men on the ticket barriers if they knew their job. He thought he saw a helmet in that direction. But the platform was long, and when a London train came in, it was easy enough to step across the line behind the red oil-lamp at the rear, and swing himself up into a compartment. It was empty, but until they were clear of West Croydon he hid in a lavatory.

The little finger of the fist that gave the punch was aching where it had caught the sergeant's belt-buckle. He filled the basin with water from the can and stood soaking his hand, watching the finger go purple.

The inspectors' room never changed, men in shirt-sleeves writing reports, men talking about villainy, all of them watched over by drawings of wanted criminals and missing property pasted to the walls. Half the officers present were idle at any given moment, but that was in the nature of the work. Even Fred Hooper, more diligent than most, had his lapses. Even if he had been working on a new Greenwich Bomb Outrage, he would have found it hard to concentrate at the same time as straining his ears to catch any gossip about Croydon.

Rumours flew around the Met in hours. As he waited for something to happen, Fred tried to remember how much light there had been for the beery sergeant to get a proper look at him. Would they trawl through the Met in search of a tall, thin detective with a bruised finger?

For a while he was afraid that some Sherlock Holmes at Central Office had already unravelled the case, and they were having Milborne Grove watched to see if he gave himself away by going there. But if they had got as far as that, he was done for anyway. He walked there from the South Kensington Underground in broad daylight, warmed by the thought of passing on good news.

A maid answered the door, looking frightened. She said Madam was not at home. Pressed, she asked him if he was Mr Tourbon.

'Why, would she be at home if I was?'

The girl shook her head. 'But it doesn't matter,' she said, 'because Madam isn't here anyway. She is not in London.'

The Tourbon chap bothered him. A tradesman? Tradesmen didn't go to front doors. A detective? No one followed him as he walked away.

It was likely he would never see Cora Crane again.

The inspectors' room was as noisy as ever. Men were arguing whether a bloodstained scarf which had been gnawed into rags by a mouse could still be used in evidence. An elderly officer, making out a report sheet, kept calling to a colleague, 'How do you spell vicinity?', 'How do you spell harelip?'

Someone said 'Croydon' behind him, not far away. It was Tom Simmons. Fred didn't move. He heard 'no proof, of course' and 'in a broom cupboard'. Someone laughed.

The inspector who couldn't spell called, 'Where did you get it from?'

'The horse's mouth,' replied Simmons.

People were wandering over to hear about the Croydon affair. Fred turned to listen. 'It may be somebody in the Met or it could be a hoax,' Simmons was saying, wrinkling his moustache with pleasure. 'But they have a fair description of the fellow, whoever he is, and they've found an artist to do a drawing. They mean to print copies for every division. We can stick it on the wall, see how many of us it looks like.'

Since the Blanche business, Fred had avoided speaking to Simmons unless he had to. He made himself say, 'I don't believe he was a police officer. No one would be such an idiot.'

'Agreed,' said Tom. 'But you must admit, it would be thrilling if he was.'

20

Instead of feeling soothed by her little fling, Cora was crosser than ever at having been driven to do something so ridiculous. It made her all the more determined to be stoical, to oppose Stephen's silence with hers, to wait until the waiting itself became a weapon that she would find some way of using to save herself.

Reynolds sent her scraps of information from New York, but she didn't know if this was because he had taken pity on her, or because he had been asked to act as an intermediary.

'Writing letters is such hard work,' Cora wrote sarcastically in her manuscript book. 'The King of Ithaca needs to save his strength. We all know his lungs weren't strong enough for the Marines. Now he appears to be having hallucinations. This is what Reynolds informs me happened some weeks back. Crane eats supper at his rooming house. He strolls down to the waterfront and what does he see? Harold Frederic, coming ashore from an open boat. Harold staggers along a rusty pier, pale as death, and *walks straight past Crane without seeing him.*

'What a pity Crane doesn't write ghost stories, or he would

have one ready-made. I have stories of my own waiting for him when he comes home, *if he ever does*. A love story. A woman encounters a police detective. She sees an officious law-enforcer. He sees a suspect. She laughs at him behind his back. They develop an acquaintance. Afterwards, she realises he was in love with her. Does that make a story? Crane is the expert.'

Cora fingered the galley-proofs and felt the coarseness of the Mexican blanket. My darling Stevie, she thought, my littlest mouse, my child, my lover, my beast, my destroyer, my almost-husband. How strange, you having that vision of Harold. Who is dead now, as you must have heard. The American papers reported it, I know, because I saw Kate gumming the articles into a Book of Remembrance. They spoke of his wife and children, but naturally said nothing about his other wife and his other children, who are deemed not to exist. Which is yet another story. Not to mention the story of Kate going to prison for killing Harold with her Christian Science, if it ever comes to that. The case is hanging over her head.

'Am I deemed not to exist?' She was writing in her book again. 'It distresses Crane that we are still unable to marry. Nobody would credit it. The world sees him as a great Bohemian. He consorts with loose women, he plays poker, he writes raw tales about men *in extremis*. But half his ancestors were preachers or lawyers, and his family are still pillars of society in New Jersey.

'All that moral striving by the Cranes, and he can't even get himself a proper wife. He blames me for not trying harder, but I went to the house and cornered my brother-in-law. I never heard any more. Captain Donald of the Gold Coast remains unsullied by divorce. I hope he has a better time with his black ladies than we ever had in Harrington Gardens. I bet he bores them as much as he bored me.'

Cora was in the study to write business letters, but filling pages in her book was more congenial. She made herself get on with the letters. Lipton's, the grocers in Kensington, were threatening legal action if their bill wasn't paid. So were Weber's, who wanted paying for stockings and underlinen bought so long ago, the fabric had gone limp. If she satisfied them, along with the others in the queue, her hoarded sovereigns would be nearly gone, with nothing left for Brede Place, the thought of which was all that kept her going. But practical Joseph Conrad had spoken to a solicitor, and told her what she should do. It was miraculously simple. If only she had known earlier, there might still have been a piano in the drawing room.

'Dear Sir,' she wrote, 'I am a married woman, and the debt to which you refer is legally that of my husband. He is in America at present. When he returns, I shall ensure that your bill is brought to his attention. I am, yours faithfully, Cora Crane (Mrs).'

Another story: an American woman in England goes to prison for defrauding shopkeepers.

Cold, wet weather sets in, and Mathilde Rudy despairs at the thought of a second English winter. On the rare occasions when there was a chill in the air in Jacksonville, the furnace and boilers of the Dream let you stand half-naked in a bedroom without freezing to death. At Ravensbrook you practically have to put your behind in the fire before you feel any benefit. As for Brede Place, everything she has heard about it makes her ill.

She remains devoted to Ma, and feels it her duty to make pointed remarks about the future, since no one else will. Undressing her employer at night, she brings the conversation round to Jacksonville, and suggests they might do worse than go back there.

'I think Mr Crane and I have progressed beyond Jacksonville,' says Ma.

Mathilde observes tartly that Mr Crane has progressed as far as Havana, for which she has three days' wages docked, not much of a punishment because these days she is lucky if she sees any wages at all. Ma isn't herself. Her scratchiness tells Mathilde that their days in England are numbered.

Adoni, who continues to keep his ears open, has reached the same conclusion, and is under the illusion that he is going with them. Once or twice he helped out at Kenley, and while he was there he saw a New York guidebook, and asked if he might look at it. Now Miss Lyon has sent it him as a present. He spends hours studying the drawings of bridges and railroad stations, practising the things he will say when he steps ashore, 'Oh boy!' and 'Gee whiz!'

Ma is up in London for the day. Mathilde is trying to keep warm in the kitchen, having a little cooking brandy and water, her back touching the stove. When Adoni comes in, clutching the guidebook, she ignores him.

He sits on the far side of the table and moves his finger along a page, reading aloud. 'On Sec-ond Street be-tween First and Sec-ond Av-en-ue is . . . words I don't know. Ma-bel Sen-try. You explain me, Auntie Mattie.'

'Ask your little friend Rose.'

'She has gone on errand. I bring my chair.'

'Keep your distance.'

Adoni slides the book across the table, holding his finger on the sentence. His beauty still distresses her.

'When I am at New York,' he says, 'I know streets like map of hand. Please, what is Mab-el Sen-try?'

'You are an ignorant dago, did you know that?'

'You have pretty voice, Auntie Mattie.'

251

'The words are "Marble Cemetery".' She mimicks him. '"What is Mar-ble Cem-et-ery?"'

'Please?'

'A cemetery is where you go when you're dead. Behave yourself when you get to New York, if you ever do, or you might find yourself in one sooner than you think.'

'I will be good American citizen. I salute flag. I will be butler for Mrs Cora in New York. Oh boy!'

He wiggles his chair around the table, holding it against his behind.

'Keep away. Bad dog! I mean it.'

'We go upstairs? Go jig-jig like in summer?'

'You are a slimy toad,' she says, but all he does is blow her a kiss and glide away.

There are problems that are never going to be solved, even by Ma. She may be smarter than Mathilde when it comes to bamboozlers who can charm your skirts off, but she wasn't smart enough to resist loving a little fellow with consumptive's eyes, wearing a shabby coat, who says he expects to be dead by the time he's thirty-five. The best thing that can happen to Ma now is that he never comes back.

Men with weak chests frequently succumb in places like Havana. Another brandy-and-water, and Mathilde is perking up. She sees them back at a new, improved Hotel de Dream, where a dignified marble bust greets visitors as they enter, the hall from Ashley Street. The metal plate reads, 'Mr Stephen Crane, Famous Author, stayed here, 1896–97.' England is a distant memory. The croupier's voice is as velvety as the southern tunes the pianist is playing. Ma goes from room to room, chatting with lawyers and real-estate men. Girls with clean medical records radiate expectation. Mathilde has solved the problem after all.

*   *   *

Brede Place had started off as the saving of Stephen, and Cora tried to go on seeing it as that because otherwise it was merely a pile of stones in the middle of nowhere. Sovereigns had been sent to persuade a builder to keep the rain out, but he appeared to have run out of slates, and more sovereigns were being demanded. The stationery she was so proud of had never been delivered by the printers, who behaved in an un-English manner and refused to part with the order until they saw their money. All she had was a proof-sheet with its imposing capital letters, 'CRANE, BREDE HILL. STATION: RYE.' The house itself was a mirage.

Kate's problems helped keep her from dwelling on her own. Cora spent days at Kenley, going through bills and other debris that Secretary Stokes hadn't bothered with, agreeing that Kate had every right to be dismayed at fourteen unpaid-for lunches at the National Liberal Club, or the borrowed servants at the borrowed villa in Ireland who were still asking for their wages. It was bad enough to die without making provision for one family. Harold had managed not to make provision for two.

When asked, Cora agreed he had been a thoughtless devil. She had to be equally willing to agree that he was the kind of man who only came once in a lifetime. Or that he was a lover who took one's breath away – 'I take your word for it,' she smiled.

Kate plunged from one mood to another. It was too early to start telling her to buck up. But when she moaned about the children, and what would become of them, Cora asked sharply if they weren't a living proof of her life with Harold, and would she rather be childless? Kate flushed and agreed. 'We could share them,' she said. 'They adore you.'

'Can you see me turning into a perpetual Aunt Cora?'

'Stranger things have happened. Will you look after them if they send me to prison?'

'They won't.'

'They might.'

'In which case, you know that I will.'

Cora was dismayed to find that her friend still believed in the Scientists. 'I lack faith, that's my trouble,' said Kate. 'Look,' and she touched a cold-sore on her lip, 'I can't even cure this. It makes me angry with myself. I need something, I don't know what.'

'An outing would cheer you up.'

'Do you remember Harold's outings?'

'Vividly.'

'Could we go somewhere by ourselves, somewhere peaceful? Just the two of us.'

'I will have a think,' said Cora, but she knew already.

Brede Place had to be confronted, once and for all. When the slowest train in England puffed into Rye, the short November day was already half over, and when Cora found a vehicle with a roof that didn't leak too badly, she urged the driver to go quicker than he said was safe along the slippery lanes.

Even on a damp afternoon, the clump of stone and chimneys imposed itself on the landscape.

'What a difference,' she said, pointing at a piece of tarpaulin flapping on the roof. 'They are getting on with the slates. Old Mack has done wonders with the garden. The hen-coop has gone.'

'No it hasn't. You can't see it for that pile of mud.'

No one was actually working on the roof. Cora banged on the door of the hut without a response.

'Look, there's a face,' said Kate, pointing up at a window. 'Now it's gone. If I was a ghost here I would be extremely bored. Having visitors must be a treat.'

'Poke as much fun as you like, you'll love it when you bring the children in the summer.' Cora put her weight against the studded door and went up the steps into her house. Her flagstones, her black beams. Mrs Mack appeared briefly in the gallery above, brandishing a broom. She descended the oak staircase to the hall, brushing feebly as she came.

'GOOD AFTERNOON MRS MACK.'

'He'm not himself, Old Mack.'

'WHERE ARE THE WORKMEN?'

'Gave himself a chill, out at all hours, putting poison down for rats.'

Either you believed in Brede Place or you didn't. Either you saw Crane astride a horse coming up from the valley, Crane safe in the study writing masterpieces – or your nerve failed, and then all you saw was a wilderness and an old house.

'HERE'S HALF A CROWN, MRS MACK.'

She took the coin, made a sudden attack on a heap of dust, and vanished through an archway.

'A phantom, obviously,' said Kate. She had a frog in her throat. When she tried to clear it she began to cough. Her eyes watered. 'It's as damp as a dungeon in here,' she said.

'That hearth's big enough to burn trees in. Anyway, you've had a cold for days.'

'I'd have pneumonia if I stayed here much longer. Living in this place isn't going to do Stephen's chest any good.'

The words cast doubt on everything. The horse came up rid-erless from the valley. The intended study above the entrance was bare boards and a smell of mice. 'If I want your advice about Stephen,' said Cora, 'I'll ask for it. You've never liked the house.'

'I'd like it well enough if you could spend ten thousand pounds on renovations. I don't want to quarrel.'

'I guess you and Harold made fun behind my back.'

The cold-sore had bled. Kate held a handkerchief to her mouth. 'I truly hope you'll be happy here. I'm sure you will.'

But something had changed for Cora. She was tired of waiting. She couldn't pretend for ever. Rain was dripping into buckets. The desolation of the house was the desolation she felt. A future with Crane was madness. He was never coming back.

The train creaked out of Rye. Kate and Cora, alone in the compartment, had put their stockinged feet side by side on a foot-warmer. 'Would you care for one each, Ma'am?' the porter had asked, but closeness was better.

Kate talked about her future, which, if it didn't consist of prison, seemed likely to consist of teaching ('Must you?' said Cora) or helping authors ('Such difficult beasts!') pursue their researches in libraries. She had done it for Harold. She liked to dredge through knowledge.

'I might join you,' said Cora gaily. Her left foot kept sliding off the warmer, so she made an inch of room by wrapping the other set of toes around Kate's. 'You do the dredging. I do the writing.'

'I suspect Stephen would have something to say about that.'

'Stephen's problem is that he has nothing to say about anything any more. I've had enough. You say you may go to America. I may go with you. Not to look for him, I assure you.'

The train drew up at a line of planks and an oil lamp. 'Romney, this is Romney,' shouted a porter, and opened the door for an elderly man, who took one look at the stockinged toes and said, 'Next compartment, I think.'

'You are depressed by the house,' said Kate. 'You'll feel differently tomorrow.'

'I've known it for weeks. The man has found himself another promised land. He has his typewriting machine, he lives in a

boarding house in Havana, and visits a whorehouse on Fridays.
I am guessing about the whorehouse.'

My littlest mouse, how could you have done it?

'It would be wonderful if the two of us had each other.'

Cora could feel the warmth creeping up her legs. 'Take it
as fixed,' she said.

21

The Croydon story took on a life of its own. What happened in the broom cupboard was widely debated at police stations, though not by Fred, who chewed his fingernails and said he wasn't interested in smut. One version featured criminal acts with a boy. Another insisted it was a girl, smuggled into the barracks by the intruder, who charged the PCs one-and-sixpence a time. Immorality was what interested the rank and file at Vine Street. Further up the line (said Simmons) they were talking about a dangerous man who had to be caught, and had begun to draw up a list of tall detectives.

Fred was giving evidence in a court when the Wanted Man poster arrived. On his return there were shouts of, 'That's him! Spitting image!' He stood in front of it, arms folded over his thumping chest. The drawing had caught his longish face, that was all. There were plenty of those in the force. The police artist, perhaps a student of Lombroso, had added a jutting brow and a thickness in the lips, which gave the face a criminal aspect.

'Better confess,' said the inspector who couldn't spell, and then another tallish detective came into the room, and there were renewed shouts of 'That's him!'

Identity parades were high on the rumour-list. Hundreds of men were going to be taken to a basement at Scotland Yard where the sergeant from Croydon would scrutinise them one by one.

The fear was like cold water around Fred's kidneys. If they had all the evidence, if 997 Jones remembered the questions, it hardly needed the beery sergeant to tap him on the shoulder and say, 'This is the man who assaulted me.' They would know already. They would find the Christian Scientists who were out on bail and trace the line of deceit, back to the woman who kissed him in Vine Street ('An officer must keep a sense of proportion, Hooper'), back to Ravensbrook, back to Milborne Grove, back to a motive.

Why was this officer, who shared his home with a sister and a canary, but who had no wife upstairs, doing favours for a woman who was lately a criminal suspect, one-time proprietor of a disorderly house? Use your imagination, members of the jury. Here is a man consumed by lust. What lengths was he not prepared to go to?

If it ever got to that, thought Fred, what would I say?

'M'lud, I never touched the lady.' (Outbursts of coughing in court.) 'No immorality took place.' (Ribald whistles from the public gallery, which has to be cleared.)

It wouldn't be much use telling the truth, that she awakened things in him he didn't know were there, because what sort of talk was that? (The judge frowns and says, 'I am giving you an extra twelve months in the jug, sentences to run consecutively, for obfuscation.')

For a week nothing more was heard of identity parades. Then Simmons approached him at the end of a night shift when both had been on duty, and asked could they have a private word.

'Be quick about it,' said Fred.

Simmons had caught him on the station steps. The first daylight was coming into the street.

'They are making a start in "K" division today, parading the lean and lanky ones.'

'I'm not interested in rumours, especially yours.'

'This isn't a rumour. This is the real thing.' The Simmons moustache had spread a bit. The lip was acquiring authority. 'I thought you might like to know.'

A postcard from Belle was on the mat when he got home. She was extending her holiday, Arding & Hobbs having agreed by telegram. 'I am drawing LOADS of English Channels,' she wrote. The card showed the Royal Pavilion and was postmarked Brighton, so at least he knew where she was.

If they were to arrest him, he wondered would they do it at Vine Street or here in the house. He had no wife to disgrace. Could one disgrace a sister? It didn't sound as bad. What would happen when he wasn't here to look after her? Would she and Violet Crumm bring forward their spinsters' arrangement for living together?

His sleep was suffering. Yesterday it was a scratching noise behind the screen that in his dream he turned into a rustling of clothes. To begin with the woman taking them off was Florence. Then she was Cora Crane. Waking, he reached for a shoe and flung it, which got rid of the mouse, but he didn't sleep after that.

Today he dreamt there was a warrant out for his arrest, and they had come looking for him in the room above Armellini's shop, banging on his door. He thought he was safe there, but Tom Simmons had given him away. Then he opened his eyes on the daylight, and heard someone knocking.

Miss Crumm was outside, in distress. 'I shouldn't have woken you when you're on nights,' she said, when he had made himself decent and let her in. 'I came to leave a note but I saw the curtains drawn and knew you were here. I have had a fright.'

She had been confronted by a couple of her 'Thomas Avertons' on sale in Streatham, where she had taken some of her river scenes to a new art dealer who catered for the local gentry. 'Your little paintings are very competent,' the man told her, 'but heavily influenced by Averton.' He had a typewritten history of the painter, 1857 to 1889, who drew scenes on the estate of the Duke of Norwich, his patron, before he died in mysterious circumstances, since when his work had been discovered by several experts and snapped up by discriminating galleries.

'I believe Mr Rukes invented it all, including the so-called experts, as a hoax on gullible dealers,' said Miss Crumm.

'I daresay he did. Why should that concern you?'

'I am part of the fraud. What happens if I am found out? What should I tell the police if they come inquiring?'

'Just the truth. You are obviously an innocent party. As we all were.'

'Um,' she said, a finger drawing circles in a scattering of flour on the kitchen table that Mrs Monge had left there.

Fred wondered how best to get her off the premises. Her chubby figure seemed glued to the chair. 'Cheer up, Miss Crumm,' he said. 'Men of that type are very plausible. No one is going to blame you for finding him, what shall I say, agreeable.'

'Don't worry, I didn't. Or he me, for that matter. It was a business arrangement, pure and simple.' She had gone red. 'I am speaking out of turn.'

'Don't be so frank if they ever do come asking you questions.'

'Leonard Rukes and I had no time for one another. It

distresses me to think that anyone would suppose otherwise.'

He wagged a finger at her, father- or brother-like. 'He did give you a slap-up celebration on your birthday.'

'I wouldn't be surprised he was out to impress Belle.'

'Why would he want to do that? She had no time for him either.'

'Wanted to change her mind? He had a high opinion of himself.' She found flour on her sleeve and tried to rub it clean, not catching his eye. 'Take no notice of me, Mr Hooper. I am upset about my Thomas Avertons. I'm anxious to know what Belle thinks about it all, but she must be in Hastings still.'

'Brighton. She's in Brighton. Here's a postcard, came this morning.'

'You never know with Belle.' She left the table at last, but only to look in the larder and say, 'Now that I have made such a nuisance of myself, shall I get your dinner ready? There are lamb chops in the meat-safe. I can boil some potatoes. It's no trouble.'

'Out of the question,' he said, but was amused to see that she took no notice, banging about with plates and saucepans.

'Am I forgiven, Mr Hooper?' she asked.

'For what?'

'Speaking sharply about Belle. I am envious of her, going off like that, sketching in new places.'

'You should have gone with her.'

'She wouldn't have me.'

Miss Crumm cooked with an anxious expression, tip of her tongue between her teeth. Fred had a feeling that she wanted to tell him something, but when she had poured gravy over his plate and taken off her apron, all she said was, 'May I look in again?'

'Very kind, although Belle won't be away much longer.'

'Then I shall have to use my discretion.'

Has she been flirting with him? Is this what flirting means? If so, it's a bit late in the day. By the time he comes out of prison, Belle and Miss Crumm will be growing old together. Fred is resigned to the future, theirs and his.

Still, the lamb chops, nicely browned, go down a treat.

At Vine Street, in the small hours, crime and punishment wait in the shadows. Rain-mist puts a haze around the blue station-lamp. Inside are wet capes on pegs and hot feet in boots. Small-coal is banked up in grates, more black than red. Fred's watch, which he still hasn't thrown in the river, says a few minutes after two. Croaks and curses come from the cells below. A shadow with long arms moves ahead of him as he strides to the ablutions. He is still a free man.

A figure is leaning forward above the wash-basin, peering into six inches of regulation mirror fixed in iron (its predecessor was nicked), doing something to his upper lip. Fred ignores him, goes to the slate-grey wall and watches his water bubble away. Buttoning up, he sees an eye in the mirror.

'Four divisions down. Only another nineteen to investigate.' The eye returns to its task. A nail-clipper is at work on the moustache, trimming it under the nostrils. 'Think they'll ever find him?'

'Get back to work, Mr Simmons.' A hesitation in the leg department keeps Fred's boots from taking his own advice. Tap drips, eyes meet again.

'I hear they're running out of steam. H.o.D. says police work is being disrupted. Sergeant Whatsit of Croydon is an ass. He said "That's him!" on Tuesday, man turned out to be a Methodist from Clerkenwell with an alibi. He was taking a Bible class.'

Fred cups his hand under a tap that says *Not drinking*

water and gulps a mouthful. He hopes he is hearing good news.

'The inquiry is to mollify them down in Croydon,' says Simmons. 'Put one tip-top detective on the case and he'd crack it. I doubt if they want that. Awkward revelations. Articles in the *Daily Mail* about rotten apples. My guess is they'll drop it. You're in luck.'

Fred's cuff is wet. The eye watches. Still Simmons doesn't turn round.

'If you've got something to say, say it.'

'There ought to be a law against women who egg us on.'

A handkerchief wipes the lip, and Tom Simmons is facing him, all smiles.

'You don't know what you're talking about,' says Fred.

'Your piece of American skirt is best friends with one of that pair of saints who killed a Mr Frederic. I did some burrowing. Our mystery man asked Constable Jones about the case. Nobody's followed that up, except me. I daresay nobody will.'

'I don't have pieces of skirt,' says Fred. He is beginning to splutter. 'You had better be careful what you say.'

'The little devils tempt us and we think, just this once, this particular bit of crackling is more than flesh and blood, etcetera. I must say, I admire your cheek, ticking me off over Blanche. But I don't bear grudges. I like a man who likes the game. We are in the same boat, you and I.'

Six a.m., smell of oil lamps on the staircases as night constables come off duty. Fred is scratching at a letter in the inspectors' room. Someone has opened a window. The rain has gone over, and redness is coming into the sky. 'Dear Sir, I wish to tender my resignation from the Metropolitan Police.'

Inspector Simmons walks in whistling, crosses to the artist's drawing of a stage villain and tears it off the wall.

'I'll bet you nothing happens. Nine days' wonder.'

Fred feels pure air on his face from the street, from London at dawn. He crumples the letter in his hand. Once in the grate, it burns to nothing.

22

A pirates' party for Barry on his seventh birthday filled the house at Kenley with small boys waving wooden swords and shouting.

'This time next year,' said Kate, 'we shall be in Chicago. Unless—'

'Unless nothing. When you go to court next week you will be found not guilty. My friend Joseph Conrad knows a lawyer who says it was a mistake you were ever charged.'

'You never heard from your friend the detective?'

'I thought I'd charmed him. Evidently not.'

Cora comforted a small girl who had been told to walk along a pretend plank and be eaten by pretend sharks.

'You are better with children than I,' smiled Kate.

'Nonsense. They see me as a soft touch. As a mother I should beat them regularly.'

'I give you carte blanche with mine. I don't want them running wild. Children can be difficult without a father. They are going to need two mothers. Will you like living in Chicago?'

'It's where you taught. We might as well live there as anywhere else.'

Their conversations about the future never progressed beyond a vague outline. Today England, tomorrow America.

A shortage of pirate hats developed, due to wear and tear. The women went into the dining room to make fresh ones from sheets of the *Times* newspaper, which was still delivered to the house under an arrangement that Harold's employers had forgotten to cancel.

When Kate gasped and put her scissors down, Cora thought she had cut herself.

'Are you all right?'

'It's nothing.' She made the hat and trimmed the edges. Her fingers were trembling. Suddenly she pulled it apart and flattened out the newsprint. 'Cora, dear,' she said, 'Donald has passed away. It caught my eye. The Lord works in a mysterious way.'

'Very mysterious.' Cora had a moment of feeling sorry for her husband, succumbing in a jungle to climate or black ladies. On a practical level, it was a pity it hadn't happened a year earlier.

'Sir Donald Stewart,' said Kate. 'Died in Algiers. Going to be buried in London. The newspaper is two days old.'

She passed the remnant of hat to Cora, who frowned over it. The Lord was being even more mysterious.

'Wrong Donald,' she said. It had been too good to be true. 'Mine isn't a Sir.'

'They must have made him one.'

'Not unless they made him a field marshal at the same time.' A child crashed against the door. 'This is my father-in-law, the one who was in the Indian Mutiny. It's not your fault. I shall buy you new eye-glasses.'

The death had evidently been reported weeks ago. The old soldier had been in Algiers for his health. Now a warship had brought the coffin back to Portsmouth, and next Saturday he was being buried with full military honours.

Already the servants would be scattering sawdust outside the house; the men were ruminating behind drawn blinds on the long life of service to the Queen; the women, at one remove from it all, were not letting the side down by showing emotion.

Kate said that the children had better have their tea before someone got hurt. The implications of a dead field marshal had to wait.

It was hours before Barry's friends had gone home, and the house was silent again. The two were in Harold's study, putting books in boxes to go back to the real Mrs Frederic, who was claiming them under the terms of the will.

The implications were that Donnie might have had time to return from the Gold Coast. He might be at the funeral.

'You can't possibly,' said Kate.

'I am still his wife. They couldn't stop me.'

'What would be the point?'

'Devilment? They might pay me to keep away.'

'I wish you wouldn't say these terrible things that you don't mean.'

'I wouldn't put anything past me. I know your state is worse than mine. You are a saint but I'm not. If I see a chance I'm going to take it.' She brushed the dust off her hands, and a grain of dirt flew into her eye. 'Can we stop packing books now?'

'I guess.'

Cora tried pulling the lid and looking sideways. The eye watered but the speck was still there.

'I can see it. Now hold still.'

Kate's fingers stretched back the lid. She brought her face up close, as if she meant to kiss Cora's nose, and something flicked her eyeball.

Cora blinked. 'It's gone. Was that your tongue?'

'Harold taught me. His mother used to lick the grit out when they were children.'

She was suddenly in tears, letting Cora embrace her. 'Forget what I said about the funeral. I know what you mean to do, beg your husband for a divorce because you still have Stephen on the brain and you think he'll marry you.'

'Love's a bit inconvenient,' said Cora, which was the only way she could think of saying that Kate was right.

In a veil and all that black silk, who would recognise her? Cora made a plan. Stage One, take the train to Aldershot. Some time ago she had been sent a printed card to say that Captain and Mrs Leopold Jenner had received the gift of a son, Bertram Donald. At midday, when she timed her arrival by trap from the station, the captain could be assumed to be doing whatever Home Forces did in the mornings.

Blinds and curtains were closed in the house, a stone villa within sight of a parade ground. Her card went in and she waited in the hall. For the moment she was undisguised, Mrs Stephen Crane on a social errand.

Norah Jenner was the youngest daughter. Cora hadn't seen her since the day she invaded Harrington Gardens. Sir Donald must have been past fifty and already a general when she was conceived, the last of eight children. Was it a duty or did he enjoy it? Cora once made a humorous remark along those lines when she was in bed with Captain Stewart, and he called her shameless. There weren't many things he hadn't called her.

'Cora Crane! How nice to see you.'

'I have come with my condolences. I heard the news while staying with friends not far from here. It must have been wonderful to have a father like that.'

'He was just Pa, an old dear. He never saw little Bertram. The doctors sent him off to Algiers, horrid place, Leo says.

269

Would you like to see him? They'd faint if they knew you were here, but a married woman can do whatever she likes, that's the law. She is a free agent, as long as it's within reason.'

A nursemaid produced him, a beribboned parcel that rested briefly in Cora's arms.

'I would ask you to luncheon, but Leo is bringing the brigade major back, and, and—'

'And they would all want to know who I am.' Cora said she must be off. She asked delicately about the arrangements. Would the women attend? Yes, said Norah, the Army approved of wives and daughters at funerals.

'If events had turned out differently, I would have been there, too, with my husband. Except that he's in Africa, I believe.'

'Not at all,' said Norah, 'he travelled to Algiers when Pa was unwell, and came back with the – came back on the warship to England. Otherwise there wouldn't be a son at all. Norman is too far away to return.'

'Of course,' said Cora. 'The infantry brigade in China.'

The trap had been told to wait. Norah stood waving at the door, almost too unladylike for a Stewart.

Stage Two, check the funeral arrangements as printed in the *Times*. Service at noon on Saturday in the chapel of Chelsea Hospital. Wreath from the Queen on the coffin. Foot Guards, Scots Guards, Horse Guards. Dead March, 'Now the labourer's task is o'er,' gun salutes at one-minute intervals, military procession down the road to Kensington for interment at the Brompton Cemetery. As Stevie said once, 'The British Army ain't entirely reliable on the modern rifle, but by Jiminy, they are hot stuff on gold lace and cocked hats.'

Stage Three, buy the funeral garb. The blackest dress, the thickest veil. It cost more than she could afford, but when you could afford nothing, it made no difference. The assistant at Marshall & Snelgrove, a man in a morning coat, said how charmed he was to be serving an American lady. He made discreet references to 'the proprieties that we English consider appropriate at these sad junctures,' among them, apparently, a mourning-fan of black ostrich-feathers on a tortoise-shell stick, a piece or two of mourning-jewellery in jet or silver, not to mention black-edged handkerchiefs, plus the very necessary black gloves, which Madam indubitably possessed, but were now available in the new high-wrist, two-button style.

'If you were on commission at Macy's,' Cora said admiringly, 'you'd be able to retire after a year.'

'Madam?'

She would manage as best she could without a mourning-fan. But there was one point he might help her with. How were family mourners allocated to the coaches as they travelled from church to burial-ground and back again? Did wives travel with husbands? Was it men in one coach and women in the other?

He was anxious to help, Madam being an American. Widow or widower travelled at the head. Sons came behind. Daughters next, if such there were, and then the in-laws.

Out of mischief, Cora tipped him a shilling, to see the distaste for the coin in his hand go backwards up his arm and into his face.

Stage Four, be patient. Visit the cemetery on Friday afternoon and find her bearings. Note the square of ground roped off, near the Great Circle at the end of the avenue, where two men are digging in the clay. Find a place where a cab can stand unnoticed, near a brick mausoleum.

On Saturday make sure that Carrie has the fires lighted early at Milborne Grove. Stand still while Mathilde devotes herself to underpinnings and over-trimmings. Catch sight of herself in the mirror, in her stockings, holding the broad hat like a vaudeville girl who is using it to tease the audience with. See, not for the first time, signs of fleshiness.

Watch the hands crawl around the clock while Mathilde, cursing like a man under her breath, does a tuck here and fixes elastic there. Tell herself she has nothing to lose. Submit to the final envelopment of black silk, and practise peering through the veil.

Too late now to go back on anything. The prearranged cab, driven by a man who had been persuaded to wear a top hat and put a black plume on his horse, arrived on time. As it took her down to the Brompton Road, she heard the minute-gun go bang, a mile and a half away, which meant the cortège was on the move. People were converging on the cemetery, soberly dressed but cheerful; it was an event, with soldiers and music. Cora saw a policeman reprimand girls who were larking about near the gates.

'Drive straight in,' she called up. They passed a line of guardsmen, and a military band with drums covered in black crape, before finding the side-path to her waiting-place.

No one was larking about in the cemetery. Even when she lifted her veil, Cora's view was obscured by crowds, and the driver had to tell her, speaking hoarsely through the roof-flap, what he could see. 'Bobbies all along the ropes, hundreds of 'em, keeping everyone back from the enclosure. Soldiers in red lined up inside. Tarpaulins by the grave in case it rains, which it won't. Would you take exception, Ma'am, if I were to partake of a boiled sweet?'

'Respect the dead, if you don't mind,' she said. Cemeteries made her nervous. It was the second she had visited that year. She admired the field marshal, who once picked a wasp from her hair and crushed it between his fingers, in the drawing room at Harrington Gardens; in the days when everyone was still trying.

Stage Five, enter the enclosure, but not too soon.

'What can you see now?'

'Something happening in the Brompton Road.'

It was ten minutes before the mounted soldiers appeared, a slow wave of black and scarlet coming down the avenue, and the heavy boom of the music. 'There's the gun-carriage,' said her driver.

'I hope you have taken your hat off.'

'I certainly have, Ma'am.'

Cora could just make out a flag on the coffin. Soldiers unloaded it in half a minute, making way for the mourners' carriages at the rear, which dropped their occupants by the enclosure before drawing up around the Circle. Cora waited till the last vehicle had gone, and paid off her cab. Now she had nowhere to hide. She walked across the grass.

Any gentleman with a top hat or wearing officer's uniform was allowed to penetrate the cordon. Cora was the only woman on her own. A police sergeant waved her past the ropes, even said, 'Good day, Ma'am.'

The unofficial mourners remained at a decent distance from the graveside, where a throng of generals and admirals blazing with medals faced the family across the broken clay. The clergyman's bands fluttered in the wind. So did wisps of sandy hair belonging to the fellow in civilian clothes who lacked a wife.

Hard to believe that she had ever been part of his life; even harder to believe he had been part of hers.

'. . . and is cut down, like a flower,' blew her way. 'He fleeth as it were a shadow . . .'

Cora kept her eye on the waiting coaches, which were ready to proceed round the Circle and leave the way they had come. If she had the protocol right, the cab that mattered was number two.

Donald had developed a stoop, or what resembled a stoop beside the poker-straight back of his mother. None of them looked particularly stricken. A people bred to reticence, Crane might have said, a grudging compliment.

She couldn't be sure which was Norah among the veiled daughters who stood alongside the husbands in scarlet uniforms, like stage soldiers.

Crane would be ravenous for detail about the obsequies of a field marshal, a rank they lacked in America. Men in plain khaki uniforms were busy with ropes and webbing, the Union flag was folded up (was it kept for the next funeral?), the coffin vanished into the earth, the clergyman threw a pinch of sand after it.

Whatever she told Crane, he would ask for more. Were there shots fired? Yes, with flashes and smoke. Who gave the order? A man shouted, 'Guards, attention! Present – arms! Order – arms! Fix – bayonets!' Rifles at the same angle went bang at the same time. And then? Then it was over. Mother and son had turned away already.

Another story: a mysterious woman pops up at the field marshal's funeral and tries to corner her estranged husband, who is the dead man's son. Do they put her in prison? A lunatic asylum? The Tower of London?

As Cora drifted towards the line of coaches, one or two mourners stared for a moment, wondering who she was. But now that it was over, the police had given up trying to exclude the crowd. Sightseers broke up the formality, provided distractions. A fat woman with a crying baby in a shawl shoved a pacifier in its mouth. Admirals and generals quickened their pace.

At the first coach, the driver had the door open. Donnie stood talking to his mother. Cora was twenty paces from them. She saw Lady Stewart shake her head. He helped her up the step and walked to his own coach, the limp as evident as she remembered.

If Cora hurried, there was time to walk between the line of vehicles, and approach from the other side. As she swerved past a tall girl they recognised one another through their veils. It was Norah. She said 'Golly!' but that was all. Cora put her hands together in a praying gesture, and Norah gave a nod.

Impossible to tell if anyone had noticed. Lady Stewart's driver was stroking his whip, awaiting instructions. If Donnie's driver saw her, he did nothing. She got the far-side door open and hauled herself up by the handrail.

The cool, dark box smelt of cloth and tobacco. He was slouched in a corner, top hat on his knee, showing a whiteness of eyes in the gloom. Cora sat opposite. Tribesmen with sharp objects hadn't worried him, so why should a woman in a veil? Perhaps he thought she was a mad aunt. She tried to read his face.

The flap shifted an inch and the driver said, 'Lady Stewart's coach is leaving, sir.'

'Drive on.' The hat fell off as they began to move. He left it upright on the floor. 'If you are who I think you are, you will please alight when we reach the Brompton Road. If you make trouble, I shall be forced to have you given in charge.'

'My dear Donnie, I'm your legal wife.' Cora got rid of the veil. 'I'm sorry about your pa.'

'If you have any decency, leave me alone with my thoughts.'

'You know why I'm here.'

'I gave you my answer years ago. Divorce doesn't suit.'

'I want to marry again. Is that too much to ask? Divorces can be arranged without any fuss. It's within your power.'

'I'm demned if I will,' he said, exactly as she remembered.

'Your brother managed to get himself unhitched.'

'More fool him. But he has his baronetcy. No one can take it away from him.' He seemed to press himself deeper into the corner. 'In a few years' time my name will go forward for a

K.C.M.G. Can you imagine what it would do to Lady Stewart to know that her son had been refused his knighthood because of someone like you?'

'You were keen enough to marry me. You couldn't wait.'

'Women like you drag men down to their level.'

Cora had forgotten the thinness of the lips and the indifferent eyes. 'You are such a smug little man,' she said. She could have struck him. Instead she stamped on his hat, a furious backstroke with her heel.

She imagined Stevie saying, 'Gee, that's enough to bring the cavalry, stamping on a man's hat.' It was a longish heel, and the hat collapsed with a wonderful tearing sound.

At least it got Donnie sitting up. Red spots appeared on his cheeks. He peered at the hat and then the boot.

'Serves you right,' she said.

Suddenly he lunged across the carriage, his hands knocking her shoulders back. Tobacco breath blew in her face. A knee was trying to work itself between her legs. She clawed at him.

'Never any decency,' he said in a curious, slobbery voice, half on top of her. Something leathery was stuffed between her teeth. One of her hands was being crushed by one of his, the other was locked under his arm.

She felt him reach back and scrabble under her clothes, grabbing at her in the same incompetent fury she remembered from the bed in Harrington Gardens. His nails scratched her thigh and tried to hurt her between her legs.

It was like being violated by a child. At the same time, being murdered seemed a distinct possibility. The weight of her clothes made it difficult to kick his vital parts. She was still trying when he shuddered and let go.

He threw himself backwards into his corner, making more of the slobbery noises. She took a kid glove out of her mouth and listened to her husband weeping. He had his head in his hands. The shoulders pumped up and down as violently as Mathilde's did when she was having one of her spasms.

Still shaking, Cora pulled a drawstring and let some light in. They were in the Brompton Road. The horse had smartened its pace. A workman on a ladder was removing crape panels that had been hung over the facade of the London Joint Stock Bank. Shops were busy; a jeweller's with electricity poured amber light over its gems and watches, brightening the pavement on a dull November afternoon.

A string of mucus hung from his nose. 'You ought to see a nerve doctor,' said Cora, without being sure what nerve doctors did.

He was mumbling apologies, but she had lost interest in him. She used the ruined hat to knock the roof and draw the driver's attention. 'Stop here!' she called, and he reined in the horse so abruptly that the cab behind nearly ran into them. Cora got out unassisted.

Heading for Milborne Grove, she removed the veil and walked proudly, despite an unsteadiness in the legs, showing off her profile for the benefit of family mourners who might pass in a cab and stick their heads out to see if it really was *that woman*. None did, as far as she could tell.

Divorce was always a forlorn hope, but the day had done her good. She walked to the Kensington Post Office and sent a cable to Reynolds for onward transmission to his client. 'Attended funeral of Sir Donald Stewart. Full military honours. Encountered a certain close relative without success. Trust you are impressed. I am still here. Cora.'

She was still there when Athalie Mills and Kate Lyon appeared at the central criminal court, and the Crown offered no

277

evidence. The public interest, said a man in a wig, would not be served by sending two deluded women to prison.

She was still there when the detective she had failed to charm appeared at Ravensbrook one evening. He wouldn't come beyond the hall, clearing his throat in the candlelight (the gas was temporarily cut off, due to non-payment of the bill), asking for her cooperation. If the police should ever question her about the unlawful-killing case, he hoped he could rely on her to deny they ever spoke of it.

'How exciting! You mean you had something to do with the charges being dropped?'

Asking questions was obviously a bad idea. He said angrily that he had been able to achieve nothing. He was a mere detective. He couldn't work miracles. His conscience was clear, but we all knew the damage that gossip could do.

'Wild horses won't drag it from me,' said Cora. 'I am afraid I took advantage of you. I had no right to.'

'I make no complaint.'

'I hope we are still friends.'

'Wiser if we are not, Ma'am.' He backed away, hit an umbrella stand and almost fell over, and whacked his hat on his head with an air of finality.

'Good luck, Mr Hooper,' she called after him. 'I mean it.'

Adoni appeared in the hall, watching mist and darkness cover the striding figure.

'Bang-bang, I shoot you,' he said.

Cora told him to get out of her sight, and he went off muttering, 'Oh boy! Gee whiz!'

She remained by the open door, listening for the train to London that Detective Hooper would catch, as she had stood listening for Stevie's train when he went off to the war. He refused to let her go with him to the station – said that railway platforms bred tears, threw his valise and overcoat into the trap, jumped up behind the driver, and didn't look back. At the time she hoped he was talking about his tears. Pretty certainly, though, he was talking about hers.

23

Belle didn't return. What was she doing in wet weather, gales blowing up the Channel? You couldn't paint in the rain, could you? Having so many things on his mind had deflected Fred's concern. He began to worry about her. She must have lost her job by now. He didn't want to make a fool of himself; kept giving her one more day before he sent a telegram asking the Brighton police to look for a missing female.

Then another postcard came to say she had been in bed with a cold. She had sent a doctor's note to Arding & Hobbs. She was drawing fishermen in sou'westers.

Fred showed the card to Miss Crumm, who looked in quite often – Belle, it seemed, had asked her to keep an eye on the domestic arrangements, such vital matters as whether Mrs Monge was sending his collars to the laundry.

Miss Crumm was philosophic about the Brighton business. 'Wouldn't worry if I were you, Mr Hooper. As usual I am speaking out of turn.'

She looked in to offer a spare steak and oyster pudding that was knocking around the Crumm kitchen. She looked in to report that her mother would be happy to do any clothes-mending that was needed. Belle gave them something to talk about.

A further postcard announced that she had a whole gallery of fishermen, and would be home by the end of the week. By the same delivery came a letter addressed to her, with a Clapham postmark, which he opened. Arding & Hobbs had sacked her.

When Miss Crumm looked in that evening with a rice pudding under a cloth, Fred gave her postcard and letter to read.

'She's burned her boats all right,' said the visitor. 'I wonder why.'

'Could she make a living as an artist?'

''Fraid not. I couldn't and I'm better than her. Pardon me for saying so.'

'She has never talked to you about her plans?'

'Says she wants more out of life, but she isn't alone in that. She had some idea of emigrating. I told her once that she was the kind of girl who runs away with a man, which made her jolly cross.'

He was shocked. 'You are not hinting she has gone off with Sidney?'

'What a wonderful idea. Does he take his cushion to the seaside, do you think, or does he borrow one from the boarding house?'

'Please be serious. Are there things she confided in you that I ought to know about?'

Miss Crumm's features were soft and rosy, but contained eyes of surprising shrewdness that he should have noticed long before.

'If there were, I suppose they'd be confidential, and I should have to think twice before telling anyone. But I have no idea what she's up to. Now, would you like me to warm up a spoonful of jam and put it over the pudding?'

* * *

When Belle showed her face, they would have some serious talking to do. Meanwhile he got on with crime and London. He was still a free man; the Croydon nightmare was over.

He was busy in the West End, looking for a fellow with a crutch who ran a gang of thieves working the omnibuses. Made his usual call in Soho – 'Are you moving in this week?' – 'Keep the mattress aired, Mrs Armellini.' Returned home in early evening, sky clear, half a moon, touch of frost in the air.

Chill down his spine at a presence in the house. Gas lit in the kitchen. Belle at the table with an inferior sketch of a fisherman and a watercolour of a jetty, 'to show you how busy I've been.' Her purse rested on top. A valise lay open by the dresser, showing stockings and a hat.

'Do close the door, Freddie. I don't want Vi seeing a light. Has she been coming round to make sure you're managing?'

Now she was there, he was more relieved than angry. Familiar curls framed familiar face. Where had she been living? A boarding house near the West Pier. He told her she must go to Arding & Hobbs in the morning and plead for her job back. Blow Arding & Hobbs, she said. So what did she mean to do? Paint and think and do something with her life. What would she do for money? She had been saving up, and typewriting girls could always find work.

'We can manage well enough,' said Fred. 'I don't entirely follow, but you are old enough to know your own mind. You're back, that's all that matters.' He reached for the valise. 'I'll take this upstairs.'

'No, don't. I'm not staying.'

'Talk sense,' he said, exasperated at last.

'There were some things I needed.'

'You're going back to Brighton?' She nodded. 'With winter

coming on? To live in a boarding house and draw fishermen? Without money?'

'I have enough.'

'Your friend Violet says she couldn't make a living as an artist, so how do you think you can? Drawing postcards for stationers? Doing portraits on the pier?'

'Don't quarrel with me,' she said. 'Please don't, Freddie. I only came because I wanted to see you.'

'So why rush in and rush out again?'

'Because if I stay here, I might stay for ever. Give me a kiss and I'll get the train back tonight and I promise I'll send you my address. Dear old Freddie, I am terribly fond of you.'

He embraced her; her face was cold; she said she must run upstairs and get the china rabbit with the spectacles because it made her laugh, allowing him just time to look in her purse and see that it contained a half-dozen sovereigns, two five-pound banknotes folded together, and a return South Eastern and Chatham Line ticket to Dover. Which was on the Channel coast but wasn't Brighton.

Then he was the detective, tracking a woman with a valise. He had waved her off at the door and given her two minutes' start, 135 yards at a female walking pace, but she was hurrying, and he had to pound along to bring her in sight, heading for Wandsworth Town station, the route he was counting on. The district possessed no cab-ranks, so she had to leg it despite the small fortune in her purse.

A change-of-appearance dodge, the kind you could get away with at night and at a distance, had had to suffice: one leather shopping-bag, empty, in his hand, one flat cap, which he kept for cycling, on his head. Railway stations were notoriously ill-lit. He made sure his compartment was well to the rear of hers, and at Waterloo, still busy, he watched her go past the flower-sellers and down the steps to Waterloo Junction, where she entered the ladies' waiting room.

The next Dover train was in twenty minutes. He emerged from behind his pillar a few seconds too early, and she would have seen him but for the smoke and steam.

Kent went by in the dark. Fred dozed off and woke to hear a commercial traveller with a case of samples on the luggage-rack, telling a chap in check trousers about a pair of newly-weds in the cabin next to his, aboard a night ferry in the summer. 'Talk about turbulence!' he said.

There had to be a man involved with Belle. The five-pound notes rattled Fred almost as much as the lies. She was only a girl, even if it was a girl of twenty-nine-and-three-quarters.

'Dover Priory!' voices were shouting. 'Dover Harbour next stop.'

She stayed on the train, and at the harbour station he watched her visit the South Eastern and Chatham steamer office, then emerge on to the jetty, behind the porter who had taken her valise, and proceed up the gangway of a ferry. Chalked boards said 'Ostend sailing, 11.30 p.m.'

Policemen standing around on the pier struck him as odd. Electric lamps gleamed on four Kent Constabulary helmets, three PCs and a sergeant. Everything he saw tonight disquieted Fred. He showed his warrant card, and the sergeant said proudly that they were after a big fish. All ferries were being watched. Being from London, Mr Hooper might even have heard of him.

'Try me.'

'It's Arthur Grimshaw, alias Leonard Rukes.'

'Name means nothing to me.'

Fred added that it was none of his business, but wouldn't they be better off keeping out of sight?

'Got other men in hiding if he sees us and makes a dash for it, sir.'

'No hope for him, obviously. I'm not here on duty, but I'll let you know if I see anything.'

Greasy water lapped the ferry. It sailed in ten minutes. Fred went on board, avoided people, watched the pier recede. They were beyond the outer lights, in a choppy sea, before he forced himself to visit the purser, to find Belle's cabin number. Even then he put off the moment, walking on the deck; pausing in the lee of the funnel, out of the wind; planning the best way to save her.

An officer went past, directing a seaman to a hatch-cover that needed securing. 'Do it in a jiffy, sir.' The seaman was solidly built, with the peaks of his jacket up around his ears, where the blond hair stuck out. Fred stood motionless in the heat of the funnel. He knew the oily voice. It was Rukes.

Handcuffs and leg-irons would be in a cupboard on the bridge. Captains had powers of arrest. The problem was somewhere else, down steep stairs, Cabin B3, tap on door, no reply, tap again – urgent now, the kind of tapping a lover might go in for. Door opens an inch, Fred gives a shove, Belle thrown backwards, ends up hanging on to shelf over bunk.

She wore a negligee of some pink stuff and her legs were bare. Black curls were loose on her neck.

'This beats everything,' she said, and began to invent more lies on the spot, a sudden urge to see the Continent, a desire not to worry him, a promise to return in a week. She pretended to be angry at being followed like a criminal; even asked him what he was doing in that silly cap, carrying a shopping-bag.

'No good, Belle,' he said. 'They were on the quay, looking for your friend. Wouldn't think of looking in the crew. Clever man, our lodger. Has he done this before? Have you? What is he doing? Setting up in Belgium?'

'He isn't what you think.' She sat on the bunk, arms wrapped across her chest. 'Business colleagues cheated him. You don't know him as I do.'

'You are the one I don't know.' He had no idea where to begin. His questions would always be the wrong ones. 'It wasn't Violet he fancied, was it?' he said. 'It was you. That's why he went for the chap on the common who made himself objectionable.'

'It hadn't started then, not as far as I was concerned. But start it did.' She folded her hands in her lap. Her shoulders were bony, immature, like a child's. 'What are you going to do?'

'Arrest him and take him back. Keep you out of it if I can.'

He knew they wouldn't let him within a mile of the case. Hard-faced men like him would grill her for hours, enjoying it all the more because of who she was. ('Sister of a detective inspector, you may have heard of him, Fred Hooper at Vine Street, good copper but accident prone, Head of Detectives had him up for misbehaving with a woman in an alley – you can't ever tell, can you?)

'You'll have to arrest me as well,' said Belle. 'If he goes to prison, so will I.'

'Do you have any idea what prison is like?'

'Bit like living in Disraeli Street and working at Arding & Hobbs, I imagine.'

'Five minutes in Holloway and you'll change your tune.'

'Do as you please.'

He tried another tack. 'Forced you to help him, didn't he?'

'Afraid not.'

'When you went to Brighton – that was for your painting.'

'Not really. We went there for a lark. I left the postcards and paid the landlady to post one every time I sent her a telegram. I didn't want you tearing after me.'

'He made you come on board tonight.'

'I've been in Belgium once already. This is the last trip. Everything's in place. We meet up in Ostend. We have an apartment in Brussels to go to. I am a lost cause, Freddie dear. If you love me, let us disappear. Nobody'll ever know. I shan't tell him you found us.'

He asked the question the interrogators wouldn't bother with. 'Why him, of all people?'

'Who else was there? Sidney the Kidney? I took to him. I can't tell you what times we've had.'

'There didn't have to be anybody.'

'A lot you know about it. You have what you want out of life.' She held her wrists together. 'I expect you brought your handcuffs. If you don't mind, I must get dressed. Can you pop outside for five minutes?'

Fred shook his head. 'Can't leave you on your own.'

He kept his eyes on the light fixed to the bulkhead, aware of her movements. Modest Flo behind the screen, long ago. Dangerous Mrs Crane, legs going like mad on the bicycle, 'Golly, this is fast.'

None of us were what we thought ourselves to be.

'I shan't stop you,' he said. 'Or him. Disembark in the morning. I shall stay out of sight.'

'Dearest darling Freddie.'

The last he saw of her was at Ostend, as it was getting light and passengers were going ashore. It broke his heart. She was on the quayside, moving fast. Her eyes swept the row of portholes but she couldn't have seen him, even if she had known which O of glass to look for.

The news, suitably disguised, left Miss Crumm puzzled and upset. Belle had dashed in and spoken of travelling to the Continent? Dashed out again? Gone for good?

He put on a brave face to go with the lies he had cobbled

together. He had to accept that Belle had gone. Nothing he did would bring her back.

'My guess would be,' he said, 'that she has taken up with an English family she met in Brighton. I can't explain the secrecy. We shall hear in due course.'

The visitor had brought a piece of boiled bacon. It was Sunday morning. Church bells had ceased. The kitchen range that Monjy had stoked up was ticking with heat.

'I'm unhappy for us both,' said Miss Crumm.

'She asked to be particularly remembered to you.'

'She did? Well it was mean of her not to call and say goodbye to me herself. She was afraid I might ask awkward questions. I'm sorry, I am speaking out of turn.'

'It's your trademark, Violet. What sort of questions?'

'I mustn't say. Has she gone off with a man? There, I've said it.'

'Who do you have in mind?'

'My lips are sealed. I have no evidence at all, and Belle has got more sense. We have all done foolish things in our time. I don't mean you, Mr Hooper. I mean me. I don't expect it's a man at all.'

'Let's say it was. Don't worry, I have no plans to try and stop her.'

'She was fonder of Mr Rukes than she let on.'

'You amaze me,' he said gloomily. 'I suppose a man doesn't notice these things. And how did Mr Rukes strike you?'

'I couldn't stand him. It was I left the note at Bermondsey market so the police would come and catch him. There, I've confessed. Now you won't ever want to speak to me again. I am an interfering woman.'

'You are a remarkable woman.'

'We don't know it's Mr Rukes. It's too awful to think about, Belle with a, Belle with a man on the run.' She had her flustered look. 'Tell me to go away and mind my own business.'

'I've got a better idea. Having brought that piece of bacon round, do the civil thing and share it with me. I could do with some company. I shall be on my own every day now that Belle isn't here.'

She raised objections, but not many, and went home to tell them what was happening.

The empty house, and knowing it would go on being empty, had got on his nerves already, and instead of thinking about the flat at Armellini's, he was waiting impatiently for Violet Crumm to return. What would Florence have to say about that? Not that he ever got much out of Florence. The boy who resembled the cornetist, the one she shed romantic tears for, was the nearest he ever came to glimpsing another side of her. But it must have been there somewhere.

Violet reappeared in a different skirt and blouse, and cooked them a jollyish dinner. He found himself discoursing about counterfeiters and cheque-smashers and confidence men, matters that seemed to interest her.

'We could take a stroll by the river,' he said. 'If you have nothing better to do.'

She took his arm as they walked by the Thames below Putney Bridge. Light rain was falling on the umbrella he held over the two of them, ensuring a closeness he wasn't used to. The disturbing hiddenness and legginess that went with Mrs Crane went with Violet Crumm in her dark blue skirt as well. He began to look ahead.

24

In the end, men were the root of the problem. Annoyance kept Cora going – that, and having Kate to talk to. Harold's case was more complicated than Stephen's because he was dead, which one could hardly blame him for. Where he had failed was in trying to keep two lives going instead of settling for one. As far as Cora could tell, his wife in London was little better off than his non-wife in Surrey.

'He sacrificed you both. I know it's a shocking thing to say, but it was a shocking thing to do.'

'You never liked him,' said Kate.

'Not true, I saw through him, but then he saw through me as well. Anyway you loved him. Nothing to do with me.'

They were in the half-emptied drawing room at Kenley. Kate had announced she was going – running, fleeing back across the Atlantic, before Christmas if she could get the tickets.

'Wait till the New Year. We'll have the holiday together at Ravensbrook. Adoni talks about dressing up as Father Christmas. Can you imagine it?'

'I lose the house in a month.'

'Stay with us as long as you like. Come tonight.'

'I don't belong in England any more.' Shivering, Kate retracted her legs, huddled on the one remaining sofa as if the tide was about to come in under the door and sweep across the bare boards. 'My mother will look after us till I find employment. Your fund has given us a start.'

'I am ashamed every time I think of it.'

Unlike the real Mrs Frederic, whose public subscription attracted enough cash to keep her going for a year or two, the wicked Miss Lyon would have been denied any charity at all without Cora's begging letters. They didn't always work. The American Women smelt misdemeanour and were not helpful, apart from Helen Hay, who sent a cheque but requested anonymity. Writers behaved better, among them Conrad. Mr Shaw the playwright sent a fiver. Robert Barr, regretting he was somewhat short of the boodle, contributed two pounds of the six he had in his bank. Cora added some of her remaining sovereigns.

The children were playing upstairs, hollow voices in rooms without curtains. The bailiffs had left the beds; it was the law. Cora picked up a dust-sheet and wrapped it around them both. Red ash in the grate pretended to be a fire. She put her arm around Kate and said, 'We could still go to Ireland in the spring. The house at Bantry Bay.'

'Lying on the bed with no clothes on and brushing off our men like bees. That wouldn't be a problem any more, would it? It's no use pretending. We shall never go to Inchgela again. Or anywhere, you and I.'

'Listen to me, madam,' said Cora, changing direction because Ireland evidently wasn't a good idea. 'You may see me in Chicago yet.'

'Fiddle faddle. You'll wait for Stephen till kingdom come.'

'Do you have any idea how angry I am? He is coming. He is not coming. He is in Havana. No he isn't, he is in New York.

Or he is in New Jersey, seeing his precious brothers. Or he is still in Havana, the other stories being false reports.'

'Angry doesn't matter. You still love him. Nothing to do with me. What does Revere Reynolds say?'

'His client is having a fire-sale of stories, is the latest. Allegedly to raise cash and settle his affairs in Cuba – whatever that means. I gather he's still there.'

'That's great men for you.'

'We could go and live in Brede Place, bring up your children there. I've kept the builders at work. The roof is nearly finished.'

'You like grand schemes. I used to envy you – very worldly, which I didn't quite know how to manage.'

Huddled together under the dust-sheet, Cora was warm for the first time. 'Did you know about me and Jacksonville?' she said.

'Of course I did. You ran a hotel where . . . men came. Harold told me. He thought it a great joke.'

'You didn't mind?'

'We had too much in common. A pair of sinners.'

Their friendship had been the best thing about England. Now Cora had to step back while Kate worked out her own future and turned into someone else. It was instructive to watch her buy one-way steamship tickets, conspire with the local carrier to send furniture off to a saleroom in Croydon without the bailiffs knowing, burn Harold's letters the day before they sailed. It was the letter-burning that made her wonder if Kate had been the stronger character all along. Cora was there when it happened, a sort of ceremony, the match flaring, and afterwards ghostly grey writing still visible on fragments. Then her friend stirred the charred paper with a stick, and it fell into dust.

At Tilbury Docks in the morning, the children's excitement papered over the goodbyes. Both women said, 'You'll write, won't you?' at the same moment. Cora didn't stay. She could still taste the face-powder after they had kissed and she was back inside the London train.

She settled down to solitude. For the first time she was alone in England. She shut herself away, more often than was healthy, with her manuscript book. She wrote nothing – what more was there to say? – and confined herself to reading passages here and there, wondering if she had the courage to do what Kate had done, and make ashes of the past.

> 'It is bitter – bitter,' he answered;
> 'But I like it
> Because it is bitter.
> And because it is my heart.'

She had no option, in the end. She waited to be incorporated in the story he hadn't yet written.

The Garnetts invited the household over for Christmas lunch. They were kindly and asked no questions. Adoni (who danced for them bare-footed) and Mathilde (who had two glasses of wine and told Mr Garnett that she admired his beard) enjoyed themselves. Cora gave no one reason to feel sorry for her. She even made them laugh with a description of Conrad and the slaughter of the sparrows. It wasn't fair either to the sparrows or to Conrad, but that couldn't be helped. She could conceal herself behind the anecdote.

The telegram, when it came, said only that the steamship *Manitou* would leave New York December 31 and was due Gravesend January 11, signed 'Stephen'. Another of his economical messages.

Cora went by herself, in case of disappointment, which was better coped with by alone. It seemed a lifetime since she took her friends there for the cricket match. Same elementary rail station, same sad conveyances in the station yard.

Trams and carts filled the street that led to the Thames, and she saw herself reflected in a plate-glass window, a figure in grey, like a woman in a tumbril, going to execution. She knew – thought she knew – that this was Crane's last chance, in which case it was her last chance as well. If he didn't come, she had no plans for the future.

The waterfront consisted of quays and piers open to the river, which was so packed with shipping in a haze of smoke that it looked as though collisions were imminent. The trap left her at the harbourmaster's office. A man in a peaked cap was in the doorway.

Had the steamer *Manitou* berthed yet?

'Search me.'

'It was due at noon. I sent a telegram to Lloyd's of London and they told me it was signalled off somewhere or other last night, and ought to arrive as planned.'

'Wait here. No one tells us anything.'

Baskets of cabbages and potatoes were being lowered into a barge with brown sails. A tug stormed by, shaving the end of a jetty. Cora's eyes burned with tiredness. When Peaked Cap came back, he said the ship had been in the river for an hour.

'Which is it?'

He peered at the shapes in mid-stream. 'Hard to tell. Liners don't berth here, you understand. She'll go up to the London docks on the tide. We get passengers who want to save an hour or two. The tender is coming up to the pierhead, so if you're meeting someone they should be along presently.'

The wind on the pier was perishing, tainted with cold mud and cold smoke. Workmen wearing coloured armbands came towards her, pulling a wagon laden with cabin-trunks and portmanteaux. Two men in soft American hats were behind, then a man and woman in swirling coats, then a child holding a nursemaid's hand. Other figures were too distant to make out.

What if he glided up like Harold on the pier at Havana, pale and unseeing, an apparition on its way to nowhere?

By the time she saw him, he was waving. Pale, certainly, but solid enough inside the military greatcoat he had brought back from the wars. She was angry at once.

'If it ain't me old darlin' Cora,' he said, and then, with his arms around her, 'Is my dog Sponge all right?'

'I could kill you sometimes.'

'Take me home instead,' said Crane.

Stephen Crane returned to England on January 11, 1899. He and Cora moved from Ravensbrook to Brede Place a month later. By the end of the year his health was failing, and after a house-party at Christmas lasting three days, he collapsed with a lung haemorrhage. He died in a German sanatorium in June 1900, aged twenty-eight.

Cora went back to Jacksonville, and by 1902 was in business with a successor to the Hotel de Dream called The Court. For a while she prospered. Following the death of her husband, Captain Stewart, in Africa, she had a brief, unsuccessful marriage that ended in divorce. She died in Jacksonville in 1910, aged forty-five.

Kate Lyon, the Christian Scientist, outlived them all. She brought up her children in Chicago, and survived until the 1940s.

30·9·04

ENJOYED THIS BOOK? WHY NOT TRY OTHER GREAT HARPERCOLLINS TITLES – AT 10% OFF!

Buy great books direct from HarperCollins
at **10%** off recommended retail price.
FREE postage and packing in the UK.

☐ **The Queen's Fool** Philippa Gregory 0-00-714729-5   **£6.99**

☐ **The Other Boleyn Girl** Philippa Gregory 0-00-651400-6   **£6.99**

☐ **The Lady and the Unicorn** Tracy Chevalier 0-00-714091-6   **£6.99**

☐ **Girl with a Pearl Earring** Tracy Chevalier 0-00-651320-4   **£6.99**

☐ **The Colour of Heaven** James Runcie 0-00-711987-9   **£6.99**

☐ **The Discovery of Chocolate** James Runcie 0-00-710783-8   **£6.99**

☐ **The Glass Palace** Amitav Ghosh 0-00-651409-X   **£7.99**

Total cost _____

10% discount _____

Final total _____

To purchase by Visa/Mastercard/Switch simply call
08707 871724 or fax on **08707 871725**

To pay by cheque, send a copy of this form with a cheque made payable to
'HarperCollins Publishers' to: Mail Order Dept. (Ref: BOB4),
HarperCollins Publishers, Westerhill Road, Bishopbriggs, G64 2QT,
making sure to include your full name, postal address and phone number.

From time to time HarperCollins may wish to use your personal data
to send you details of other HarperCollins publications and offers.
If you wish to receive information on other HarperCollins publications
and offers please tick this box ☐

Do not send cash or currency. Prices correct at time of press.
Prices and availability are subject to change without notice.
Delivery overseas and to Ireland incurs a £2 per book postage and packing charge.